JANETTE OKE
&
T. DAVIS BUNN

The Meeting Place

BETHANY HOUSE PUBLISHERS
MINNEAPOLIS, MINNESOTA 55438

Books by Janette Oke

Celebrating the Inner Beauty of Woman
Janette Oke's Reflections on the Christmas Story
The Matchmakers
Nana's Gift
The Red Geranium

CANADIAN WEST

When Calls the Heart *When Breaks the Dawn*
When Comes the Spring *When Hope Springs New*

LOVE COMES SOFTLY

Love Comes Softly *Love's Unending Legacy*
Love's Enduring Promise *Love's Unfolding Dream*
Love's Long Journey *Love Takes Wing*
Love's Abiding Joy *Love Finds a Home*

A PRAIRIE LEGACY

The Tender Years *A Searching Heart*

SEASONS OF THE HEART

Once Upon a Summer *Winter Is Not Forever*
The Winds of Autumn *Spring's Gentle Promise*

WOMEN OF THE WEST

The Calling of Emily Evans *A Bride for Donnigan*
Julia's Last Hope *Heart of the Wilderness*
Roses for Mama *Too Long a Stranger*
A Woman Named Damaris *The Bluebird & the Sparrow*
They Called Her Mrs. Doc *A Gown of Spanish Lace*
The Measure of a Heart *Drums of Change*

DEVOTIONALS

The Father Who Calls *Father of My Heart*
The Father of Love *The Faithful Father*

Janette Oke: A Heart for the Prairie
Biography of Janette Oke by Laurel Oke Logan

By T. Davis Bunn

The Gift
The Messenger
The Music Box
One Shenandoah Winter
The Quilt
Tidings of Comfort & Joy

The Dream Voyagers
The Presence
Princess Bella and the Red Velvet Hat
Promises to Keep
To the Ends of the Earth
The Warning
The Ultimatum

By Janette Oke & T. Davis Bunn

Another Homecoming
The Meeting Place
Return to Harmony
Tomorrow's Dream

"Blessed are the peacemakers;
for they shall be called
the children of God."

Matthew 5:9

JANETTE OKE was born in Champion, Alberta, during the depression years, to a Canadian prairie farmer and his wife. She is a graduate of Mountain View Bible College in Didsbury, Alberta, where she met her husband, Edward. They were married in May of 1957, and went on to pastor churches in Indiana as well as Calgary and Edmonton, Canada.

The Okes have three sons and one daughter and are enjoying the addition of grandchildren to the family. Edward and Janette have both been active in their local church, serving in various capacities as Sunday school teachers and board members. They make their home near Calgary, Alberta.

T. DAVIS BUNN, a native of North Carolina, is a former international business executive whose career has taken him to over forty countries in Europe, Africa, and the Middle East. With topics as diverse as romance, history, and intrigue, Bunn's books continue to reach readers of all ages and interests. He and his wife, Isabella, reside near Oxford, England.

PROLOGUE

Lieutenant Andrew Harrow clicked to his horse and moved down the trail to a break in the trees. In the distance, smoke rose from what he knew was Fort Edward, his destination and his home. His heart beat like a drum calling to quarters. But whether his excitement came from seeing his home again, or dread over the news he carried, Andrew could not tell.

After four long days of marching through primeval forest, the first sight of his home village made the blood thrum through his veins. Yet danger lurked nearby, and the reports he carried were equally ominous. War was brewing in the home countries, and though a broad ocean separated England and France from this peaceful land, he and his countrymen might well be caught up once more in the sport of kings. Such a time was not ideal for making plans to wed. But as the colonials were wont to say, the world kept turning whether they liked it or not. Andrew's wedding day was soon to come.

His horse tossed its head, as though it too could feel his anticipation. Andrew ran a hand down its withers, patted the sweaty neck, and murmured, "Not long now."

He turned at the commotion of two dozen soldiers in full kit rounding the bend behind him. "Sergeant Major!" he called.

"Sir!"

"Ten-minute water break. See the men keep their weapons at the ready."

"Ten minutes it is, sir." The ramrod-straight man with bristling mustache stomped about and roared, "Water boy!"

The heavily laden wagons clattered into view. Andrew pressed his knees into the horse's sides and moved away from the soldiers and the clamor. The noise level was a major difference between new arrivals and those who had served longer in the colonies. The seasoned colonials learned from the natives and the forests. They moved with such stealth that a battalion could pass without disturbing the birds.

But these were soldiers fresh off the boats from England, and they masked their nervousness with noise. The forests and the empty reaches had already left their mark. Four days they had traveled since disembarking, and in that time they had not seen a soul. Such emptiness was unheard of back home. Here in the provinces of Acadia, however, only the thin strip of land between the sea and the forests had been cultivated. Farther inland the interior was all mystery and danger. The Micmac Indians who lived there had never been counted. Not even the number of their villages was known.

Andrew now rode a ridgeline of hills steep enough to have been called mountains in his native Somerset. But here they were mere shadows to the spine rising in the heart of this strange land. Stranger still that he, Andrew Harrow, younger son to the seventh earl of Sutton, would have come to call this land home.

Andrew lifted his hat and ran a grime-streaked sleeve over his heated brow, his gaze taking in the full sweep of land exposed to his view. Under the morning sun, the earth descended like giant steps, and each level told a story. Below the forested hillside spread the broad ledge of cultivated land. Scores of farmhouses dotted the meadows. Smoke curled from countless chimneys, and faint cries of animals and children rose upon the gentle June breeze.

A village of stone and wood lay directly beneath him, a village they would do their best to skirt. Andrew's eyes moved across the lanes and market square, but he saw no signs of danger. No matter how eager he might be for what awaited at the end of his journey, still he studied the terrain like the soldier that he was.

The village of Minas below him was French. Nowadays the French were rumored to be allied with the Micmac Indians, and together they posed a possible threat. Or so his generals claimed. Personally, Andrew was not so sure. Two years he had been stationed in this scarcely tamed land, and neither the French nor the Indians had signaled any threat at all. Not within his territory. Andrew had discovered that as long as he treated both with respect, they responded in kind. But such attitudes were called treasonous by his superiors, and he had learned to keep his opinions to himself.

"Beg your pardon, sir, care for a drink?"

Andrew turned in the saddle. "Thank you, Sergeant Major." He accepted the heavy metal dipper and drank deeply, then flung the remnants toward the trees and handed back the ladle. "Much obliged." A foot soldier lifted a dripping bucket to his thirsty horse.

The sergeant major, new to the garrison but a ten-year veteran of the New England colonies, pointed with his blade of a chin. "That a Frenchie village down below, sir?"

"Minas, yes." Andrew nodded toward the scattering of hamlets surrounding Cobequid Bay. "Almost every second village you see here is French."

"Seems quiet enough." The officer sniffed as he stared down the steep slope. " 'Course, you never can tell with them Frenchies. Sneaky, so I've been told. Bad as the Injuns."

Andrew bit back a sharp retort. It would not do to publicly rebuke the man, not for stating the belief shared by almost every member of the officer corps. "Prepare the men, Sergeant Major."

"Sir!" The man stomped away, shouting, "All right, you lot, on your feet!"

Andrew pulled on his reins and swiveled in his saddle to check the seven high-wheeled wagons, the only ones capable of managing the muddy trail. The men assembled to either side with another contingent fore and aft, weary and footsore.

Andrew turned back around, raised his hand, and let it fall.

The sergeant major shouted, "Foooor-ward, ho!"

The wheels creaked; the tin plates rattled upon the cook wagon; the soldiers shuffled and muttered and coughed and marched. Andrew knew them all by now, not just by name but by noise and habits. He liked to bring the new troops in himself. It gave him an opportunity to test their mettle in the field.

When the trail jinked around a steep curve, their destination finally came into view. Once again he felt his heart rate surge. There, off beyond the river and more fields and farmhouses, Fort Edward rose stolid and stern and safe, and beyond it the village of Edward itself. Andrew squinted against the morning glare, trying to make out the stone cottage at the village entrance. The one where the love of his life lived and awaited his return. No, he could not quite make out the individual houses, not yet. But the search alone was enough to bring a smile to his lips. Catherine was there, and she waited for him. He was as sure of that as he was of his own name.

A sudden boom caused his horse to rear, and the mules pulling the wagons started their noisy braying. Andrew quieted his horse as he searched the horizon. He spotted a cloud of smoke rising from the fort's cannon.

The sergeant major trotted up beside him. "Trouble, sir?"

"Not at all." Andrew pointed beyond the land's final shelf, out to where billowing squares of white indicated a ship of the line sailing up Cobequid Bay. He called to the troops behind them, "Easy now, they're just signaling to an incoming ship!"

As though to confirm Andrew's words, the ship responded with a booming reply of its own. Andrew spotted the signal flag below the Union Jack. "Press the men hard, Sergeant Major," he urged. "We need to arrive in time to greet the governor's representative. General Whetlock himself sails in that vessel."

Andrew spurred his horse on ahead. He was eager to arrive, to see Catherine again. Almost a month he had been away, a month of disturbing news and unwelcome developments. He could not help but cast another watchful glance at the French village below, as though some enemy lurked there unseen.

North of the New England colonies stood the disputed lands of New France, settled for a century and a half by people who had named the region Acadia, their "beloved home." The British had come soon after. Building upon the strength of their southern colonies, they battled the French here as they had in Europe for over six hundred years, enemies ever.

Now, in the year 1753, the lines were firmly drawn. A man was either French or English, and though the villages were but a stone's throw from one another, most inhabitants would go an entire lifetime without speaking to the other side. Certainly there was some contact in the markets, but those who did not travel—and most did not—lived in a state of constant suspicion and fear. They avoided open contact with people who were considered enemies because they were strangers. Villagers whispered rumors and grim warnings behind secured doors. On both sides, raw fear haunted their days and troubled their sleep with terrifying night-mares, knowing that they might be the ones to be conquered and displaced.

Two nations of hard-calloused farmers and crude-crafted village shopkeepers lived side by side and never knew the other. They vied for possession, hoping their troops would somehow protect them from the other. Praying to the same God, imploring His help to make them the victor—the un-disputed owner of the territory.

Andrew shook his head and turned away. Strange how he could be filled with so much joy and so much worry, so much happiness and so much concern, so much love and so much alertness for battle.

It was almost enough to tear his heart in two.

CHAPTER ONE

Catherine Price watched the world unfold outside the carriage window. She felt such joy she could scarcely contain it. So many events of magnitude were coming together in her life, it was enough to make a girl raised on the rough frontier believe that she had been transported into some magical fairy tale.

Fort Edward kept just one carriage, usually reserved for the king's representative, the provincial governor. But the general had personally invited Catherine to dine on board a ship of the line. It was the first time an official invitation had been addressed to her, the first time Catherine was not going just as her father's daughter. The written invitation had read that General Whetlock, the regimental commandant recently arrived from England, requested the pleasure of her company on board the vessel *Excalibur* for a banquet in celebration of the sacking of Fort

Louisburg.

Her father sat ramrod straight beside her, pride showing in spite of his efforts to appear nonchalant. John Price had served in the King's Own Fusiliers for eleven years, until a French cannonade had injured him and cut short his career. He deeply missed the pomp and circumstance, the honor and the glory. No matter that he now served as the provincial notary, answering only to Fort Edward's senior officer and the governor in Halifax. John Price had never forgiven the French for ending his rise within the military, and he loathed them to a man.

The carriage rocked like a boat in high seas as the trail descended and forded yet another stream. The woman seated across from Catherine sniffed her disdain. "I do not see why on earth we must suffer through this endless journey. The ship is almost close enough for me to reach out and touch it."

"That may be so, ma'am." John Price's voice was as stiff as his bearing. "But there is only one docking station between Fort Edward and Chelmsford. We must make for that in order to meet the ship's boat."

Mrs. Priscilla Stevenage sniffed even more loudly. "Even a provincial town such as your own, sir, should be able to afford a proper docking facility. Why, our new capital of Halifax is but a few years old, and already we have a decent rock-lined harbor."

"I daresay you do," John Price said, a red flush creeping up from his collar. "Since the fleet must winter there and at Annapolis Royal."

"Then why on earth can't a fort as old as yours—"

"Mud, ma'am. Good, rich, fertile mud." He waved an angry hand out beyond the open window. "The very same mud which allows this *provincial* town to feed not only its own citizens but Halifax and Annapolis Royal as well."

Though Catherine did not wish to say anything at all to the woman seated opposite her, she realized she had no choice. To remain silent would mean seeing the evening ruined before it had properly begun. She patted her father's hand, then said matter-of-factly to Priscilla Stevenage, "The Cobequid Basin has the highest tidal surge in the world. Twice a day the waters rise twenty feet, and descend the same amount."

Clearly Mrs. Stevenage had no interest in being instructed by Catherine. Her thin lips pursed in disapproval. "I fail to see why that makes it necessary for us to make this horrid trek just to reach the general's ship."

"Because at low tide, such as now, the

tidal basin is full of shallow ponds and mud so thick a man can sink out of sight and vanish." Catherine held on to her patience with great effort. Her beloved Andrew had once paid court to this woman. *Before he had met me*, Catherine comforted herself. Even now, after marrying an older officer stationed at headquarters, it looked as though Priscilla Stevenage remained bitterly resentful that she had lost Andrew. She was supposedly visiting Fort Edward to accompany her husband to this honored occasion, but Catherine was certain the woman had made the journey to see who had won the man she had once endeavored to claim for herself. Andrew's brief courting of Priscilla had been at his superior officer's suggestion, but he had soon realized that he did not want to pursue the relationship. Rumors suggested that Priscilla remained furious over this rejection.

Catherine kept her voice calm as she went on. "The French found a way to build dikes and reclaim much of the land. It is the finest farmland in the world, so rich it will grow anything. But to reach a vessel anchored in deep waters, it means we must build a pier out far enough to span the unclaimed muddy land."

"Only thing the French ever got right," her father muttered. "Building those dikes."

Priscilla gave another sniff, one of many mannerisms Catherine was swiftly learning to dislike. But before the woman could open her mouth and cast another barb, Catherine spied a familiar figure on horseback coming down the trail toward them at a brisk pace. She cried, "Here comes Andrew! Oh, I knew he wouldn't miss this evening!"

Normally the adjutant of a minor garrison like Fort Edward would not be invited to dine with a visiting senior officer. But Andrew had been acting commandant of the Fort Edward garrison since the colonel in charge had been stricken that spring with a severe fever and taken by barque to Halifax. That, plus the fact that Andrew's father and the general had been friends back in England, had resulted in the evening's invitation.

The young lieutenant reined his horse up close to the carriage and doffed his hat. "A very good evening to you, Miss Catherine," he said, bowing slightly toward her as she gazed at him from the carriage window.

"Welcome home, Mr. Harrow." She wished there were some way to hide from the others, to give him a proper greeting after the weeks apart. But all she could do was put everything she was feeling into her voice and eyes. No matter that the woman across from her was shooting daggers her way. Catherine motioned graciously to the other woman and went on, "Of course you know Mrs. Stevenage."

"Your servant, ma'am." Andrew gave a small bow, then turned to Catherine's father. "I bring you greetings from the Annapolis garrison, Mr. Price."

"Excellent, my young fellow. Excellent. You had a good journey?"

"Uneventful, save for the wretched state of the roads. Almost lost one wagon to a mud slide and another to a panicking mule." Lieutenant Andrew Harrow had to bend over to meet John Price's gaze. Which brought his face quite close to Catherine's. She resisted the urge to lean out the carriage window and kiss him then and there.

Even her father, who was as scant with his praise as he was with laughter, called Andrew Harrow a rare breed. The young man was not particularly tall, yet held his slender frame so erect that he seemed to tower over men half a head higher than himself. He wore his raven hair long and full, tied back tonight with a dark red ribbon the color of his dress uniform. Not for Andrew Harrow the stuffy confines of a powdered wig, not even on a night when he was to dine in the general's company. He held to the confident strength of a born leader and kept his men's ready allegiance with deceptive ease.

But it was neither his strength nor his heritage that had caused Catherine to love him, though in her heart of hearts she had to confess to liking both immensely. Andrew had a kinder side, a light to his pale blue eyes which seemed to grow in intensity whenever they were together. She loved that gentle light and wished for nothing more than to dedicate herself to strengthening it all their life long.

Andrew gave her a look then, one which seemed to say that he too was caught by the thought of reaching for her. Catherine knew a thrill of sudden fear that he would cause a public spectacle, but he gave her a mischievous smile before rising up tall once more in the saddle. "I'll just ride ahead to make sure the ship's boat is ready."

Catherine watched him spur his horse on, then dropped her gaze to her lap. She did not need to glance across to know Priscilla Stevenage was rewarding her with a look of sheer venom. A smile kept threatening to rise from the warmth of her heart and spread across her face. Not even Priscilla Stevenage could rob this day of joy.

Despite a naturally sour expression, the general obviously was putting himself out to make the evening pleasant for his guests. For Catherine, who had never been on a naval ship before, all was new and exciting. Priscilla Stevenage's sophisticated demeanor could not hide the fact that she was vastly impressed. The ship had been assigned to General Whetlock, co-commandant of all British forces stationed in Acadia Province, by Governor Lawrence himself.

The ship's decks had been holystoned until they gleamed a soft honey gold. Every rope was plaited with perfection, every railing freshly painted, the brass fittings polished until they shone. Even the cannons gleamed dull and ruddy in the fading sunlight. The crew who had manned the general's jolly boat had all worn fresh-starched white trousers and straw hats with ribbons fluttering in the evening breeze.

The ladies were lifted to the deck in what Andrew had called a bosun's chair and piped aboard by two fresh-faced youths, then greeted by the general himself. They were led to the aft stateroom and directed to carefully arranged places about the glittering table. The stateroom and the meal were much grander than Catherine had expected to find on board a ship. The cleanliness of everything surprised her as well. Andrew had said that the general, a friend of his father, would do them proud. But she had never expected to find such a welcome, and in such distinguished surroundings.

Catherine was so overcome that the meal was almost finished and she still had not managed to find her voice. But no one seemed to notice, since most of the talk swirling about the table was of war.

"I take my hat off to you, sir," the general declared to Catherine's father. "Keeping close watch over this garrison's supplies, locked in a backwater colony with the enemy for neighbors, that is one assignment I would run from. You have your work laid out for you, I daresay."

"Major Price served in His Majesty's forces for over a decade," Andrew pointed out.

"Well I know it. The notary of Fort Edward is highly spoken of in Halifax and Annapolis Royal both. The governor is well served to have you, sir. Well served."

John Price's expression did not change, but Catherine could see the flush on his cheeks and knew he was pleased. "I'd give my good leg for the chance to go back into service, I don't mind telling you, sir."

"Now, now. Ten years and a wounding

you've managed to survive is more than enough service for any man." The general wore long muttonchop sideburns, which were almost as white as his powdered wig. He was a large man with a booming voice, commanding the table with the ease of one born to rule. "Plus I might add that the service you continue to grant the Crown here and now is valued most highly."

"You are too kind, General."

"Not so," the general argued. "With the storm clouds gathering, there will be honor for all, no matter how they serve."

Priscilla Stevenage's husband, a broad-faced lieutenant with glittering green eyes, demanded, "Have the latest dispatches reported anything more?"

"Nothing except what any man with his head attached correctly would expect. War is coming, mark my words," the general said heavily. "The king of France is allying himself with anyone who is willing to put pen to paper. Princes in Spain, dukes of Sicily and Sardinia, even the ruler of the Ottomans, if rumors are to be believed."

Catherine did her best to ignore the discussion. Talk of war disturbed her greatly, especially when it dealt with the French. She was born and raised in the province of Acadia. This was the name given the land by the original French settlers who had arrived over a hundred years before the English had landed. For as long as Catherine could remember, there had been talk of this war or that, always far away, and always against the French. Yet she had lived under the shadow of Fort Edward all her life, with the French village of Minas so close she could see the rooftops from the fort towers. And there had never been any trouble with her unseen neighbors. Not ever. Though she had never laid eyes on a Frenchman outside the markets of Cobequid Town, she could not call them enemies. Mysterious, yes. Threatening, no.

She cast a glance around the room, taking in the darkened beams and the silver candelabra. The light flickered and danced over the silver and gold plating. The general's table was a broad slab of aged oak, polished with beeswax so she could see her reflection in its surface. Great iron hooks in each corner revealed how the table was raised and latched to the cabin's ceiling when not in use.

Her reflection twinkled back at her from a score of surfaces. The center of the table was lined with gold and jeweled ornaments, all of them polished until they shone like perfect mirrors.

Catherine wondered if it was as evident

to the dinner guests as it was to her that she was a provincial lass. She had sewn her dress herself, using drawings from an English journal and a bolt of the finest material brought last season from England. She wore it off the shoulder as the magazine had indicated but felt a bit uncomfortable with this, even though the June night still held to a bit of chill. She resisted the urge to reach up and lift the ruffles. Instead she touched her burnished brown curls and drew them forward over her shoulders. Her hair was her finest feature, she felt. That and her amber eyes, which were almost the identical color.

But the talk remained upon battles past and those yet to come. Priscilla Stevenage, the other woman at the table, sat across from her husband and offered supporting comments whenever he spoke up—which was rather often. Catherine found the voice of Lieutenant Randolf Stevenage to be particularly grating. A weak chin and flaccid features seemed an ironic contrast to his loud and aggressive manner. Catherine and Andrew exchanged glances when Stevenage had made a particularly belligerent comment. She knew what Andrew's feelings were about the French.

But the others at the table seemed utterly at ease with savagery and conflict. Suddenly the gold and silver gracing the table lost its glitter, and Catherine saw it for what it was—booty from previous battles. Prizes won at the cost of blood and suffering and fear and death. A flash of shivering premonition seemed to hold a trace of her own future.

Andrew leaned forward and murmured, "Are you cold, Miss Catherine?"

"No, I'm fine." She managed a smile and took strength from his concern. He was such a good man. Other women might have pursued him for his title and his dashing looks, the raven black hair and eyes the color of a winter sky. But she saw in his care and understanding all the other qualities which she loved most and which she vowed to nurture all her life long. The gentle nature he strived to hide from the world, the intelligence and the questing spirit, these were prizes far richer than all the gold in all the ships in all the world. Her smile rose to fill her gaze, giving to him all she could not put into words. Not there.

The general's voice boomed from the table's far end. "Miss Price, I fear we have bored you with all our talk of conflict."

"Not at all, sir." She hoped her sudden flush was hidden by the candlelight. "I am honored to be included among your distinguished company tonight."

The general smiled for the first time that evening. "A proper lady, with manners of one highborn. I shall report as much to Lord Harrow. Have you ever met the earl?"

"Alas, sir, I have never been to England."

"That is England's loss, my dear. One soon to be remedied, I hope."

To Catherine's relief, the table's attention was drawn away from her by the arrival of dessert. The general's two servants brought in steaming platters of bread-and-butter pudding, spiced with cinnamon and other scents of distant lands. They wore their hair in long tarred pigtails and had gold earrings. The man who served Catherine had a most remarkable design upon the back of his right hand. Inked into the very skin, a serpent coiled up his wrist and disappeared into his uniform's starched sleeve. As he put down the plate in front of Catherine, the serpent seemed to writhe and hiss at her. Another shiver coursed through her.

The general's attention returned to her after the servants had bowed themselves out. "What manner of activities keep you occupied, Miss Price?"

Despite the battery of gazes directed at her from every place around the table, Catherine was able to keep her voice even. "I keep my father's house, sir. My mother died when I was very young."

"She also helps with my records," John Price added, pride coloring his tone. "A finer hand with a pen and figures you will never find."

"A lady of talent and good sense." The general gave a ponderous nod and turned to Andrew. "I hear you are to be congratulated, young sir."

"Your words are perhaps a bit early, General, but I thank you nonetheless." Andrew reached across to clasp Catherine's hand. "I have indeed asked for Miss Price's hand in marriage, and I am happy to say that she has accepted, and her father has kindly granted his approval."

A chorus of murmurs rose from about the table. The general banged his knife loudly upon the surface. He rose to his feet and proclaimed, "Our ship is honored to be graced with your presence and your news. I am sure my officers will join with me in wishing you both a long and happy life together."

Chairs and benches and boots scraped as the men rose and joined with the general in saluting the pair. Only Priscilla Stevenage remained seated across from Catherine, her haughty stare and manner distancing herself from any well-wishing.

Catherine lowered her gaze in embarrassment at all the attention. This brought her again face-to-face with her reflection on the table, and for some reason this disturbed her even more than the other woman's cold gaze.

CHAPTER TWO

Louise Belleveau stood before the small pier glass in her bedroom and brushed her hair with forceful strokes. The dark hair beneath her brush crackled and sparked, as though catching her nervous fear. Henri Robichaud had been delaying for almost a month, arguing that they must wait for the proper moment. Something this important, he repeatedly told her, something which would change the course of their lives forever, needed the right time. But with everything that was happening, the perfect time might never come. Today would have to do. Henri must tell her family. She would insist on it.

She put her brush down, but her hair continued to fly at the edges in the dry air. The loose strands accentuated the anxiety reflecting back at her from the glass. Impatiently Louise gathered the long hair and contained it tightly in her fist. Though Henri preferred her to wear it free, shimmering and flowing with each movement of her head, today she would wear it modestly tied back in a ribbon. There was so much else to worry about now, she could not be concerned about her hair.

She lifted a blue ribbon, but it seemed too plain, so she added to it a yellow and a white. She had done this so often she did not even need to watch her fingers as she braided the three ribbons together and then lifted her arms to tie them into place at the back of her neck. Her dress was homespun, as was almost every garment worn by men and women alike in Minas. The English blockade had halted almost all trade with French ships for three long years, and while the markets of Cobequid and Annapolis Royal would accept some French-grown foods and handcrafted goods, there were far more pressing needs for their meager store of silver shillings than English cloth—not that anyone in the village would choose to wear anything British during the current siege.

Louise plucked at the starched white blouse which emerged from the neck and shoulder straps of her dress, lining up the blue-and-golden floral pattern of its apron. This garment was the finest she had ever made, the homespun tightly woven from threads as close in size and weight as she and her mother could manage, then dyed a lovely sky blue. The buttons up the front were carved by her brother from elk horn, and the silver pin by her lapel had been brought over from the old country by her great-great-grandmother. She took a deep breath and lifted her chin against the uncertainties of this day and the future. She looked almost as nice as any of the English ladies she had seen at market. But no such thought could halt a trickle of fear from racing down her spine.

Her gaze remained locked upon her own face, especially her eyes. She should be happy this day. A lifelong dream was soon to come true, one she knew would please her parents. But she did not see happiness reflected in her face. Only the worry, the nagging unrest over what might lay ahead.

Perhaps this was normal. Perhaps every woman faced distressing thoughts at such a time as this. Perhaps it was simply part of growing up, to feel concerns about Henri, about the day, about the future. But Louise had always envisioned this day holding laughter and celebration and perhaps even a fiddler and dancing.

Still, despite Henri's hesitations and her own worries, she knew they already had waited too long to break the news. Louise turned from her bureau, straightened her shoulders, and started for the door. Today was the day, no matter what.

Their home was built in the manner of French farmhouses in the province of Brittany, from where her ancestors had come over a century ago. The roof was high and steep and fell in protective shelving over the main house. The windows were small and shuttered, meant to allow in light yet guard from winter winds. A sturdy, spacious home, it was older than her father and so big that Louise had a room all to herself up under the eaves. She unlatched the door and started slowly down the stairs, wondering how she could ever think of living in any other home than this.

"Finally!" Her mother bustled from the kitchen, her exclamation in the French tongue sounding sharp in the midst of her busyness. "So, you decide to grace us with your company, after everyone else has worked their fingers to the bone. What kind of daughter is this?"

Louise's eyes moved from the flushed face of her mother to check the expressions of her two cousins and her aunt, who followed closely behind the matronly figure. Their faces betrayed nothing of their feelings.

"I was up before dawn making preparations for the meal," Louise replied, her voice so low her mother did not hear. The words were intended for the cousins. "I waited until it was almost too late for my bath."

The aunt's expression softened into a smile as she passed and murmured, "You are a good daughter, my dear. All the village says so, and your mother knows it well."

The words were a gift, and they did much to ease the shadows Louise had carried downstairs with her. She moved into the kitchen and picked up the final two bowls from the long central table. As she moved toward the door, a familiar figure stepped up. "Here, let me take one of those."

"I can manage." Her tone was more abrupt than she meant, and for an instant she heard echoes of her own mother. She glanced at the man she had loved since childhood and thankfully found only his familiar smile. "Oh, Henri. I'm so worried."

"I know you are," he whispered. He lifted a bowl from her hand and planted a quick kiss on her cheek. "But you were right, what you said last night. I must find the words today."

Yet his finally agreeing to speak did not give her the joy she hoped for. Instead, it only gave rise to all her other concerns. "If only things were different. All this uncertainty . . ."

He did not deny her words, nor echo her wish, but for an instant his normally cheerful gaze mirrored her anxieties. Then the familiar grin which danced through her dreams resurfaced, and he said, "I offer you the strength of my love."

It was the perfect thing to say to quiet her fears and give her back a feeling of optimism. He was good at that. The entire village knew that Henri had endured a lifetime of woe in his scant twenty-one years and had thrived despite it all. Even the tightest-lipped villager agreed that if any man was worthy of happiness and good fortune, it was Henri Robichaud. *Worthy*. Louise raised her chin and straightened her shoulders, determined that she would do right by this good man. Starting today. She followed her strong and stalwart man through the front door and over to the garden table.

Their arrival was greeted by a raucous welcome and knowing glances between the family members already gathered. An uncle, one who had joined them from across the bay, called, "It's Louise! Look, everyone. See, the village's most beautiful girl has decided to join us!"

Another uncle, her father's older brother, grinned broadly and showed toothless gums. "Your eyes are worse than mine. She's a girl no longer."

Her father's wide girth expanded with his evident pride. "True words, brother. We indeed have a princess in our midst!"

Louise's cheeks burned and she lowered her eyes at the extra attention. She came up beside her mother with the bowl. When the woman turned to accept it, her mouth was compressed into the thin, tense line she always wore when preparing a meal for guests. She opened her mouth to speak, and Louise knew it would be something about how hard it was to live in the same house with a would-be princess. But today when her mother glanced at her, dark gazes touched and spanned the distance of age and time. Louise's mother remained silent, and her eyes turned soft as the sunlight filtering through the sheltering trees.

Louise allowed her mother to take the bowl, then moved around the table to sit between her father and her younger brother. Her mother did not look her way again as she ladled out the steaming fish soup. She did not need to. Louise remained caught by all she had seen in her mother's gaze.

She found herself recalling a time from

long ago. Louise had been swinging upon a limb that even now reached out overhead. The apple trees which offered shade to this summer table had been planted by her father's father, and the limbs were twisted and gnarled by more than sixty hard Acadian winters. They had been perfect play areas for an adventurous young girl. But one day she had slipped and fallen, scraping her arm upon the table's corner. Suddenly blood was everywhere—on the ground, her dress, her hands, her face. She had run screaming into the house, terrified by the pain and the blood. Her mother had rushed up and swept Louise into her arms. Such strength had been found there, such comfort. Her mother had bathed the cut, all the while singing about a cat and a little girl and a moon that came down for tea. And suddenly the wound had not hurt so bad, and the fear had been banished. Louise had been able to sit and watch her mother probe the scrape, extracting a long splinter before tightening the clean white bandage. Then her mother had kissed the cloth and smiled and said, "There, I have taken all the pain away." And the little Louise had replied, "But it still hurts." So her mother had taken Louise's little hand and placed it upon her own heart, and said, "Then you must put it all inside here, and let me carry it for you."

Her father glanced over and demanded, "What's the matter, daughter? Is the soup not to your liking?"

"Oh yes, it's fine, really." Louise swallowed the lump of bittersweet memory and picked up her spoon. Why she would think of such things today, when all around her was more than enough to think about already, she did not know.

Her father smiled at her. Then his gaze lifted to the horizon, and his face tightened until deep lines stretched out from his mouth and eyes. He pointed with his spoon and asked his brother, "Did you cross in front of that British ship today?"

"Aye, that we did." Louise's uncle had the same strong face as her father, but it was set on a body that looked stretched upon the tanning rack. All sinew and stringy muscle, he was a man who ate little and spoke less. "Forty-eight guns and a general's flag."

"Fifty, Papa," chimed in Louise's young cousin. "You forgot the two stern chasers."

"We paddled right by the bowlines. Sailors leaned over and shouted something. Glad I didn't understand them."

Louise glanced at her youngest brother's face. Philippe traveled twice a year to Annapolis Royal to trade the farm's supplies and had picked up quite a bit of English. He had taken the family's fishing boat across the bay to bring back his uncle's family and would have heard what was said. Philippe was flushing with remembered anger, and he muttered, "Something foul."

"What business does a general's ship have down Cobequid Bay?" Louise's father mused aloud. "It's like watching a winter storm come crawling along the cove."

All the table turned from their food to look out over the naturally terraced landscape and down to where the Cobequid Bay stretched silver and blue beneath a cloud-chased sky. Their home stood at the village's edge, upon the first bank of cultivated land. Behind them rose rank after rank of forested mountains, from which they took both game and wood. Before them stretched the finest farmland any of them had ever heard of, land so rich it could grow almost anything, even within Acadia's short summer season.

Down another level spread the muddy tidal flatlands. Over the previous hundred and fifty years, the industrious Acadian farmers had built so many dikes they had reclaimed almost half the land. The dikes were long earthen barriers, standing higher than a man and running like ramparts in lines over a mile long. They truly were fortresses, standing stalwart and firm against the strongest tidal flow in the world.

At low tide, such as now, the deeper waters of Cobequid Bay seemed so narrow that it could almost be traversed on foot. Yet for many months each year, there was no way to cross to the other side except by circling all the way to Cobequid Town at the bay's far end. The muddy bogs became treacherous and impassable, laced with ice and unseen pits, and the central currents flowed so strong they kept ice from forming even during the most bitter of freezes. Which meant that through the long winter season Minas remained mostly cut off from the other French villages along the bay's opposite side.

This first summer family gathering was supposed to be a festive time, a moment to taste the cider pressed and jugged last autumn. A time of sharing the news of family and offspring. An opportunity to hear all that had happened during the long hard winter, and discuss the crops and plans for the growing season to come.

But this year, the news from beyond the bay was so worrisome there was little time given to anything else.

Louise's father was the head of the clan, and thus was the spokesman with the authorities in Cobequid Town. Her uncle demanded, "Jacques, have you heard anything more?"

"Nothing but what we all know. The English hold our Fort Louisburg. And the new edict stands as written. All Frenchmen in Acadia are required to take an oath of allegiance to the English king or forfeit all lands."

The loss of the small and isolated fort had long been expected. Even so, the oft-repeated news cast further gloom upon the table. Fort Louisburg was fifteen days' hard march from Minas, but with the general's gunship resting in tranquil Cobequid Bay, it might as well have been just around the southern point.

Louise's grandfather spoke in a voice creaky with age. "You won't remember this, but it has all happened before. Back before you were born they took one of our outposts, then made the same threat about oaths of allegiance. Every time there is war in Europe, the soldiers here make such noises."

"Maybe so," Louise's father replied. "But we've never had a general's ship come this far up the Cobequid before, have we?"

A man in clerical garb at the far end of the table spoke up for the first time. "I fear what Jacques says is correct." All eyes turned his way. The parish vicar was a good man, tall and learned and loved by all. Jean Ricard seldom joined in political discussions, one of the differences which separated his leadership in this Protestant Huguenot village from the priests in nearby Catholic towns. "I have traveled up to Cobequid Town as well, and spoken to the canon. At his request, I might add."

This was news. Years could come and go between meetings of their Huguenot vicar and the Catholic priest of Cobequid Town. "What did he tell you?"

"That the war may well move across the waters this time. That the English are bringing regiments up from the colonies of Massachusetts and New York, headed for the inland fortresses around Quebec."

Despite the warming sun, the mood at the table darkened perceptibly. Louise wished for some way to escape. Normally when talk turned to politics and threats from afar, she left the house. Today, however, she was unable to move. The news she waited for Henri to announce kept her firmly planted. She lifted her gaze to the last remaining apple blossoms overhead. As she did, a tiny golden shape flitted into view, a miniature hummingbird that poised before a blossom and drank in the space of a heartbeat. Such fragile beauty, such fleeting charm. She shivered, caught by the impression that she was struggling to hold to a happiness as delicate as those invisible wings.

She looked back at the group around the table in time to find her mother watching her. Marie Belleveau shared her daughter's dark eyes and strong features, but her countenance bore the wisdom of family and the years. Her gaze probed deep and drew from Louise the tears she had felt threatening all day long.

Their eyes unlocked, and her mother stood. "Enough!" The sharp word struck the table like a sword. "I tell you, enough!"

Even Jacques, who had lived with his wife and known her stormy moods for twenty-eight years, was taken aback. "What is it with you, wife?"

"Do we invite the English soldiers into our parlors? Are they people we would stop and talk with on the street?" Normally Marie Belleveau wore her dark hair long and braided, but today, being a feast and a gathering, she had drawn it up under her white formal bonnet. The starched hood formed a curving frame for her flashing eyes. "Then why must we make room for them here at our table? Why must they be our constant companion on a day when we are supposed to celebrate the summer?"

A stillness greeted her words. Then Jacques cleared his throat and said, "Marie, my dear, there is trouble. . . ."

"Not today, there isn't!" She waved expressive hands as though to gather up the laden table with its cluster of family and friends, the nearby cheeping birds and blossoming trees. "Show me trouble. Where on this day is there trouble except in your talk?"

It was the vicar who cleared his throat and said, "Madame Belleveau, you are correct in what you say. I ask your forgiveness for having brought such news to our celebration."

That their pastor himself would accept fault caused them all to pause. Silence reigned through the soup and on into the main course of roast goose, until Jacques cleared his throat and said, "Marie, you have done yourself proud once more. This is a feast fit for the king's table."

Smiles and relieved agreement broke out around the table. All clearly were glad to have peace restored.

Mother and daughter exchanged a long look, then Marie replied, "I could not have done it without Louise's help."

As the table's attention and compliments again turned her way, Louise's eyes sought rescue from the far end, down where Henri sat with the younger cousins.

But Henri remained focused upon someone farther down the table. Henri was perhaps the most popular man in the village, despite his lowly position. For his eyes shone with strength and calm confidence and something more. He seldom spoke, but he greeted the world with an invitation to make him smile, to laugh out loud. Henri must have felt her eyes on him and glanced back at her, a single nervous flicker that she would have missed had she not been watching him so closely. She knew this occasion was hard for him. Even so, it was something only he could do.

Henri nodded to the silent urging in Louise's glance and rose slowly to his feet. He stood there, clearly nervous and alone as attention turned his way.

Then he looked down the table to where she sat watching him, and his eyes cleared. His dark eyes were deep and full of all the mysteries of their future together. He gave her the smile that was for her alone, gentle and caring. And it gave her the strength to breathe.

Henri faced her father and let out the words in a quick rush. "Papa Jacques, Louise and I wish to wed."

Once more the table was shocked into

stillness. Louise clenched her hands, bunching up the sides of her embroidered dress. *That is not the correct way*, she wanted to cry out. She wished she could pull his words from the air and plant them back in Henri's mouth.

Henri glanced her way again, only this time she gave him a look she had learned from her mother. Stern and uncompromising, willing him to gather himself and try yet again.

Henri straightened his broad shoulders and forced himself to say the traditional words, ones brought from the old country and used for generations beyond count. "Father Belleveau, I hope—I hope that you know me and know my worth."

"I do indeed." Jacques Belleveau puffed his girth with obvious pleasure at Henri's proper correctness. He nodded ponderously to the smiling table. "A finer man I have never met."

"I love your daughter, and I have asked her to bind our futures together, to become one until—until the end of time." His stumble on the last phrase was rewarded with a murmur of encouragement from everyone at the table. Henri took another breath and finished with the customary petition, "I ask the blessing of Louise's father, our chief elder, and of all the clan."

Jacques Belleveau rose and drew his daughter up with him. The arm which settled around her held a strength so familiar and comforting that more tears filled her eyes. Jacques boomed, "Daughter, do you love this man?"

She wanted simply to nod, keep her face lowered, and hide her tears from view. Yet if Henri had the strength to endure the public spectacle, so too did she. When she raised her face, she found her mother staring up at her, and once again Louise recalled earlier difficult times and her mother's newly offered peace. Louise took a long breath and said the words she had heard said by women of her clan for as long as she could remember, "He is the one for me and for my life."

"Then you both have my blessings." Jacques Belleveau reached out another arm in invitation to Henri, combining the traditional benedictions on this union from his roles as father and clan elder.

The young man stumbled as he stepped over the bench and was steadied by a grinning uncle. When Henri joined them, Jacques intoned the words, "May you join as one. May your roots dig deep into this fine land, may your children stretch out across the years and the fields and the time beyond time."

Louise watched Jacques embrace the shorter Henri with fierce pride, knowing he had always had a special place in his heart for this young man. His voice boomed as he allowed his joy to shine with the words and the sun and the day. "May the Lord shine His light upon you. And may you be blessed with many sons!"

The laughter and the cheering died gradually away as Marie Belleveau rose to her feet. Even for Louise, who knew her mother as well as anyone, it was hard to predict what the woman would say.

Marie clasped her hands across her fine apron and raised her head so that the bonnet no longer masked the light in her eyes. She did not look at Louise, but rather at Henri. And she said in a voice meant for the entire gathering, "Henri Robichaud, I have known you your entire life and watched you grow from a tragedy that would have crippled most men. I have watched you become a man who is a mark of pride for the parents who are no more." She stopped then and turned to her daughter with eyes that sparkled dark and calm. But her words remained for the man and for the table. "It will give me great joy to invite you into our clan and our home. When you hear me call you son, know it is a word I use with pride."

The cheer that rose was one of unbridled joy, for Marie was a woman known more for her caustic tongue than words of praise. Louise felt her fiancé grasp her hand and draw her around the table to where they were both embraced by Marie Belleveau. Louise was bumped and jostled as people made room for them to sit together at the table. She heard a call for music and another call for a toast, and then listened as the pipes and fiddle and accordion started off on a merry tune.

All the while Louise wondered how it was that her mother had known all along what the day was to hold.

Henri's strong hand squeezed her own, and she raised her gaze to meet his. His voice low, he asked, "Did I do it well?"

"You did it perfectly," she said, glad for the music to mask their words. "I am very proud of you."

"You know I am not one for speaking before others."

"It makes what you did even nicer."

He grinned his special smile, the one which filled his eyes with that passion for life and for her that stirred her soul. He started to say something else, but hands reached for Henri's shoulders, drawing him up and

51

around to accept congratulations.

Louise smiled in response to the well-wishing she scarcely heard. Then her attention was caught by the scene down below their orchard and their celebration. The general's ship sat in the middle of Cobequid Bay, blocking the waters with quiet menace. Despite the joyful music and her friends gathered here on this brilliant day, Louise felt a shiver run through her frame. It seemed as though the ship was a warning lurking upon the outer edges of her day.

CHAPTER THREE

Tinny strains of music floated through Catherine's window as she prepared her father's evening meal. It was one of the many chores that defined her day. Only now the tasks held a special poignancy, because it was only three weeks until she would no longer be the one to add comfort and order to her father's world.

Though it was the middle of June, the breeze drifting through her window carried a hint of chill. Still she did not close the shutters, preferring instead to tighten the shawl about her shoulders. The air held the fragrant spices of blooming trees and the music of songbirds. The sun descended toward the western hills, turning the Cobequid waters to gold. Catherine could just make out the general's ship, a somber shadow cut from the waters and the light. Even in the safety of her home, she was conscious of the threat it represented, resting there in the calm waters of her homeland. She shook her head and went to stoke the fire. Her father would soon be home.

The door creaked back on its leather hinges. "Daughter?"

"Good evening, Papa." Catherine used the towel to wipe the flour from her hands. "How was your day?"

"Passable. Fair and passable." He stopped in the alcove and used the metal staff to draw off his muddy boots. He watched as she picked up his house slippers from beside the fire and brought them over. "I saw your young man at dockside. He was on his way out to the general's vessel."

Catherine's face flushed at the mention of Andrew, but she kept her poise as she extended her hand to her father. "Here you are."

As he fitted on the fur-lined slippers, her gaze lifted to glance out the open front door. The ship filled the waters and the evening with a brooding menace. "I won't be sorry to see the last of that," she murmured.

"Eh?" John Price straightened and followed her gaze. "Strange for you to say such a thing, daughter. Especially as the general has offered to convey his commendation of your marriage to Andrew's family in England."

"I can't help how I feel." She sighed as she wiped her clean hands on her apron and walked back to the kitchen. "Did Andrew say how long he would be?"

"The lad will be there as long as the general requires his presence." John Price limped with a heavy tread across the raw planked flooring. "General Whetlock is under direct orders from Governor Lawrence. That he would send for Andrew at all can only be good for the lad's career."

"I wish the general and his ship were gone." Catherine regretted the words as soon as they were spoken. Her father could turn hot and sharp at the drop of what he considered a single improper comment. He was a good father but stern, and his anger was never too far from the surface. It was said about the garrison that John Price excelled at his work precisely because of these qualities. He could make the most recalcitrant drover move lively and could squeeze the truth from a stone.

But today he awkwardly shuffled to the

fireplace and stood looking down at the fire. The old war wound had left him with one leg slightly shorter than the other, causing him to rock back and forth as he walked. John Price said to the flames, "Your mother did not like the ships either."

Catherine's hands stilled over her work. She could not recall the last time he had spoken of her mother.

"She used to call them harbingers of doom," John Price continued. The hearthstones glowed ruddy and bright, and the light reflected upon her father's features, turning his features old and sad. "She said that whenever they appeared they trailed the flag of war behind."

Catherine forced herself to move, to reach for a mug from the wall hook and pour a cup of steaming cider. She walked over and said softly, "Here, Father. You must be parched."

"Thank you, daughter." He lifted the pewter mug to his lips without raising his gaze from the fire. When he had sipped the hot brew, he went on, "It will be a lonely house when you have gone."

She tried for a cheerful tone. "I shall only be just down the lane. You know Andrew has taken hold of the old Elton place." Her laugh sounded strained to her own ears. "That should keep the parish carpenters busy for years to come."

"Yes." He drained the mug and handed it back, his eyes rising to fasten upon her face. "You cannot imagine how much you have come to resemble your mother."

"I wish I had known her."

"No more than I do, child. She was the finest woman God ever made. She . . ." The gaze dropped back, as though memories were too heavy to keep aloft. "When the fever took her the second year after you were born, I thought for certain I would never make it alone. You were so tiny and there was so much I didn't know."

"You did a good job, a fine job. The best anyone could have."

As though John Price had not even heard his daughter's words, he continued, "Thank God for our neighbors. The village wives took turns with you through that first winter. It seemed that none of them would allow us to be on our own. Then the Widow Simmons offered to help out. You remember her, of course."

"I think so." She had memories as fragile as winter sunlight of a woman whose face was seamed and ancient. Yet whose eyes had been bright and clear, and whose hands were always open to receive her.

"Mrs. Simmons lived in the room off the back, where your mother and I . . ." John Price turned and limped over to his chair. He lowered himself into the seat and stared again at the fireplace flames. "She stayed with us until her chest grew foul. I think that was your fifth year. She went and lived with her son after that, until she departed this life the next midwinter."

He was talking to the fire and not to her, Catherine realized, allowing the memories to rise and drift with the crackling blaze. "Then the rector's wife decided to set up our little school. That was a blessing, I don't mind telling you. You were so excited to be off to school, so eager to go in the mornings I could hardly hold you to tie the sash on your dress."

Catherine used a swift gesture to clear her eyes. She did not want anything to disturb these recollections. Normally John Price lived as though the past did not exist. Even to her simplest questions as a little girl he had sharply replied that nothing could be gained from dwelling upon what once had been. So she stood, scarcely breathing, quietly wiping her eyes only enough that she could see her father clearly.

"You were handling the broom before your little hands could even reach around the handle. Following the charwoman about the place, copying her motions. Learning to cook from the neighbors. Even the garrison cookhouse woman had told me how you had pestered her with questions until she couldn't remember whether she was coming or going."

His ruddy features stretched into a sad smile. "The rector's wife liked to tell me how you would energetically take on your lessons, until you were sitting with the children twice your age. Smart, you were. Smart and quick and eager to help your old papa with the housework. I was sorry you had to grow up fast, but there was little I could do about it. Your mother was gone, and I watched you try as hard as you could to take her place, even before you knew exactly what it was you were doing."

He looked at her then, but Catherine was not sure he was seeing much beyond his own memories. "I hope Andrew realizes just how lucky a man he is, taking you to his home."

Catherine found enough of her voice to reply, "I think he does."

He returned his gaze to the fire and the past. "It's a shame your mother will not be there on your wedding day."

"Thank you, Father." The words seemed so inadequate, but nothing of their quiet life together had prepared her for this chance to say all she had on her heart and mind. How his gruffly abrupt ways had forced her to work hard, ever hoping for a word of approval. How she had missed the woman she had never known, how her heart had ached for the touch of a mother. How even seeing a villager carrying a child or smiling over a crib had sometimes brought tears to her eyes.

Since the words could not be found, she took refuge in the work that had shaped their life together. She reached into the back of the corner shelf and drew out the last jar of the previous summer's fruit. She used the knife to break the wax seal and announced, "We'll have your favorite dessert tonight, Father. Plum pudding."

The room behind her was silent for a long time, quiet enough for the sounds of merrymaking to drift over from the distant French village. Finally her father murmured, "Your mother would be very proud of you, Catherine. Very proud indeed."

She didn't even notice the tear that dripped from her chin into the pudding.

Andrew heard the music rise from the French village as he stood against the ship's railing. He did not care much for ships and the sea. Far too confining, with four hundred and fifty men crammed into a vessel less than two hundred paces long. With the cannonballs well stacked and the smell of gunpowder everywhere, it was impossible to move far from the stench of war on a ship of the line. The burly, tattooed sailors with their long pigtails might be jolly jack-tars and the backbone of the British Empire, but Andrew was far more comfortable ashore. Ships like this always reminded him of his departure from England and all he had left behind forever.

"Ah, Harrow. Summoned yet again?"

Andrew stifled a groan and turned a blank face toward the approaching officer. Lieutenant Randolf Stevenage had long considered Andrew a rival, and not just over his new wife's affections. Stevenage's father, a regimental commandant, had granted his son officer status through the ancient right of ancestral assignment. Stevenage held a resentment bordering on loathing for the more capable younger man whose position had been bestowed on merit.

Andrew calmly replied, "The general sent for me, yes."

Randolf Stevenage leaned his bulk against the railing. A year of eating at the governor's table in Halifax had further padded his already substantial form. "Come tomorrow, you'll be using a mite more respect when you address me. I've been promoted to captain."

Andrew was far from surprised. Stevenage's ambitions were matched only by those of his new wife, Priscilla. Though Halifax was four days' hard ride from Fort Edward, and the Stevenages had been wed for less than a year, already the rumors of greed for power were filtering back. "Permit me to offer my congratulations."

"Kind of you." He smirked out over the waters. "Yes, the governor decided his new adjutant required a bit more authority behind his orders."

"So you're to remain stationed in Halifax?"

"Indeed. There's trouble afoot, and the governor wanted the best man possible for the posting." Randolf Stevenage squinted out to where music rose in the distance. "What is that confounded racket?"

"It sounds like a celebration of some sort. It appears to be coming from the village of Minas."

"Ah, of course. Those Frenchies will

dance at the drop of a hat." He turned his back to the music and the peaceful scene. "Speaking of celebrations, that's quite an attractive little lass you've found for yourself."

Andrew could trust himself only with "Thank you, sir."

"Not at all. Not at all. Astonishing how such a rose could grow from these muddy colonial climes. But there you are. No doubt you will manage to train her in time." Stevenage stared at Andrew's face for a moment, and a note of satisfaction crept into his voice. "Of course, these colonials can be such a stubborn lot. But you've had years of training menials, haven't you? No doubt you're up to the task."

Andrew was saved from checking a superior officer by the general's booming voice. "That will do, Stevenage."

The heavy man forced his girth off the railing. "Sorry, sir. Didn't hear your approach."

"No. So I noticed." The general's stony gaze did not waver. "For your information, I found Harrow's fiancée to be a most remarkable young lady. It bodes well for the new acting commandant of Fort Edward to have shown such discrimination in his choice of a mate."

"Yes . . . that is—I beg your pardon, did

you say—?"

"Yes, I said 'commandant.' Ah, the governor neglected to mention that, as you were not party to that discussion, were you? No." The general swiveled his gaze like a pair of gray gun barrels toward Andrew. "Word of your work as acting commandant found its way back to Halifax. I am happy to report that the governor feels, and I quite agree, that you should be granted a further nine months to test your mettle. Of course you will be granted the rank of captain, subject to your successful completion of these new duties. Of which I have no doubt."

General Whetlock's cold gaze returned to Randolf Stevenage. "Naturally, you would like to be the first to congratulate your fellow officer."

Stevenage forced the word through a constricted throat. "Congratulations."

Andrew could not fully hide his elation at the news. "Thank you."

"Now then, Stevenage. Be so good as to allow me to have a private word with Harrow here." The general grasped Andrew's arm and led him up to the quarterdeck, the private domain of every ship's commander. When they stood by the higher railing, the older man said in a conversational tone, "This area strikes me as holding a strong inclination to frigid storms. Even here in June I smell the coming snow, if you catch my meaning. Tell me, young Harrow. What is it like here in the twilight of winter?"

"Cold, sir." Andrew was truly grateful for the general's gift of a moment to collect himself. "Uncommon cold."

"That I can well imagine." An eye that looked to be experienced at judging men fastened upon him. "And yet you choose not only to serve here but make it your home."

Andrew looked out over the bay a moment. He held his tongue more comfortably this time. The general knew his family, so there was no need to speak of his older brother, the new earl of Sutton. It had been his beloved father who had seen the coming sibling conflict, and when he had grown ill that final time had ordered his younger son to depart for the colonies. The king's law was clear on this point. The splitting of noble estates was expressly forbidden. The land, the house, the vast majority of the family's wealth, all was destined for the elder son's hands.

And still Andrew's jealous brother had considered him a threat.

Andrew's father had done the best he could under the law's constraints. A commission in the King's Own Regiment and a stipend established in his name granted Andrew a career. But Andrew had been banished to the colonies—there was no other word for it—and instructed never to return. Andrew had accepted the edict because it had been his father's final request. "I hope you understand, Andrew," he had gasped out on his deathbed, "this is for your protection."

Andrew turned back to the general and replied simply, "This is indeed my home."

"Yes, well. On to business." The general turned and started pacing across the holystoned deck. "As you know, Fort Edward is our only bastion between here and Annapolis Royal, four days' hard ride to the southwest."

The general motioned a torch-bearing sailor to enter the quarterdeck and light the two lanterns. Their glow joined with light from the rising moon to dispel the dusk. "The governor has requested I make this journey up Cobequid Bay to ensure the roads stay well patrolled. Those men you brought in, your new troops. What did you make of them?"

"Raw recruits fresh off the boat from home, sir. English farm boys, most of whom have never handled a musket before."

"Well, you are expected to whip them

into shape, and be swift about it."

Andrew gave a short nod, but he took the opportunity to voice the doubts that had accompanied him all the way back from Annapolis. "England is four thousand leagues distant, sir. Surely the conflict cannot engulf us here."

"Can and will, Harrow. Can and will." The general stomped to the portside railing and stood staring out toward the glimmering lights of Minas, warm and inviting. The sound of cheerful music drifted over the water. But the general's tone remained cold and battle hard. "The trouble may not reach us this year. Perhaps not even next. But it is coming, you mark my words. It is most certainly coming."

CHAPTER FOUR

Catherine's fingers tugged gently at the strings of her bonnet. She wished she could push it back onto her shoulders and let the slight breeze blow through her hair and cool her flushed face. But she feared being seen, even on this remote trail. Some patrolling British soldiers would be scandalized to see a young woman out walking without proper head covering.

Though it was a warm day, that was not

the only reason the blood raced through her veins and flushed her cheeks. Tomorrow—tomorrow was her wedding day. It was finally arriving, close enough now for her to feel the long wait at last coming to an end. She really was to become the wife of Lieutenant Andrew Harrow. Her cherished cedar chest, filled with bed linens and kitchen stock, was at the very moment being delivered to their recently acquired quarters. Her personal belongings would accompany her after tomorrow's ceremony.

Yet more than impatient agitation had driven her from the confines of her father's house. On a recent market trip with her father she had spotted a secluded meadow, west and south of town and two ridges higher than the village. It had lain well off the trail, hidden almost entirely by the surrounding forest. Through the greenery of branches she had caught glimpses of bright flower patches. Her father had been busy guiding the two-wheeled cart over the rough hillside trail. She had not mentioned her discovery at the time, but had secretly promised herself that soon she would return to explore it on her own.

She had been totally entranced by the secret spot and found herself thinking of it by day and dreaming of it by night. She had not been able to get back to it before now, just a day before her wedding. She hoped there would still be flowers to decorate the chapel, maybe even her veil.

As she climbed, Catherine imagined the changes that took place in the secret meadow with the advancing of each day's hours. The sun rising over the trees and streaming in at high noon, making the entire sheltered world enriched by a golden glow, then fading to the soft, shadowy blue tints of early evening, and then on to a mysterious wonder-world lit by the mellow moon and flickering stars of night. Catherine caught herself hoping that no one else knew of its existence. It had seemed an almost ideal, ethereal place. She longed to claim it as a place she might escape to, even after she was married. She yearned for a haven, one removed from the rumors and ill-tidings which disturbed her happiness.

Catherine's step quickened along with her pulse. Would the meadow really be as magical as she had envisioned? Was it still there? Was it owned by another? She hoped with all her heart that it could be claimed as her own.

She hadn't told her father or even Andrew about her destination. John Price had merely nodded absentminded assent when she had said she was going to gather flowers for her bridal bouquet. She had not divulged that the meadow she sought was a good distance from the little village. She knew he might object to her traveling so far alone. Not that there was any real reason to be concerned. It was rare indeed that the Micmac Indians came so close to the settlement. In her entire lifetime, Indians had not entered the village more than three or four times. Occasionally she saw them fishing the tidal basins, but normally they preferred to hunt and fish farther from the white settlements. Nor had Catherine ever sought association with the French. But neither had she been given any personal reason to fear them. Still, she knew that her father, especially with the renewed war rumors, might hold to an entirely different view.

She couldn't wait to fill her arms with the brilliant colors of meadow flowers. They would not only grace her wedding bouquet but would lift her heart to beauty, giving her an inner strength that she knew she would need to be the wife—and perhaps one day the mother—that she should be.

Her thoughts naturally turned to Andrew, and her cheeks flushed even more deeply. How she loved and admired him. She longed to be all that he thought her to be. She wanted to be a part of his world. To understand his thoughts. To share his deepest feelings. Much of himself he had shared with her. She loved him all the more for it. But when it came to matters of his calling—his duty as a king's soldier—he seemed closed off. Apart from her. When she tried to draw him out in conversation, he seemed reluctant to speak. Women were not to concern themselves with military matters, he had kindly told her on one such occasion. But, she had objected, they were not just military matters, they were matters that would affect each and every member of the small settlement, and more importantly, they would greatly affect the life and safety of her future husband. And as his wife she wished to be a part of every facet of his life.

He had squeezed her hand and smiled. "And so you shall be, my dear," he had insisted. "You shall pack my provision kit and kiss me good-bye and be waiting with a light in the window for my return." Though she sensed that was all the information about his chosen career he was willing to divulge, she knew that his eyes had warmed with appreciation at her concern. He had seemed to be proud that his wife was genuinely interested in the affairs of state and how it affected her community as well as the man she was to marry.

Catherine supposed she must be satisfied with the areas of his life that he was presently willing to share. Perhaps in time she would win his complete trust, and he would open the details of his life more freely.

She slowed her steps, feeling a sudden hesitancy. At long last her meadow was to be explored. She was about to step into the meadow from the shadows of the protective forest. She took a deep breath. Would it be as she had imagined?

She swept aside low-lying branches of a willow tree and stepped past, her long cotton skirts pulling at the green of the bushes. *Yes*. The meadow was as beautiful as she had remembered. And no one was about to disturb her solitude.

Surrounded on all sides by towering trees, the glen extended before her like a great outdoor cathedral, canopied by a sweep of glorious sky. Birds flitted across the arch of blue, calling to one another. A large gray squirrel granted Catherine a chirping welcome.

She couldn't help but smile as she moved forward, letting the branch swing back into place like a door closing behind her. She was alone among flowers and birdsong and lazy-drifting clouds high overhead. It was exhilarating. Breathtaking. She sank down on her knees and buried her face in the closest bank of blossoms, breathing deeply of their fragrance. Then she lifted her eyes heavenward and spoke from a full heart. "Thank you."

The words surprised even herself. She was not accustomed to spontaneous, heart-felt prayer. Her prayers had been learned. Structured. Repeated in a formal litany. But her overflowing heart could no more have stifled her gratitude to God than her hands could have kept from reaching out to the nearest flowers. "I will have the most beautiful bouquet a bride ever carried up the aisle," she whispered to herself. But she did not hurry to collect the dainty blooms. She wanted time. Time to enjoy the luxury of this world set apart. Time to feel the warmth, the strength, the hope that this new place of peace instilled in her heart. This was exactly what she needed to refresh her soul.

Again she spoke quietly. "Mama, if you were here, if you could be with me today, I feel this is exactly the place you would have taken me. This place of serene calm, of beauty. I'm so glad I found it."

Catherine shifted her position to sit among the meadow grasses, her long skirt tucked up under her legs, her fingers trailing gently through the flower faces on either side, a smile slowly tilting the corners of her mouth. Though the setting was new to her, she felt wonderfully at home.

Empty basket in hand, Louise Belleveau crossed the small footbridge over the river's narrowest point and made her way up the hillside. The main trail leading along the ridgeline was far too risky these days. British soldiers seemed to be everywhere, their horses stomping and blowing, the saddles creaking and muskets rattling. Though she could not understand the words, their voices always sounded angry and harsh. Louise gave no thought to the Micmac. She had been taught to consider the Indians her friends since childhood. Well, not friends exactly. Allies. The thought of meeting a small hunting party in the woods brought no flicker of fear. The British soldiers, though, were another matter entirely. Her father had often solemnly cautioned her and the rest of the village against unnecessary contact.

Henri's warning had been far more personal. When she had once spoken of her love of such forest walks, his eyes had darkened and his normally jovial tone had vanished entirely. "Take great care, *ma chérie*," he had cautioned. "They are not to be trusted. Even the eye of an uncivilized Brit can see that you are a beautiful woman."

Louise was secretly pleased that he was so protective. It made her feel much more confident of her safety and of her place in his heart. Even so, she had no intention of forsaking her walks. But she did pay far more attention than ever before. For Henri.

Now she walked quietly through the trees, eyes and ears alert to any movement, any sound about her. Henri had once joked that she moved through the woods like a Micmac. Like a silent shadow, he had said. Louise smiled at the recollection.

In spite of his natural reserve, Henri had said many things to her that sent her heart racing. She could hardly wait for the ceremony of the morrow that would finally bind her to him for a lifetime. It had seemed so long in coming that she had often chafed in impatience. "I will be an old woman before becoming a bride," she had complained at one point when Henri still seemed to be stalling. But now the actual day was close—tomorrow. Tomorrow when the birds began their morning song, she and Henri would be preparing themselves for the sacred vows. Louise wanted the house and the chapel filled with flowers to add to their celebration of the occasion. She knew exactly the place to find them—the meadow on the hillside overlooking the village.

Since the day she had discovered it, Louise had visited the meadow whenever she could slip away. She had fallen in love with the solitude and the peace it offered. The highland glen was a wonderful place to draw apart. To close her eyes and pretend that all the uncertainty, all the troubles that seemed to wreath the entire village like blue curling smoke, did not exist. In the meadow she could shut it all out. Quiet her thoughts to concentrate only on good things. Her future life with Henri. The children that she hoped to one day have. She wanted the first to be a boy, just like his father. She would be so proud to cradle Henri's son.

Her cheeks flushed at the thought of being a wife and mother, and she quickened her steps and hurried through the shadows of another grove. In her anticipation, she almost lost her caution, so she checked her steps and looked carefully into the sea of green before advancing farther into the meadow.

Yes, she was alone as usual.

Her mother would scold if she spent too long on her errand. Louise could hear her clicking off the anxious words. *Have you no idea how many things remain to be done to be ready for the wedding guests? You think that food prepares itself? Maybe the wild turkeys will climb into the ovens of their own accord.* Louise smiled again. It was true. There was much to be done. She had been working hard since before daybreak. Even so, her mother had been working even harder. Louise tried in vain to imagine her mother slipping away for a bit of respite during the day.

With her conscience getting the better of her, Louise began quickly to gather armloads of flowers for her baskets. As much as she longed to linger, to quiet her heart and prepare her mind for what was to come, she must get home to help finish the wedding feast preparations. With the rising of another sun, family and friends would be streaming into the simple but spacious house, spilling out under the trees in the yard, boisterous and merry and ready to celebrate her joy in becoming Madame Henri Robichaud. She must finish her quest and hurry home.

A hint of movement to her left brought Catherine's head up quickly. Her first thought was that she had unwittingly invaded a bear's territory. Her pulse raced even faster as she imagined another human stealthily moving near. Actually, she had heard nothing and seen no one. But then she had been wrapped in her dreams, oblivious to the world around her. She slowly rose, her head swiveling around, eyes searching as her feet prepared for flight.

Catherine's frantic gaze fell upon the form of a young woman moving across the meadow, filling her arms with flowers. Even at this distance Catherine knew by her dress that she was Acadian. A Frenchwoman was sharing her meadow. Catherine felt a keen flash of disappointment, then resentment. What right did a French villager have to be here? This was a British meadow.

Catherine momentarily let her gaze move down the hillside, sweeping the plain, the coastline below. To her surprise, she discovered that both villages nestled below. The British settlement of Edward with its outlying fort on the one side and the French village of Minas on the other.

Catherine turned back to the approaching French girl. Indeed, she was probably her own age, barely eighteen, quite pretty in a pixyish sort of way, with dark hair flowing about her face. The flashing dark eyes never left the flowers growing among the meadow grasses as she reached for one after the other. She wore a long-sleeved dress of simple homespun, with an embroidered apron, and a starched white bonnet hanging down her back. Such clothes would have identified an English lady as coming from peasant stock. Yet on her the garb seemed appealing and unaffected. She was close enough now that Catherine could hear her singing softly to herself as she walked, probably some little French ballad.

Catherine had once spoken and read French so well her teacher had stopped instructing and merely urged her to continue with her reading and writing. Yet the books had been packed away for years, and now she could only catch a word here and there of the French girl's merry song. Something about a French maiden, loved by a daring cavalier.

The girl was approaching the center of the oval-shaped meadow. Catherine realized that it was only a matter of minutes until she would be discovered. Should she move forward, greet her? She did not wish to startle the girl as she herself had been. But certainly she should make her presence known.

Slowly and deliberately she took a step forward, her eyes never leaving the oncoming singer. Just as she thought, the simple movement brought the dark head up. The song stilled on the lips, the eyes threw an anxious look her way. The woman stopped in midstride. The two stood several feet apart, flowers on their arms, a startled, questioning expression on each face. Still and staring at each other.

The French girl was the first to move and break the silence. With a slight nod of her dark head, she spoke one word. *"Bonjour."* Her voice was soft. Musical. Catherine found herself hoping she would say more. When she didn't, Catherine murmured, "Good morning." She offered a tentative smile of her own and followed up with a nervous, accented "Bonjour," and a dip of her head.

Then each girl moved off in opposite directions, totally absorbed in completing the gathering of bouquets. As Catherine left her side of the meadow she glanced back over her shoulder. She saw only a brief glimpse of dark hair and the flash of skirt as the other young woman disappeared into the greenery of the forest.

CHAPTER FIVE

The first day of July dawned with a sky etched by just a few clouds, enough to lend depth to endless shades of blue. The fields, growing tall and fragrant, lay below forested green mountains standing like protective sentinels beneath the sun's glow. The distant waters of Cobequid Bay sparkled like a mirror. By midday the entire village of Minas had turned out for the wedding of Louise Belleveau to Henri Robichaud. It was a tale made for generations of winter fires, a story to warm the hearts of young girls as they dreamed of their own days to come in the sun of romance and love. How a girl lovely enough to capture the heart of any French nobleman had instead given her heart to one of their own.

When his peers were still delighting in childhood games, Henri Robichaud had been forced to mature beyond his years. His father had gone first, dead of a fever that one summer had swept away almost a third of the village. His mother had followed only two days later, so soon that their burials had taken place the same afternoon. Poor Henri, only twelve years old, faced further trauma on top of tragedy as his family's crops threatened to rot in the fields.

Louise drew her thoughts back to the present with a little shake of her head and allowed her mother to straighten her dress and retie the wedding bonnet with its long satin bow—the only satin to be found in the entire village. Her embroidered dress was cut in time-honored style, falling loose and long so she had to grasp it in one hand as she carefully stepped down the stairs. The stairs to her home, the only home she had known. Louise felt a gentle constricting of her heart as she moved down one step, then the next, knowing that she was walking into her future. One which beckoned to the longing in her heart, yet included many unknowns.

As she pushed through the front door of the Belleveau cottage, she saw villagers she had known all her life smiling and murmuring a welcome. Beyond this crowd was yet another throng, one larger still and made up of neighbors from surrounding villages and hamlets. A mist veiled her eyes, making their faces indistinct. Her vision was dimmed by all the bittersweet emotions swirling through her heart and mind.

Louise had known since her eleventh year that she was going to marry Henri Robichaud. And there he was now—she could just make him out as the crowd parted before him, making a path up to where he stood in his new dark coat and white shirt. She felt more than saw his beloved smile, the one which had never diminished, never faded, even during those first years of struggling mostly on his own.

As Louise continued walking toward the familiar form, she thought she saw villagers point at Henri and murmur traces of the famous story. How Henri Robichaud had slaved through that first summer alone. Almost every family in Minas had lost someone to the fever. Louise could still remember the sadness in her own home over the tiny basket by the fire, the one which had remained as forlorn and empty as her parents' gaze. And because the sadness was so total, and most were hard pressed to manage their own harvests, few had the strength or the time to offer more than a word of sympathy about young Henri Robichaud's plight.

But Henri had not asked for help. Not even when the first chill winds of September arrived, and his family's fields remained only half cleared. Those who were aware of it had admired the young boy for trying so hard, but they also assumed he would be forced to leave the house and fields and go to live with relatives or to work for another farmer.

It had been Louise who had passed by the Robichaud farm that fateful day and found Henri collapsed in the field. She had run home for her father as fast as her eleven-year-old legs could carry her. Together they had gone back, only to see that the young boy had struggled to his feet and returned to his harvesting. Now, as Louise walked on through the happy throng, she remembered that time as clearly as if it had happened only yesterday. Her father had plucked the hoe from Henri's hands, then stared down at a handle sticky with blood. Her father had turned over the boy's palms to see the flesh scraped and torn. The boy had tried to pull away, but he had scarcely enough strength left to stand. Henri had stared at the bewildered older man and said simply, "This is Robichaud land." And then he had fainted a second time.

By the same fever which had robbed Henri of his parents, Jacques Belleveau had been made clan elder. One of his first edicts was to ask for help to save the Robichaud farm and bring in the harvest. The vicar, newly arrived to take the place of the previous pastor, who had not survived the epidemic, had silently joined in alongside Jacques and Louise, clumsy in his efforts but strong in his silent urgings to give aid and comfort to the young lad.

Somehow the community's sharing of

this particular hardship had helped to lift the pall of sadness and loss which had settled upon the village. The winter had come and gone, and with spring there was a readiness to face the future once again. That next season of planting and harvesting had found many willing hands to help Henri with his work. And over the years to come, Henri Robichaud had repaid the village a hundred times over. Strong and cheerful, he had grown up ever ready to lend a hand to whoever needed help, free with his gifts of game and fish and fruit and strength. All the village counted him a friend.

Louise's pounding heart returned her attention to the present. The vicar waited just beyond Henri, Bible in hand. His broad-brimmed hat and his best black cassock were in direct contrast to the warm, approving smile. From those hard beginnings Pastor Jean Ricard had grown to be a welcome part of the village, a true man of God with a heart for Acadia.

To the one side of the vicar, the girls holding the traditional marriage pole waited in giggling anticipation. The flowers Louise had gathered from the highland meadow formed a colorful crown at the top of the pole. Long ribbons shivered in the fresh breeze to be gathered after the wedding ceremony in the lilting maidens' dance.

Henri's eyes met hers in a silent message for her alone, and he stepped up beside her. The vicar turned and led the assembly up the hill to the white chapel. The Minas church, in a field of bluebells and buttercups, was the village's oldest building, dating back to the earliest days of their settlement. A low stone wall rose behind the church, marking the boundaries of the village cemetery. Some of the headstones were so old that time and winter winds had erased the names of those who rested there. Louise took in a deep breath of the summer air, and thought there could be no finer wish on this most wonderful day than to live her life among family and friends, to be the wife of Henri Robichaud and raise their children, then die and be buried here in the heart of Acadia.

As Louise trod the familiar path to the chapel entrance, she caught sight of a group of men standing by the cemetery walls, staring northward, up beyond the Minas River to where smoke rose from the English settlement. She felt a flash of irritation. How could they think of disturbing this perfect day with talk of worry and troubles?

Henri must have felt her stiffen at his side, for he moved forward until his face filled her frame of vision. His dark eyes sparkled with joy. Louise looked deep, and she found there a promise that filled her being with answering joy. She was to be married to Henri, the only man she had ever cared for. She would be Louise Robichaud. She turned her attention back to the chapel and its simple lime-washed walls. *Here is safety . . . here is home* was in the smile she gave to her beloved.

CHAPTER SIX

The birds chattered outside Catherine's window, yet not even their laughing chorus could hold her attention. She was so full of swirling emotions she could not even rise and dress. She could have plucked any emotion under the sun and said, "Here, yes, this describes my heart." Yet none of the words would have described it fully.

Brilliant summer sunlight streamed through the open window, falling upon her wedding dress where it hung on the wardrobe door. Her father had purchased a bolt of the palest blue satin she had ever seen, the color of a rain-washed sky an hour before dawn. The village dressmaker had spent days and days sewing lace upon the neck and sleeves and fashioning a long lacy train down the back. The shoulders were puffed in the proper fashion of London circles, at least according to the latest journals from England.

Catherine hugged herself with excitement and fear. She hoped Andrew would find her *striking*. She had thus heard an officer describe a visiting English lady. Catherine wanted to be *striking* for Andrew, especially today. She wanted to show that she, a girl raised in the colonies, could be a suitable match for an English officer, and one to the manor born.

Andrew rarely spoke of his past. The little he had said left Catherine certain that he had burned his bridges when he had come to the colonies, and would not be returning to England. There had been a few words about the death of Andrew's much-loved father and an older brother entitled to the family legacy and estate. No, Andrew was no longer welcome in England. Much as she would have liked to have seen the Harrow castle, Catherine was not sad. Acadia was her home, Edward the village where she hoped to live out all her days. And with Andrew by her side.

Even so, a small shiver raced through her. She could not say why she felt so fearful and uncertain. The air was warm and fragrant, the birds were singing, the village beneath her window already filled with festive sounds.

Perhaps it was not fear of this day at all. Perhaps it was of the days to come. A life outside the home she knew and loved. A life with a man she loved, it was true, yet there was so much she did not know.

Another shiver touched her frame. Yes, that was it. She was frightened of all she did not know about the days and years to come. As though even this brilliant day was touched by shadows of a future beyond her ken and control.

Her gaze moved to the Bible resting on the corner table. Catherine could scarcely even reflect on the cover without thinking of her father. John Price was a religious man, in a somewhat cold and rigid manner. He had ordered her since she was a little child to read the Bible and memorize passages. "Know the law of God," he had often commanded. "Know the law."

Yet the day's promise of a new chapter in her life granted Catherine a new perspective on her father. Perhaps because she was truly leaving, because this night and all the nights to come she would sleep beneath a different roof, she could look at him in a way she had never known before. Much of her young life had been fashioned by such orders, she now realized. Her father was a rather distant and self-engulfed man. Though he truly cared for her, he had never been able to express those feelings. She tried to remember when he had actually spoken about love for her. And she could not recall a single time.

Since the death of his wife, John Price had probably not even realized that he should try to tell Catherine he loved her. The acknowledgment of this brought a soft knell of sorrow to her heart, but just a little. In this newfound understanding was also a growing ability to forgive. Catherine's gaze rested upon the Book. Her father had always insisted that she be morally upright, that she be a good daughter and a good member of their church. But because of his rigidity, she had not found any personal relationship to his legalistic religion.

She reached out and drew the Book into her lap. As she opened the leather-bound cover, she wondered if in truth she had not kept herself from something precious. Her new discovery about her father, about herself, seemed to be urging her not just to look at things differently, but to grow beyond what was comfortable.

She had viewed God in terms of her father and his coldness. She realized that now. The Bible had been a source only of rules, of warning.

But she needed something more than that now. She needed timeless wisdom, direction, yes, even comfort. She was facing marriage without a mother to turn to. Her father was caught up in the habits and the focus of his life, and she needed a place she could turn with all her fears and her doubts. Scraps of phrases she had heard from the Book all her life, yet not really listened to, now seemed to take on a life of their own. "Ask, and it will be given. . . ." "Come unto me. . . ." Catherine felt a burning come to her eyes. She had not missed her mother so much since she had been a little child.

And yet just glancing at the pages seemed to whisper to her a quiet promise. One she had never been able to hear before. One which invited her to grow beyond herself and see the Book anew. Perhaps here in these pages she might find what she so longed for, guidance to help her through all the mysteries and unknown experiences to come.

The church bell began to ring. Catherine sat upright as though awakening. The bells were ringing for her, and she was not even dressed! She rose to her feet and put the Bible in the tapestry bag she would be carrying with her this night. As she reached for her wedding dress, a warm sense of comfort grew in her heart. She felt as though she had done something very right, very good, in that simple action of recognizing that the Book would be a part of her future life.

Andrew had warned her about it, explaining in his patient way that it was a tradition for British officers and a necessary part of the ceremony. Even so, when Catherine passed through the gates to the Anglican chapel and saw them for the first time, she hesitated midstride.

The soldiers of Andrew's company were formed into two long lines flanking the walkway. Their red-jacketed uniforms and parade hats made them appear almost as tall as the trees that shadowed them. Their muskets, held aloft with pikes fixed upon the end, sparkled in deadly brightness in the noon sun—an unnerving limbless forest through which Catherine must walk in order for her long-awaited day to begin.

Andrew had been at his gentlest when he had explained the rite as old as the regiment itself. An officer's new wife was granted a salute by the men. Much as he knew she would prefer otherwise, they were obliged to carry through this military custom of long standing. After listening in resigned silence, Catherine offered but one objection: "It feels as though I'm being forced to marry the regiment as well as you." To her dismay, Andrew had not contradicted her.

But there he stood, the love of her life, tall and slender and handsome in his gold-bedecked uniform. His hat was tucked under one arm. His eyes locked with hers, and though a smile would be appropriate in front of his regiment, Catherine saw the warmth that could not be hidden in his pleased and eager gaze.

Out of the corner of her eye she caught sight of Captain Randolf Stevenage and his wife, Priscilla. Another harsh vision for her marriage day. Andrew had said that the governor in Halifax was doing them both great honor by sending his own adjutant to add an official blessing to the day's events. But her husband-to-be had not sounded as though he believed his own words as he had spoken. Priscilla stood there in the sunlight, watching Catherine with an expression as unreadable as stone.

Catherine turned from the silent couple, straightened her shoulders, took a deep breath, and proceeded toward the military passage. Her legs felt as though they could scarcely support her. She focused every shred of her attention upon the man she loved with all her heart.

Two young girls walked before her, scattering petals of wild flowers Catherine had brought back from the highland meadow. As they started the procession between the ranks of soldiers, a man with a bristling mustache and chestful of medals whipped out his saber and swung it to within a hairsbreadth of his nose. He shouted, "Troop, present *arms!*"

The soldiers stamped in forceful unison and slapped their muskets out before them. The flag bearers lowered their staffs so that the regimental colors and the symbol of the British sovereign formed a brightly colored canopy under which Catherine would walk.

One of the flower girls whimpered at the strange noise and the towering men. Catherine offered her a comforting smile. *For Andrew. I will do this for him.*

Next to Andrew stood the Anglican vicar, and next to the vicar was her father. John Price's normally stern expression softened as Catherine's eyes locked for a moment with his.

The glorious July sunlight dappled through the soldiers and muskets and pikes and flags as it would through tree branches. Catherine took a firm grip upon her flowers and her smile and willed herself forward. And her Andrew was standing there, becoming nearer with every step.

Finally she was there and Andrew touched her arm, filling her with renewed strength and purpose. Then her father tucked her arm through his, and they stood and waited until Andrew and the vicar and the villagers all had entered the chapel. She barely noticed the sergeant major's shouted orders and the sharp rapping of boots and arms as the soldiers paraded away. Catherine focused her attention upon the lovely young faces of the flower maidens, seeing there the hope and the excitement she had always dreamed this day would hold.

Then her father spoke words she heard but did not truly understand, and Catherine knew it was time. She turned her face to the sun and accepted its light and warmth and beauty. This day was her dream come true.

As she entered through the church doors on the arm of her father, trumpets sounded. Andrew had told her of this as well. Two silver trumpets flanked the church entrance, so long their bells crossed overhead, and their long, colorful tassels framed her entrance. The chapel received the sound and shouted it back, so that the entire sanctuary reverberated with clarity and joyous power.

Here in the church almost the entire Fort Edward community was present to greet her, standing in honor of Lieutenant Harrow and his bride. Here the aisle she walked was bound by friendship and the ties of a lifetime. She found her smile coming more readily, springing from the gladness of a full heart. And there again at the aisle's end stood the man she loved, answering her smile with one of his own.

The days and nights of wondering how it would be to stand before the vicar and be joined to another for a lifetime, of hoping and yearning once she had met this man beside her, all of it combined into a single moment. Catherine scarcely seemed to have time to breathe, it happened so swiftly.

Then the vicar smiled at them both and said the words she had dreamed of for so long: "I now pronounce you man and wife."

CHAPTER SEVEN

Berry basket in hand, Catherine climbed the steep trail leading up and away from the village, warmed by the memory of breakfast and the talk with Andrew. The early September sky was as overcast and dull as the bay down below her. The brisk wind smelled not of the coming rain but of winter. As though each leaden day was merely a forerunner of the long cold months soon to come.

But today it did not matter. Today she was comforted by the fact of being Mrs. Catherine Harrow. She had been married two months and two days, and already it was hard to recall another existence. Her earlier years seemed to belong to someone else entirely.

Andrew was off now on another patrol. She had stood at the door of their cottage and waved her handkerchief as he had led the patrol down the winding lane and out of the village. She had felt proud, not only because of the way he had sat tall upon his shining steed, with the scabbard gleaming and the flags fluttering and the men lined up behind him. Her heart had been filled by their discussion at the kitchen table and by Andrew's special farewell gift.

Catherine arrived at a level place in the trail and paused to catch her breath. She turned and looked back, pleased at how high she had already climbed. To her right, the church steeple pointed its solitary finger toward heaven. The town of Edward spiraled out tightly from the church, upon lanes that rose and fell along the uneven terrain. She could see her own little cottage there, and she felt a warm sense of pride, and of belonging. Their home.

The lane broadened as it left the hamlet and approached the fort. Although Fort Edward was only an offshoot of the much larger Annapolis Royal garrison, still it seemed quite large enough to her. The outer bastions were of local rock, heaped into triangular escarpments three times the height of a man. These had been covered with sod, then grass, so that now it looked like a hill which had risen in unnaturally straight lines and clean angles. Within the outer walls rose stone-and-log lodges, narrow and long. Her gaze lingered upon the garrison's supply house, where her father worked. As he often did, he had joined them for breakfast that morning, something which had not pleased Catherine, since it was Andrew's last meal with her for a while. But upon John Price's departure their special discussion had begun. So Catherine was now glad for the interruption.

John Price noticed nothing amiss with her initial welcome, and saw no reason not to linger over his cup of hickory-laced coffee. He was very proud of his new son-in-law. "I see from the duty roster you're off again today."

"East to Cobequid Town, a stop at the Chelmsford fort, then on up around the bay's northern side. We've had word of some bandits raiding the Tatamagouche Road."

"More Indian nonsense, no doubt. Allied to renegade Frenchies, you mark my words." Subconsciously John Price stretched out his leg and kneaded his old wound. "How long will you be away?"

"Ten days, perhaps twelve." At this Catherine had turned away, busying herself at the dish basin and trying not to think about the lonely days ahead.

"I must tell you, sir," Andrew added carefully, "that we have no concrete evidence the French are taking part in these disturbances."

"Only because they're slippery as eels, the lot of them." Price clattered his cup down upon the saucer. "The French are our natural enemies."

"Not here," Andrew murmured.

"Here, there—it makes no difference. The English have fought the French for nigh on four hundred years. You of all people should know that."

"I do know it very well, sir." Andrew had adopted the formal tone he often used around his father-in-law. "I only question it in the very special circumstances of Acadia.

The French have lived here on Cobequid Bay for over a century and a half, and in all that time there has never been any conflict between their settlers and ours. Yes, we have battled their fortresses, but the settlers and the villages have remained—"

"Enemies now and enemies for all time," Price barked. "I can see them now, them and their foppish ways, gathered in some hall and plotting our demise."

"Sir . . ." Andrew paused, then said simply, "No doubt there is some truth in what you say."

"Of course there is." John Price rose from his chair and headed for the door. "Well, I shall let you get on with your preparations. Good day, daughter. Thank you for the repast."

When the door had shut behind him, Andrew said quietly, "And his is the opinion of almost every officer in my regiment."

Catherine turned back, not at the words but the sadness in his tone. "Will there be—war?" She stumbled over the dreaded word.

"There already is. Not here, but in the homelands." Speaking thusly seemed to tire him. "The latest dispatches are full of new conflicts. France is up to her old tricks, encroaching on British territory, bombarding Gibraltar, making false accusations in the courts of our allies." Andrew looked at her with helpless eyes. "I had hoped and prayed none of this would touch us. I hope it still." He shook his head. "I can't think of a single Frenchman here in Acadia who is an enemy."

She did not know what to say. The talk of war, even one separated from them by a storm-crossed journey of four long months, troubled her so. Catherine crossed the room and settled into the chair still warm from her father's presence. She reached out and took her husband's hand.

When she did not speak, Andrew said softly, "Tell me what you will do when I am away."

"Miss you," she said, and felt hollowness creep higher in her chest.

"Tell me," he said, softer now. "Let me carry with me an image of where you will be and what you will do. It makes the parting go easier."

She looked at him, smiled into that familiar face, and shook her head. "I will clean up the breakfast dishes and sweep the floors and then watch through the window for you to pass."

"Ah, good. I shall make it a point for the parade to be as smart and polished as a new penny."

"I shall go and stand on the porch and wave my handkerchief," she said. "Even though it will hurt and worry me to see you go, I will give you a smile to carry with you."

"In my heart," he said and raised her hand to kiss it gently. "What then?"

"Then I will come back and sit right here to read the Bible." The words were easily spoken, somehow lightening the burden of her coming sorrow. "I find great comfort in the Book. It tells me that God is here with me when you can't be. And I will pray for you. At least in this way I am helping to bring you safely home."

Andrew's gaze joined hers to look at the Bible by the window. In the gray light of a cloudy morning the leather cover gleamed soft and warm. "I've never given much thought to the Book outside Sunday gatherings. The sight of you reading by the fire of an evening . . ." He hesitated, searching for the right word. "It has warmed me."

"Me as well." She had wanted to tell him all that had been growing within her but felt as though it was still too new, too fresh to fit well with words. "I don't know if I have ever really understood the Book before, not with an open mind and heart." When that felt inadequate, she added, "Somehow I feel as though I am reading it for us. For our marriage."

Andrew did not question her as she half expected. Instead he nodded slowly, then said, "Perhaps when things calm during the winter months, we can read it together."

"I would like that," she said, her heart full of love for this man. "Very much."

He nodded again, but his gaze remained absent. "All I really know of the Bible is how it fit into my family's tradition."

Catherine waited a moment, then asked, "What was it like inside your family, Andrew?"

"Cold. Especially after my mother died. You know about that, of course."

She nodded but said nothing. That much Andrew had spoken of. When he was eleven, how his mother had died giving birth to a little girl who also had not survived.

"After Mother passed on, Father retreated even further from me. He lived for his horses and his hounds. I was sent off to boarding school, where I stayed until I reached my seniority. My brother hated my being around. It was one of the defining parts of my life, like the sun rising in the east. He hated me, and I was happier being away. Especially after Mother passed on."

For the first time Catherine thought she could ask questions. Now it seemed as though there was not so much pain in his eyes and voice. As though within their marriage he felt the same distance from his past as she did from hers. "It must have been hard, though, giving up a castle and all the servants and such a rich life," she commented.

"I do not miss it a whit, not an instant. A castle is no more than a tomb of many rooms when there is only coldness and anger."

"Your father must have loved you."

"Oh, I'm sure he did, in his own way. But Father was as trapped in tradition and as bound by his past as your own father is by his feelings for the French. I hope I am not offending you when I say that, my dear."

"No. It is true. Sad, but true."

"Since marrying you I have begun to see how these same chains of tradition have trapped me as well." Andrew was speaking more slowly now, his brow furrowed with the effort of seeking his way through unfamiliar terrain. "There is so much of my life I never bothered to question until now. For generations beyond count, the younger Harrow sons have all gone into the military. Their portraits decorate the front staircase of Harrow Hall. They make up one of my clearest childhood memories, climbing the stairs at night, followed by the fierce stares of these men, with their medals and their prancing horses."

Catherine remained caught by two words that she quietly repeated: "Harrow Hall."

"Of course I attended Eton, and then did a brief stint at Oxford. Every Harrow minor—that's what the younger sons were called. Harrow minors. We all followed that course, and straight from there into the King's Own." His gaze had turned as bleak as his voice. "It is only now, when I sit by the hearth of my own home with my own wife, that I find a need to question this road. One chosen for me by others, long before I had a power of choice of my own."

His candid speech granted Catherine the chance to say what had long rested in the dark recesses of her own heart. "When I think of your family and all you once had, sometimes I feel so inadequate." She could not help but glance around their simple little cottage. "I'm just a colonial lass, I was taught by the vicar's wife, I've only been to Halifax twice in my entire life, I've never seen England, I don't—"

"Catherine, my dear sweet angel, look at me." His eyes were startling in their clarity. Nothing but truth could exist within his gaze when he stared at her as he did now. "I have never felt as complete, nor even dreamed that I could know such happiness, as I do here in the home you have made for us."

Catherine carried the warmth of those words with her the rest of the way up the trail. The River Minas was split into a series of streams that she could easily cross. The babbling water seemed to agree that yes, of course, she missed her husband. But she was also happy. There was nothing unusual with feeling the two emotions at the same time, sorrow over his absence yet blissful over how their lives were joining.

The trail meandered through trees as ancient and gnarled as time itself. Roots crabbed about the stony soil, then dug through rocks with stubborn determination. Beyond the old growth there came the sound of a merry waterfall, which invited her to stop for a drink. Then she moved over the final rise and stepped into the meadow. The berry bushes were across the meadow, just where she remembered and just as full as she had imagined.

But to her surprise, there was another figure pulling at the ripe fruit. The same

Frenchwoman Catherine recalled from her last visit, the day before her wedding. With Andrew's words about the Acadia French people in her mind, she walked across the meadow, her hand raised in greeting. The young woman looked kind and lovely. It seemed not only natural to walk toward her, it felt right. Only later did she wonder at her boldness.

"Hello!" She smiled at the way the young woman stood, her openly curious eyes as dark and brilliant as her hair. One hand was poised halfway to the bush, like a blackbird balanced upon the branch, ready to take flight at the first hint of danger.

But Catherine carried no danger with her. Just gladness at seeing another person there, a young woman with the same love of nature and of wild berries as herself. She sought the phrases from the French she had learned in her lessons, worried that in this moment she would find nothing at all to say.

The tall grasses and few remaining autumn flowers swished against her skirt as she drew nearer. She saw that the young woman's lips were stained with fruit she had been eating as she plucked. Catherine smiled at the sight of that face, full of life and mystery.

Catherine said her first complete sentence to a Frenchwoman. "I desire to bid you good day," she managed in French, then switched with joyous abandon to English. "Isn't it a wonderful morning?"

The flashing eyes crinkled in merriment, and the young woman's delightful laugh, like bells, joined with Catherine's.

CHAPTER EIGHT

Some days after her encounter with Catherine in the highland meadow, Louise found herself with her housework done and a yearning for the season's last fruit. Wondering if the frost had denied her a final picking, she bundled herself into two shawls. The clouds were heavier than Louise had seen in months. They spread flat and featureless just above the hilltops, as though their burdens were too great to hold at accustomed height. The next time the clouds released their load, she knew it would be snow. The past three nights, temperatures had fallen low enough to freeze the ground by morning. Louise stepped carefully over rocks made slick with rain, her breath coming in steamy puffs.

Yet even with winter's quiet warning at every turn, Louise could not feel disappointment. It had been a good summer. Very good indeed. Despite the rumors of distant conflicts and the constant political worries, she had busied herself with the task of making a cozy home within Henri's farmhouse, and she usually managed to ignore such talk.

But it was difficult to shut it all out when every trip through the village brought alarming news to her ears. In the leather-smith's shop, she would hear of more warships arriving at the Halifax harbor. In the chapel gardens, there were rumors of English soldiers camped near one of the few remaining French forts. At a meeting of the clan elders, there was talk of soldiers closing the market road to any French attempting to trade at Annapolis Royal. And on and on it went.

Louise had watched her mother's reaction to it all and seen that her fuming had done little but silence the men whenever she was around. The men were justly concerned about their families, their livelihoods, even their lives. They could not help but discuss, analyze, and dissect each piece of information that surfaced. And of course the bearer of such items of information always received his moment in the sun. Louise had seen how the man with the latest news could stand for a moment in a light all his own, puffed up with the importance of having something to tell.

As the summer waned, Louise had found it increasingly easy to put the worries out of her mind. Henri helped enormously. Her beloved husband lived to smile, to laugh. To turn her thoughts to more pleasant things. He did not permit these bad tidings any significant place in his world. Or in hers. Her *husband*. Louise stopped to shift the basket she carried to her other arm. Such a wonderful word. One she had heard all her life, but now one she was beginning to understand.

Now there were so many words like that, ones which had come to hold entirely different new meanings since her wedding. Such as *home*. Life in Henri's little cottage was a constant source of joy. The house itself had shouted its forlorn need of a woman's touch. She had spent most of the summer bringing order to what had before been merely a place for a bachelor to eat and sleep.

She remembered that first time Henri had shown her around the cottage. He had been so worried, so afraid of what she would think. The place had been scrubbed and polished and swept, but all his efforts had only highlighted its bare and tattered state. Henri had apologized continually while she had walked through the three rooms and looked at the plank bed with the corn-husk mattress,

the single cracked mug and one set of utensils, the two blackened frying pans. He had
been so astonished when she had turned to
him and flung her arms around his neck.
"What are you on about?" he had cried. She
had laughed into his ear and replied, "You
have given me a dream come true, a home I
can make from beginning to end."

There also had been the need for a garden. The first one of her own. It had taken
time to plant and cultivate. Now she was
looking forward to winter. Henri would
complete the harvest in a few days, and then
he had promised to help her. Together they
would finish making the cottage a home.
Their home.

Louise held the basket in front of her as
she came to the narrowest jink in the trail.
The earthen jar she had placed in the basket
rolled about the bottom. She had felt a little
silly, but the idea of bringing a little gift had
seemed right as she was leaving the house,
and it seemed right now. Just in case. The
lady of the smile. That was how she remembered the pretty Englishwoman. As she
crested the first rise, Louise found her heart
warming at the memory.

From here the trail ran straight and true
along the lower ridgeline, until opening into
the meadow. She knew this section well. She

had been coming here since she was old enough to walk and hold her father's hand. And yet she had never been inclined to show it to anyone else. It had been such a surprise to find the woman up there, not once but twice. A stranger, an Englishwoman, in what Louise had come to consider her own private meadow.

But what a smile the woman had given her. "A heart in full bloom"—that was an expression she had often heard her father use. The Englishwoman had been dressed in clothes finer than anything found in Louise's entire village, finer even than her own wedding dress, and for a walk in the forest. And the way she had walked, so upright and correct, just like all the illustrations she had seen in her father's tattered journals. Back when she was a child, before the English blockade had closed off news and books and journals and materials from France, Louise had loved to look at the pictures of places and people from far-off lands. Her father had taught her to read from those pages. Now the pictures were yellowed and crinkled from years of use, the sheets torn from the binding and the words almost memorized, yet read over and over nonetheless because there was nothing new. When the Englishwoman had appeared, she had walked forward with the queenly bearing of characters lifted from the pages of Louise's childhood.

Yet the Englishwoman's smile had shone with warmth and clarity, as though none of the troubles between their two nations had ever existed and they had been friends for life. The thought stopped Louise just at the point where the trail opened to greet the meadow. Could she ever be friends with an English lady? What would Henri think? What would her father say? How would the villagers treat such news?

Then she stepped through the thicket, and there at the meadow's edge stood the English lady. Only this time, it was she who stood with hand poised by the berry bushes, eyes wide and startled by Louise's sudden appearance. And it was her lips which were berry stained.

After a pause, their laughter mingled in merriment over the bushes. "I have seen infants who eat more neatly!" Louise finally was able to gasp out.

"Slowly, please to speak more slowly. My French, it is terriblest in the world." But her smile was just as sweet, as Louise recalled. "I have more to be placed in my mouth than my basket."

"And more still upon your face, mad'moiselle." Louise confidently walked forward, as though they were acquaintances meeting upon the lanes of Minas, rather than strangers separated by a river and language and history and a world of woes. "I am called Louise Robichaud," she said with a little curtsy.

"My name is Catherine. Catherine Harrow," she said. "Madame, not mademoiselle." Catherine responded with her own curtsy and spoke very carefully. Obviously, she was searching hard for the French words. She motioned to the bushes with a berry-stained hand. "The frost has—what you say—finished them."

"The frost, yes. I feared it would be so."

"But they are still . . . tasty."

Louise nodded, reaching for a berry that she popped into her mouth. "So you are married?"

Catherine's eyes brightened as she nodded. Again the smile, the sense of sharing more than two strangers should ever reveal to each other. "I am married this summer past."

"I as well!" Louise smiled at her own memory and said, "I was married upon the most beautiful day in all the year, the first Friday in July."

Catherine's eyes widened further. "July, the month after June, yes?"

"Just so, madame. Every summer it is the same."

Catherine stared at her, two stained fingers touching her chin. She said words in English, then struggled to say, "That day . . . that day I marry also!"

The news stilled Louise's outstretched hand. "Surely you are jesting with me."

"At three o'clock after the midday. The number one Friday in July. The most beautiful day of the summer."

Louise put down her basket. "I heard your wedding bells just as we were sitting down to our own celebration."

"And I hear your music also!" Catherine clapped her hand to her cheek and said something in English.

"I beg your pardon, madame. I know only a few words of market English from my trips to Cobequid Town." Hand on hip, Louise cocked her head to one side and managed the English words, "Non, non, zee eggs, zay are two shillings a douzing."

That was enough to break out in further merriment. The two young women shed their baskets and retreated behind hands. But the laughter was not easily stemmed, and the hands dropped in defeat with the last of their reserve. The pair of them laughed until tears streamed down two faces.

When they stopped for breath, they turned to stand side by side and gaze down over their world, at the land falling away from the meadow in a series of grand tiers. Beneath the solid blanket of gray, the river's many fingers gathered and grew to a strong silver ribbon. From this height, the two villages seemed more joined by the waters than divided.

Louise was the first to turn back. "What is your husband's name?"

"Andrew."

Louise noted that simply his name seemed to bring the English lady both joy and concern.

"He comes home this day, or perhaps tomorrow. He travels to Cobequid."

Louise wondered if this Englishman would be happy to know his wife was speaking with a Frenchwoman. She could well understand if he would not. She herself had no idea how her own family would react to such news.

"I wish to make him a . . . a welcome cake." Catherine shook her head. "Please, excuse my French. It is horrible bad."

"It is far better than my English, madame."

"You must to call me Catherine. Please."

"Catherine." Louise returned to filling

her basket. She had so many questions she wanted to ask this lovely woman. So many things it would be nice to know. But did she dare? Just from Catherine having spoken her husband's name, she could feel the centuries of hostilities back in place. Perhaps the man had something to do with the fort. But he could not be a soldier. The thought was enough to still not just her hand but her breathing. *No, surely not a British soldier's wife!*

"Something is wrong?"

"It's nothing, I just pricked my finger." The words were spoken so swiftly that she was certain Catherine had not caught her alarm. Even so, each woman now concentrated on the filling of her basket. Louise's hands moved at a blur, and soon the basket at her feet was full of gleaming berries. The soft ones would cook up nicely for preserves to brighten a winter meal.

She started to say the polite farewell of two strangers. But she was stopped by Catherine's warm expression.

Louise did not need to ask what caused the interplay of emotions on her companion's face. As soon as she turned fully about, she understood. The season's first snowflakes were drifting gently down, soft and delicate.

Catherine murmured something in English.

Louise said, "Excuse me, madame . . . Catherine?"

"Oh, is nothing. I say only that it is lovely but comes too soon."

"Oh yes, every winter it is exactly the same with me. The summer is wonderful here—why could it not stay just a little longer?" Her heart was suddenly sparked by a desire to share mysteries and delights she would not have dreamed of talking about with another stranger. But here, standing shoulder to shoulder as winter's veil drifted down upon the meadow, she felt that a discussion of the weather was probably all they could safely manage.

Catherine's sigh matched her own as they picked up their baskets. "I must be going before trail is . . . lost to me."

Louise remembered the gift. "Oh, just one moment, Catherine!" Gently she pried up the cloth at the base of her basket and reached down one side. She pulled out the corked clay jar and extended it to Catherine. "This is for you."

"For me?" Once more Catherine's eyes widened with astonishment. "A present for me?"

"It is nothing. Just some maple syrup flavored with my mother's special recipe." A touch of apple cider, a trace of refined ginger added as the maple sap was boiled down. Words Louise was certain Catherine would not understand.

Hesitantly, the Englishwoman reached out and took the jar. "But . . . I have nothing for you."

"Do not be concerned, Catherine." Louise found it possible now to sort through the confusion in her heart and mind and bring out something worthy of a winter's farewell. "It is in return for your own gift, that first day we met. Your lovely smile."

CHAPTER NINE

Catherine sat in a circle of women to which she had been welcomed for the first time and tried hard to concentrate on her piece of the quilt.

If the Edward community agreed on anything that November, it was the strength of the winter. Nobody could recall one which had arrived with such early severity. Since those September flakes had floated down out of the skies, the snows had stopped only long enough for the sky to clear and permit an overnight freeze to pounce like a hawk on its prey. When the clouds reformed, it was without the thaws that traditionally loosened winter's grip, at least momentarily. The winds had come, hard and bitter and straight from the north. Unyielding and fierce, they were called lazy winds, for they would blow straight through a person rather than go around. January winds in November. And staying. Like the snow.

Though the sky was finally clearing from yet another snow, still the wind blew so fiercely the ice pellets struck the shutters like tiny hammers. They beat upon the glass, timed to the wind's hostile growl. Catherine stared out the window nearest her chair. She shivered and drew her shawl more tightly around her shoulders.

"Andrew will be fine, my dear," Mrs. Patrick, the vicar's wife, murmured from the seat beside Catherine's. "How long has he been making these patrols?"

"Five years." Though she had been married only four and a half months, already the other women of the village were treating her as a woman, as an equal. "This will be his sixth winter."

"So. And not once has he lost a man, not even a horse." Mrs. Patrick nodded over her needle. "Andrew Harrow is a careful man and a good officer."

"And handsome." The Widow Riley

cackled over her corner of the quilt. "You've got quite a prize there, missy. If I'd been fifty years younger, I'd have given you a right run for your money, I would."

The cackle was repeated, and Catherine smiled with the others working on the quilt. Such activity was a chance for the village women to meet and talk and draw strength from one another during those months when winter chills mostly kept them indoors. She was not totally sure if she was pleased to be welcomed into the housewives' circle, rather than relegated to the corner of the hall reserved for unmarried girls. But in her heart she felt a bit of pride. Her life was now inextricably entwined with Andrew's. The thought made her back straighten just a bit as she plied her needle through the woven fabric. But she did wish there was *someone* in the group her own age. All the younger wives were also new mothers and had infants at home to take their time and attention. *But my turn will come soon*, Catherine thought with cheeks turning pink.

The Edward community great room was a long affair, running almost the entire length of the northern wall of the town hall. A great fireplace flanked the western expanse, large enough for those who were chilled or elderly to step into its warmth.

Light flickered and danced from the flames on the faces of the village's younger children playing games on the floor in front of it.

"When is the gallant officer due back, dear?" asked a neighbor who had known Catherine all her life.

"Tonight, at the latest tomorrow." Catherine did not raise her head. She was still learning the complicated stitching, and it required all her attention. Which was not altogether a bad thing, she decided. "He couldn't be certain with the snows so heavy so soon."

"Seems sure to stop, at least for a bit." Widow Riley made a pretense of sniffing the wind, though all that could be detected in the close hall was smoke and melting tallow from the candles. "But not for long, you mark my words. This will be a winter for tales to our children's children's children."

As though in confirmation, the wind rattled the shutters with another fistful of icy needles. Widow Riley nodded sagely, her fingers finding their own familiar way even as her eyes gazed at the fire. "I remember such a November as this." The voice, coarsened with age, grew soft. "Seven years of age I was, perhaps eight. Ice formed almost the whole way across the bay, it did, and wolves came down from the hills almost every night, snarling and howling about the lanes like it was their village and not ours."

The children looked up from their play. Another old woman, a grandmother who was watching the children, joined them in listening, nodding to Widow Riley's words. "You were seven. Three years younger than me. I remember it too."

Fingers gradually grew still about the edges of the quilt. Widow Riley did not notice, for her own failing eyes had returned to the needle. "Saw my first Indian that winter. Three days after Christmas, it was, I remember it as though it was yesterday and not nigh on seventy years ago." The crackling of the fire was all that filled the pause.

"The week before Christmas it had snowed every day, a snow so thick a body could get lost within reaching distance of his own front door," the story resumed in the quavery voice. "The fort had just been built that very summer. My pappy, he was one of the first English settlers to till this land, he didn't hold to having soldiers so close at hand. Not until that winter. The young lads were kept busy shoveling and clearing the trails from house to house, farm to fort, hitching chains and drag-poles to horses and walking them back and forth, day in and day out. Carving valleys through drifts so high they looked like mountains to my young eyes. Walking from my door to church for the Christmas service was like hiking through white canyons taller than my pappy."

When she stopped to rethread her needle with trembling fingers, a young voice finally piped up, "What about the Injun, Miz Riley?"

She turned and squinted at the watchful faces. "What's that, young'un?"

"The Injuns." This time a half dozen voices joined the first. "You saw 'im," and "What happened?"

"See 'im I did. See and touch both."

Catherine waited with the others as the widow counted her stitches, her fingers moving at a snail's pace. And she had the sudden impression that Widow Riley had known all along what effect her story would have.

"Three days after Christmas, I woke to the first clear dawn in what seemed like years. I was the first out of bed those days. Moved a sight more sprightly than I do now, and I took pride in being the one to light the fire and warm the cabin. I had to use the tinderbox that morning, for the ashes were stone cold—see the things I remember? I chipped and chipped and finally drew a light, and I blew on the tinder until I was near red in the face. By the time I got that fire drawing strong, I was all in a lather. So I took the bucket from the kitchen and went out to gather snow, since the well and the creek had both been froze for nigh on three months. Well, I'm here to tell you, I threw back the door and walked straight into the biggest, foulest-smelling man I'd ever seen in all my born days."

When she stopped yet again, a tiny voice piped, "Did he eat you?"

"No, child, I still got all my fingers and toes—the Injun didn't eat me. Though he could have, for I fell back straight onto the ice and just sat there, too astonished and scared to even draw a good breath. And he didn't move neither. A stiller person I've never seen, not one who ain't been laid out for the final wake. Tall and dark and strong. And hungry. I remember that clear as the day itself, how his cheeks were sunk in so far they looked like caves a squirrel could've used for his winter sleep.

"But I couldn't lie there forever. I finally got my wits about me enough to realize I was looking a real-life Indian square in the face. I leapt to my feet and hollered like a stuck pig, then raced back inside. Straight back to the bed I shared with my sisters, and I leapt in there and burrowed deep as I could go, screaming all the while."

A child cried, "What did he want, Miz Riley?"

"Food, child. He was starving. Whole Micmac village was down to almost nothing. Which was passing strange, for there ain't much better a body for seeing the winter through comfortable than a Micmac Indian. But the summer before they had not had much in the way of game. We didn't have much food either, since the summer's crop had been bad, but we gave 'em what we could." The widow sewed on for a time, then said, "For three years after that we didn't have a single attack on our market wagons. Not a single solitary one. Only good thing that came out of that winter, far as I can recall."

"Hmph," the grandmother by the fire snorted. "I wouldn't have given them nary a thing. Thieving Injuns, the lot of them."

There were a few nods from about the quilt but most frowned at the words. Mrs. Patrick gave her head a single shake, nothing more. Widow Riley kept on with her sewing, commenting only, "Maybe things were different back in those days. The times, they surely do change."

Catherine completed stitching in her

square. She rose to her feet and brushed the threads from her skirt. "I must be getting back. I have some supper preparations to make in case Andrew does return tonight, so I bid you all a good afternoon."

Smiles and murmurs followed her to the door, and Mrs. Patrick rewarded her with the words, "You are making into a good wife, Catherine Harrow. Andrew should count himself among the fortunate."

The compliment kept her warm throughout the walk along meandering snowbound lanes. The sky had cleared and the wind died, but now the temperature was dropping sharply. Though the sun was an hour and more from slipping behind the western hills, already the air bit sharp and hard on her face.

These few afternoons each week spent with the village women meant much to Catherine, especially when Andrew was away. As she hurried down the lane toward home, the new-laden snow rose like delicate white dust behind her. Catherine found herself recalling something she had not thought of in years. Back when she had been a very little child, a woman of the village had been banished from the church for a winter. She had never been told the reason for it. But now, when she was struggling with the new experience of running a home and living with a man, she truly understood the need for the company of other women. Though the unfortunate woman's name had long passed from memory, still Catherine felt a pang of sympathy and sorrow for what must have been an excruciatingly lonely winter.

In the months since her marriage, she felt as though her whole life had undergone transformation. Not just her home, but her body and mind and heart were all being changed to fit around the presence of this man. She recalled from Scripture the passage about two becoming one, and felt the wonder of this anew. Catherine glanced at the surrounding white hills and sent a swift little prayer lofting upward. *Bring my husband home safely.*

She was doing more and more of that these days, little words of entreaty or thanks. In the past, her prayers had remained locked into the same traditions as the rest of her worship, dictated by the church and formed around the attitudes of her staid and rigid father. But for three months now she had been studying the Bible every evening, joined by Andrew whenever he was not away on sorties and duty. Though much of what she read she did not understand, still there was a sense of slipping free of thought patterns and negative perspectives she had scarcely recognized before. God was still very much a mystery, but His presence seemed closer. Close enough to speak with whenever worries or joys, fears or love, emotions of all kind filled her heart to overflowing and she needed someone in whom she could confide.

She quickly went into the house and lit the candle she kept burning in the window whenever Andrew went away. Part of her said it was an expensive folly, what with the cost of tallow. But day or night, whenever he came home, she wanted him to see the glimmer of the light that was burning for him and him alone.

She completed her chores as quickly as possible, then glanced out the window. The day's final light turned the shutters into sheets of solid gold. She peered through windows already frosted with the cold of coming night but saw nothing except the sunset's gleam. Catherine walked to the chair by the fire and tried not to look at the empty seat across from her. She picked up the Bible from its place on the small table. Though her mind could scarcely take in the words, she found her mind and heart returning to peace as she read. She watched the flames dance in the fireplace for a time, knowing she should rise and eat her own lonely supper, but not yet willing to accept that Andrew would spend yet another night in the hills away from her.

She placed the Bible back on the table and reached beneath its covering to the lower shelf, drawing out another book. She felt a quickening of her breath as she opened the pages. Even as she worried over her husband sleeping out in such cold, she could not help but feel a little thrill.

Yet there was another sensation as she began to whisper the long-forgotten words and phrases aloud, a slight chill which flickered across her heart. Catherine stopped her repetitions and nodded once to the flames. She did not want to have any secrets from her husband. Somehow, someway, she was going to have to tell Andrew.

Her gaze came back to the window and saw that the daylight was nearly gone. Once more her heart spoke the silent prayer. *Bring my husband home.*

Andrew reined his horse in near the crest of the ridge. His steed halted gratefully and stood blowing great plumes of white so thick they looked like froth from the sea. He slid from the horse's back, flipped the reins around a tree limb, and waited for the others to move up.

This time there were only four in his patrol, all mounted. He had selected the best of the new recruits who had arrived that previous June. He could now trust these men in particular to move with stealth and react to his hand signals as readily as they once would have obeyed the sergeant major's bellows. Without being told, they tied their horses where the trees would mask them, then unstrapped their muskets and moved at a crouch up to where he waited.

The garrison contained only sufficient horses for the officers and a select group known as outriders. These men were intended to function as scouts and messengers, roles with prestige and the promise of swift advancement through the ranks. This was their first foray with the commandant, and the sense of new pride shone from four earnest faces.

Carefully Andrew moved from tree to tree, showing through example how they should use whatever cover winter provided when approaching exposed space. The closer they came to the knoll, the lower he crouched, until he moved onto the rocky mound on his knees. He scouted the horizon carefully, then motioned the others to join him. One by one they approached. There was no flashing or clinking of metal this time, for all exposed buckles and buttons had been blackened, all knives and utensils wrapped in burlap. Regiment regulations were put aside, for this was not the parade ground at Windsor Castle. This was Acadia, and silence was by far their greatest shield.

The four of them crouched and watched and waited for their commander to speak. Andrew stared out over the white waste of winter shimmering in frozen splendor under the setting sun. It was hard for him to imagine that anything living could exist here except a frozen desert of brief days, long frigid nights, wind, and snow.

He turned to the men and said, "This is your enemy. Not the French, not the Indians. Winter. Never turn your back on it, never think you have conquered it, not even for a minute. It is a fatal error."

They nodded in somber understanding. From these heights the world stretched out white and stark, countless hills pointing snowy peaks toward a gradually darkening sky. Though the wind had died, the night would be bitter cold. Andrew had already decided he would try to make it back to the fort that evening.

Swiftly he sketched out the points of interest—where the trails emerged from around lower bends, points where Indians had been spotted in previous hard winters, places where bandits had planted ambushes—though none of these since he had taken over watch of this region. He was striving to teach these men to track the trackers, to stop danger before it happened.

One of the men pointed to where the snowy landscape fell in gradual stages to join with Cobequid Bay. From their aerie they could see twelve, perhaps fifteen villages along the frozen shoreline. The man asked, "Beggin' your pardon, sir, but which of them hamlets is Papist?"

"Almost none of them," Andrew replied, not at all sorry to have the question asked. "Almost all the Frenchmen who have settled this region are Huguenot."

That brought a murmur of surprise. "They's Protestant, sir? Those Frenchies?"

"To the core." Andrew could have told them more, information he himself had gathered from journeys to towns up and down the valley. How the Huguenots had broken from the Catholic church in France, just as the Lutherans had in Germany. How they had suffered persecution so harsh they had fled to lands all over the world. There were even Huguenots in England now, sheltered by the breakaway Anglican church and good English law. More still in Switzerland with the Calvinists, many others here in the northern colonies, even some with the Ottomans, if rumors were to be believed. Andrew looked down at the peaceful setting, wondering if a stranger could tell which houses belonged to the English and which to the French. He added quietly, "The same as you and I."

"Don't seem right," one man muttered.

"The sergeant major, he said all Frenchies suffer from a severe case of genuflection," continued the first man with a wry grin.

"The sergeant major's humor sometimes goes amiss. No, almost all of this region was settled by French fleeing persecution because of their religious beliefs." He stretched out a hand, pointed off to the south. "The first major Catholic enclave is Cobequid Town itself, at the very tip of the bay. Unfortunately, the canon there considers himself responsible for all this region, although many of these villagers have never even met him. He is a troublemaker, not because he chooses to be Catholic, but because he chooses to be militant. He is a man who lives to stir the pot of politics and twice has urged his villagers to rise up in opposition to the English fort at neighboring Chelmsford."

Andrew turned his attention back to the region directly below them. "But these Huguenot villages have never responded to any call to arms, not even ones coming from the French king's own envoys. They are an independent lot, from what I have heard. They have a loose council of churches, but each vicar stands alone. Much like our own way. They even call their vicars by the same names we do—reverend, pastor, preacher. Or so I've been told." He felt a familiar tension over the injustice of being neighbors and presumed enemies. "Which is why the English have asked them to swear allegiance to the Crown and be done with it."

A moment's pause, then, "So why don't they do it, sir?"

Because those addle-headed officials in London had insisted on putting in a clause stating that the French might be forced to bear English arms, Andrew wanted to say. The French had no more interest in fighting on the side of the English king than they did with the French. Yet because of this horrendous error on the part of English politicians four thousand leagues away, the French had refused to sign the oath, and were thus branded as enemies.

But all Andrew said was, "We have been in this region for almost fifty years now, and our settlers for twenty years more. In that time we have fought the French army twice and attacked their forts on four different occasions. Never have the local villagers taken up arms. Time after time the French government has called upon them to fight alongside the soldiers. But they have resisted. As I said, they are an independent lot. They farm their land and mind their own business."

He paused to let that sink in, then went on. "Remember, we are here to preserve the peace and protect the innocent." And he added to himself, *If only I could convince my fellow officers and the officials in Halifax of this simple truth.*

One of the men demanded, "But what if there's war, sir?"

Andrew pushed himself half erect and started back down the knob. "Then may God help us all."

It was an hour after dark by the time he had seen the horses to the stalls and the men back to their barracks. His heart quickened as he turned into his own lane and caught sight of the candle flickering in the window—for him. He paused outside his door for a moment to collect his thoughts and emotions. The risk of war was real; he knew that as well as anyone. As acting adjutant, he had access to the reports filtering down from Halifax, and the news was ominous. What disturbed him most was his own helplessness.

But he tried to put that all aside as he pushed through the door and caught sight of his wife bounding to her feet from her place by the fire. "Andrew!"

"Catherine, my dear." His arms enfolded her.

"Oh, Andrew, I had given up any hope of seeing you tonight." She held him with a strength he could feel through his greatcoat. "I am so glad to see you. I was worried."

"Why should you be worried?" He peered down at the shining brown hair and tried to see the beloved face pressed hard against his chest. Andrew had the fleeting thought that if he were to die at this very moment, he would be able to part from this earth as complete as he had ever been. "We were just out on an ordinary sortie. I have done hundreds of them."

"I know, I was silly. I told myself not to

be concerned. But it is so cold and getting colder." She looked up at him. "That must sound rather foolish."

"It sounds delightful. I never knew what a pleasure it could be to have someone fuss over me." He plucked at the buttons on his coat. "Let me get this off so I can greet you properly."

"Oh, of course, look at me, what kind of greeting is this, keeping you here in the doorway." Hasty fingers helped him with the buttons and the scarf and hat, then she bent to help him ease off the high boots. "Come, take this seat by the fire. Are you hungry?"

"I could say that seeing you is enough food for my soul," he teased, "but I truly am hungry. Especially after days of trail fare."

"I would like to think that my countenance is enough to nurture both body and soul," she retorted, her eyes glinting with mischief, "but I do have some stew I can heat for you straight away. And dough I had set aside for bread tomorrow that will nicely make into biscuits."

"Thank you, my love," he said, easing into the chair. He picked up the book from the floor. "What on earth is this, Catherine?" he asked in astonishment.

Slowly she retraced her steps. She said very quietly, "A French grammar."

"I can see that. Why would you study that?"

Her arms folded across her middle, her hands clasped her elbows and held tight. "I used to be quite good at French when I studied it as a girl."

Andrew took a deep breath and kept his voice even. "So you just decided to return to your studies, after all these years?"

"Yes. Well, no." A hesitant breath, then, "I have met someone. A young Frenchwoman."

He leaned back in his chair. Of all the things he might have expected to hear upon his return, this certainly was not among them. "Here in the village?"

"No, of course not. Up in the meadow. The first time I saw her was the day I went up to pick our wedding bouquet. She was there for flowers as well." A smile lit her face. "Her wedding day was the same as ours, Andrew."

"Remarkable."

She didn't seem to notice any sarcasm in his laconic response. "I've seen her twice more," Catherine said, her voice gaining animation as she added to her explanation. "She gave me the syrup you enjoyed so. She is a lovely young woman, so nice, I think about my own age. We tried to talk together, but my French was so rusty it was the very heart of frustration." She stopped, eyes searching his face. "Are you—are you angry with me?"

"No," he said slowly, unsure how he felt but certainly not angry.

She twisted her hands together. "Please don't tell me not to see her again, Andrew. Please."

"No, I won't do that." Though for the moment he did not quite understand why. The logical step would have been to forbid it. But he could not bring himself to do such a thing, even with the possible jeopardy he would be in with his superiors. "But you must be careful."

"She is no danger to me. Of that I am certain."

"That's not what I meant. Word of this can't get out, Catherine. You must be extremely cautious. The garrison would view this in the worst possible light."

"I understand," she said solemnly.

He was as curious about her fervent desire to see this Frenchwoman as he was about the woman herself. "Tell me about her."

"I don't have much to tell. I don't even know for certain if I will ever see her again." She turned back to the kitchen and he followed, settling himself at the table. As she prepared his supper, she recounted the three meetings with Louise, lingering over the last time. "I wish I could have found the words to talk with her. Really talk."

Andrew watched her face. "Why is that?"

"Just think about it. I have lived all my life in this village, separated by only a few miles from Minas, and I have never set foot over there. I've never even spoken to the French, unless it was by chance in a market." She whirled to face him, cheeks flushed with emotion and her wooden spoon waving in the air. "Imagine, Andrew. Wouldn't it be wonderful to know what they think, how they are, *who* they are? These are our neighbors."

He thought about her words and found, to his surprise, that the strongest emotion he was feeling was pride. "Yes," he said quietly. "Yes, it certainly would."

CHAPTER TEN

After Christmas, the land of Acadia remained deeply imbedded in the winds and snows of winter. People added extra garments when venturing forth, and piled the firewood a little higher beside cabin doors.

The Minas widows nodded with the wisdom of experience as they gathered in front rooms full of children and grandchildren, repeating to all who would listen that this would be a winter to remember. A chilling foretaste of things to come.

But Henri Robichaud did not mind the winter at all. The cold had never troubled him as it did others, not even when January descended like a frigid beast of ice that filled the world with bleakest howls. Perhaps his stocky build helped him stay warm. Or perhaps it was as Louise said, that he did not give himself a chance to grow cold since he labored from morning to night. This too was true. He loved to work. He loved working almost as much as he did eating. And he loved laughter better than both combined.

Since his marriage to Louise, winter had taken on yet another special meaning. The long nights were no longer lonely. Loneliness had been etched so deeply upon his soul that now, with his beloved wife to fill their home with love and light, he noticed its absence more keenly than he had ever known its presence.

He had tried to explain this to his wife the night before. Finding him seated by the hearth staring deep into the fire, she had been sure something was wrong.

"No, nothing is wrong. Not in the least." His mother tongue, spoken quickly, carried no hint of sharpness, yet the French words did not have the same soft, musical tone as when Louise spoke.

"You were sitting there like a statue. I don't remember ever seeing you so still for so long."

He told her the truth, though it was hard, and harder still to meet his wife's query with anything other than his customary smile. "I was thinking of my parents."

"Oh, Henri." She drew the other bench up close enough to hold his work-hardened hand with both of hers. "Do you miss them?"

"I can hardly remember them." He tried for the smile, but here and now it was false. And he wanted nothing false between Louise and himself. Not ever. "But somewhere inside me there is—there is a little boy. And this waif, he does miss them—terribly."

The words silenced her. They sat together for a long moment as he continued to stare into the fire. The flames crackled and the logs hissed, as though whispering to him that this was the time to speak. He might never talk of this again, and it was good to speak his heart. Here, with this wonderful woman, it was good.

So it was that Henri finally spoke the thoughts haltingly. "I think there has always been a hollow point at the center of my soul, the place where my parents must have lived. And it is here and now, in the home I love, at night when the work is done and I have been preparing for sleep, that I remember the empty basin. Only here. Only at night."

Louise did not speak for a while. Then she said, "Sometimes I think that one reason you work so hard is because it keeps your mind occupied. Does that sound harsh?"

"No, it sounds true." But he spoke to the flames and not to her. The truth was easier to bear when he knew the fire would take the words first, releasing them both from the shadows the words contained. "It sounds so true I have spent a lifetime trying to flee from it." His voice was very low.

"I am sorry, my beloved. I did not mean to sadden you."

"It is not you who has brought me this sadness. It is life. I have always been afraid of looking too deeply into the past. I have run from memories—in laughter, in work, and in the company of friends."

Louise stirred, gripping his hand more tightly still. "You have never spoken like this before."

"I have never even thought like this before." He was more amazed than she, not only at the words, but at how easy they had come. "I feel as though your love has freed me, Louise. Freed me to look back at those lonely years."

"Oh, my dear, dear husband."

Suddenly there was a burning to his eyes, and a pressure building in his chest and rising up that clutched at his throat. And it took all his mighty strength to press it down, gaze upon her face, and say in a hoarse voice, "I think I can look at it all and understand it now, because the emptiness is no longer there." His tone lifted as he finished. "The caverns of my heart have been filled again."

Walking the winter lanes and hearing the snow scrunch beneath his boots, Henri wished there was some way to take back all he had said the night before. He was most comfortable with silence and a smile. The questions which had no answers were best left unspoken, and confessions were best whispered down a dark well at midnight. That was one of the few things he recalled hearing his mother say, and this philosophy had formed a vital part of his life.

But the thoughts had been spoken. There was no way to take them back now. Henri called a cheery good morning to a neighbor and turned down the lane leading to one of the hamlet's more distant farms. The day was so quiet he could hear a dog barking in the English village beyond the River Minas. Then the lane fell into a cul-de-sac, and the drifts of snow began spilling into the tops of Henri's boots.

The Duprey farm rested upon a knobby butte sticking far out toward the bay like a giant earthen whale rising from the frozen mud flats. All was white in this wintry world, and silent. Too silent. There was no smoke rising from the Duprey chimney, and no sign of movement. Henri quickened his step.

Closer still he could hear the bawling of the cattle, a clear sign that all was not well. He hallooed the house and was relieved to be answered by a quavery shout from within. Henri stomped his feet upon the porch and pressed against the latched door. He shouted through the thick wood, "Can you rise, Gerard?"

"Wait, wait, I am coming." The voice was hoarse, the footsteps scraped heavily across the floor. Finally the door was flung back. A man, stooped and flushed, leaned against the jamb. "Henri. Our prayers have been answered."

Henri answered with his customary grin. "You sound like a bear waking early from winter."

A woman's voice called feebly, and the man turned to cry, "It's Henri Robichaud. I told you someone would come."

Henri moved past the man into the house. The front room was scarcely warmer than outside. He could see his breath as he piled the few pieces of kindling still in the woodbox in the fireplace and struck a spark on the tinderbox. "How long have you been without heat?"

"It went out sometime yesterday. We didn't know when we would get more wood. The wife, she tried to do all the work herself and did her back in, just like I said she would. She had to crawl back from the cow shed. And me—" Gerard stopped to cough, a wracking sound that went on and on, bending him over almost double.

"Go back to bed," Henri ordered. "You've got the croup. Anybody in their right mind can see you shouldn't be up."

"But the cows—"

"I'll see to the cows after I get something hot into the both of you. Go back to bed, I say."

Louise had told him that Gerard had

come down with a terrible cough and fever, which had laid him out flat for the first time since he was a boy. All this she had learned from his wife. It was the way of their village, to know the state of all their neighbors and all the clan, as far out as the roads remained passable. But then the wife had not been seen for some days, too long as far as Louise was concerned.

There was little enough in the larder, a strip of side meat and meal and some dry bread. Henri's face drew down into an unaccustomed frown as he thought of how the two older people must have spent their Christmas. Even over the sound of frying bacon, he could hear the old man coughing from the back room. Henri poured the meal into boiling water, set the bread in the bacon grease to soften, and called, "I'll have Louise come by this afternoon with some proper food."

The woman's voice was almost as feeble as her man's. "You are a prince among men, Henri Robichaud."

Henri felt his face flush at the words. He had never managed to accept compliments well and had no idea what to say in response.

Thankfully there came another rapping on the front door. Henri turned to see the vicar, Jean Ricard, enter and say, "I should have known you would make it out here before me." He called to the back room, "How are you, Gerard?"

"Better, now that I know my cows will be—" He concluded with another furious spate of coughing.

When the noise had died down, his wife told the vicar, "I just said that Henri is a prince among men."

"A prince," the vicar agreed, stepping over to the fire and warming his hands. "Indeed."

With all the attention Henri found the room growing too close for comfort. He handed the skillet to the vicar and said, "You see to their meal, vicar, and I will tend to the cattle."

The woman's voice followed him out the door. "A prince among the angels!"

The cattle's bawling had grown louder since he entered the house. Which was no surprise if they had not been milked since the previous morning. He entered the barn's sweet warmth and shucked off his coat. Swiftly Henri lost himself in work he knew well—milking the cattle, filling the water trough, mucking out the stalls, spreading out new straw and feed. Normally when his hands were busiest his mind was quietest. That was one of the things he loved about work, how he could spend hours straining his body, then seem to come awake from a long slumber and not recall a single thought that had occupied him all day. It was somehow refreshing, this ability of his to place all cares to one side through labor.

Today, however, he found his mind drifting back to the conversation he'd had with Louise the night before. And from there it went on to what he was doing here. It was not as though he did not have a full day's work at his own farm. Especially now, when Louise had a list as long as his pitchfork of things she wanted seeing to around their home before the spring thaws. *Their home.* The words were still new enough to send a little shiver through his muscular frame. *Their* home.

For as long as he could remember, Henri had filled his free hours—and some hours which were not free at all—helping people around the village. It was only now, as he worked down the long series of stalls with their moaning cattle, that Henri had an idea as to why. As he walked to the last cow but one, he was struck afresh by the thought that somehow his marriage was waking his mind as well as his heart, permitting him the ability to see inside himself. Part of that freedom he had talked about with Louise last night. He was not sure how he felt about this. Not at all.

But the awareness was not to be denied. He leaned his forehead against the cow's side and squeezed the milk in rattling streams into the pail, and he knew why he was willing to be the friend in need to all the village. It was because they were the only family he knew. The only family, in fact, that he could really remember.

The cattle seen to, he then turned to the other animals. He had fed and watered the horses and was about to see to the chickens when Jean Ricard pushed through the big outer doors. "Do you need a hand?"

"You are just in time, Vicar." Though Henri had known the man almost all his life, he still felt uncomfortable around the pastor. Jean Ricard seemed to share Louise's ability to see what was masked by his smile. "I've just finished all the work."

"It is good of you to help out like this." Vicar Ricard walked over and watched Henri gather up the last of the eggs. "I'm sure you have a hundred things going begging at home."

"A thousand, Vicar, a thousand." Henri kept his grin firmly in place. "But who's going to thank me for doing what I always do around the house?"

"I don't know what the two of them in there would have done on their own." Jean Ricard had deep-set eyes and a gaze that seemed able to peer inside Henri's mind. "Do you know what they are saying about you around the village these days?"

"I've got more important things to do with these short winter days than listen to village talk, Vicar."

"They are saying that maybe Henri Robichaud is preparing to step into the shoes of the clan's elder."

Henri froze. "What?"

"Marrying the daughter of Jacques and Marie Belleveau, seeing to the needs of those who cannot cope with winter on their own— they say it could be a strategy of a man with an eye on his father-in-law's position."

Henri's laugh was forced. "That is the most foolish nonsense I have ever heard."

"Is it?" The dark eyes probed deep. "I know that you are not seeking the title. And it is precisely because you do not want it that you could indeed make a perfect elder."

Henri worked his mouth, but no sound came. Finally he managed, "Vicar, you don't . . . I can't be the one to make clan decisions. You—I'm . . . I'm not a thinking man. I do with my hands, not my head."

"Yes, you are correct." There was no

151

guile to the quiet man, nor moving away from his intent. "But your wife possesses the finest head in the village."

"Vicar . . ."

"You have heard the passage, the two shall become one? There is no reason why you cannot rely on your wife's wisdom, just as she relies on your strong arms and good heart. Learn to trust your wife, and learn to pray to God with her so that you both are filled with His eternal wisdom." The vicar waited. Then he turned away, saying, "It is time to prepare yourself for what may be presented to you, Henri. Whether you want it or not."

CHAPTER ELEVEN

As Catherine picked her way along the muddy lane that May morning, it appeared to her that spring was the most troublesome of seasons, the one hardest to love. She had read the English sonnets to spring, about warm breezes scented by fields strewn with wild flowers in full bloom. Whoever wrote those verses had never seen an Acadian spring, she decided. The wind still held icy teeth, no matter how determinedly the sun shone. Even on cloudless days, such as this morning, everything remained wet with the snow and ice melting from every surface, and the world was filled with the sound of dripping. Stepping beneath a tree was fraught with peril, as the topmost limbs seemed to hold their final snowy burdens for just such an opportunity, flinging them down upon the unwary with dank abandon.

The children seemed to suffer most in spring. Or perhaps it was that Catherine's first year of marriage had brought a new awareness of children. She noticed that after they had been cooped up for weeks and months on end, they were bursting with energy, hard to hold down. Yet the wind was knife edged, the world still muddy and wet. So many of the village's small noses seemed to be running, so many eyes rheumy and puffed with fever. It pained her to see them suffer, and a new ability was being borne within her heart to care for those small and fragile angels.

The path was treacherous as she climbed the steep hillside. By the time she arrived at the first stream, her skirt was rimmed with mud. Catherine paused at the final turn before the path moved into the thicker forest to stare out over the village and the bay. She tried to tell herself it was a foolish trek. The snows had scarcely melted, and there would not be the slightest chance of finding either flowers or berries. Even so, when she turned back to start up the final rise to the meadow, she could not help but smile in anticipation.

Louise pushed back her long hair with a hand freed at last from winter mittens. It was so good to be released into fresh air—even if it was still very chilly. Her eyes drifted upward, noting the sun that shone down with muted warmth. It held great promise, but the still-sharp wind blew away any strength to really warm the world beneath. But spring would come. It must win over winter, Louise reminded herself. God had promised that season would follow season.

With that thought firmly in place, Louise quickened her step. It was much too early to be visiting the meadow, but she couldn't resist. None of the plants had begun to unfurl new leaves—but she had to go. Had to push free of the little house, beloved though it was, and stretch her legs and her cobwebbed mind once again to include more of the world in which she lived.

The long, hard winter had brought reminders of winters past to the older residents of Minas. Elderly ladies had snuggled more closely to the fire, tongues wagging with oft-repeated tales of earlier struggles and what had gotten them through. Louise was not used to being so confined. She chafed as Henri bid her stay by the fire's warmth lest she take a chill. Even as milder weather finally reached them, Henri worried that she might return home with icy feet and skirts, or suffer one of the village's many ills.

So when Henri eventually gave in to her entreaties, it was with suppressed jubilation that Louise finally took to the hillside path.

Many times over the long, wintry days she had thought of the young Englishwoman. Had she fared well over the winter months? On a few occasions she had found the young woman's name creeping into her evening prayers. She flushed and wondered what her parents would think of her praying for the enemy. What would Henri think?

But Louise could not make herself see Catherine as the enemy. Louise saw her as another young woman, much like herself— seeking to make a home, loving her new husband, searching in her own way for a chance to make their world a better place for the children they hoped to one day have. No, she was not an enemy. But did she dare to think of her as a friend? She was, after all, English, and the English and French had been enemies for decades beyond count.

With a determined sigh, Louise pushed the thoughts of enemies and warring aside. She crossed the small creek that now flowed with the renewed vigor of spring melting. It took all her concentration to keep her feet firmly planted on the crossing log as she eased her way across the stream. If she wasn't careful she would be returning home completely sodden, just as Henri had warned.

Lithely she jumped the last few feet, landing on firm ground, pleased with herself for outwitting the rushing water. Overhead a bird sang. The first birdsong of spring. Louise smiled. Surely their winter ordeal was behind them.

The meadow was just ahead now. Louise's steps quickened. Was it possible that the young Englishwoman would also have felt the need to refresh her spirit at this spot that was special to both of them?

Louise's eyes quickly scanned the leafless meadow bushes. She felt a moment of keen disappointment. Why had she even dared to hope? It was much too early for anyone to stir so far from the home fires simply for an outing. A breath of spring air.

And then Louise's dark eyes caught a slight movement at the meadow's far edge.

Something was there. Someone.

Louise watched without stirring, trying to determine just who shared the meadow with her. The figure was bundled warmly in winter wear, sitting sedately, silently, on a fallen log. Was it—? Not a soldier. The figure was too slender, not tall enough to be a man. And then the head lifted, turned toward her, and after a moment's hesitation a mittened hand rose in greeting. "Bonjour" came the lilting cry across the meadow.

They hurried toward each other, eyes alight with the joy of meeting.

There was no hesitation in Louise's embrace, but she could feel Catherine's English reserve at this new experience. But Louise held her in the French fashion, cheek to cheek, and knew when Catherine relaxed.

Louise smiled and moved back a pace. Both were speaking at once. Expressing relief at finding the other, asking about the winter's toll on the other's village, voicing the fact that it was so good to be free at last from winter's clutches.

When they stopped for breath, they smiled at each other, timidly now as mutual realization of their unguarded reactions began to sink in.

"Your French," Louise enthused, "it has grown with the winter."

Catherine answered with a soft laugh. "I have been practicing and practicing. I do hope that it has made improvement. My little French grammar is near worn through—yet I do not remember if I pronounce things right."

"It is much improved. I only wish that I could speak the English tongue with such competence."

Catherine blushed. "Thank you for such a—a compliment. You must be free to correct me—when I make an error."

Louise nodded. "If you wish," she responded.

"Oh—I do. I will never learn otherwise. The grammar books—they do not give full instruction. One must have a real teacher."

Louise laughed and lifted the hem of her muddy skirt. "Then I will be your tutor. Happily so. But look at me. A muddy tutor I am, to be sure."

Catherine's laughter echoed Louise's as she looked down at her own hemline. "Well, you have also a muddy pupil, so we are—what do you say?—the same."

Louise gave her the French word for "even," which Catherine carefully repeated. Then Louise moved toward the fallen log from which Catherine had risen. "Let's sit down," she prompted. "I do not have much time, and there is so much to say."

Time. Louise wished with all her heart that the time would not pass so quickly. She had counted the days until this meeting might take place. Now that it had, she was sharply aware of its brevity.

"You say there has been much sickness. In our village, too. It will end now—with the coming of the warm sun again. It always does."

Catherine nodded. "I hope you are right. It has been a very difficult winter for many in our village."

"A winter hard for the beasts and the men as well," Louise agreed. "Our horses are lean and shaggy, their bones showing through."

"My husband worries nearly as much about his animals as he does about his men," Catherine agreed. "Andrew says we need the spring grasses for the stock to gain strength again."

"How is your Andrew?"

Catherine's cheeks flushed as she said, "He's been fine, but very busy. He's not had one bout of ill health all winter. I tell him it is his determination and concern that keeps him healthy. He is always thinking of others. And not enough about himself." Catherine held up two mittened hands and chuckled

159

softly. "See me. I am still in woolens. Andrew's orders. He wouldn't let me out of the house unless I promised to dress for the dead of winter."

Louise joined the laughter. "He sounds like my Henri," she responded. "I have just now—this day—been given permission to leave those scratchy things behind on the shelf."

"I hope I soon will have such freedom of movement. I am tired of being bundled so I can scarcely breathe."

"Yet," spoke Louise, "it is nice to be cared for. It makes one feel—so special."

"Loved," responded Catherine as two sets of eyes met and softened in unison.

"Loved," repeated Louise. "We are very blessed to be loved. And by such wonderful men."

Catherine nodded. When she spoke, her voice was soft with emotion. "I do not know your Henri," she said, "but knowing you, I am sure that he is just as you say. Very special. Very wonderful. It is too bad that we meet at such a time—that our husbands will not have a chance to share a friendship simply because . . ."

"Because our two countries have declared that we should be at war," finished Louise sadly.

"Yes."

"It is outrageous," said Louise, her feelings so powerful that it drove her to her feet. "What have you ever done to me? What have I ever done to you that we should be enemies? And Henri and Andrew? Why should they not be friends? Because some distant rulers somewhere dictate the way it should be, should we listen?"

Catherine's hand came down gently on the other young woman's sleeve. "We cannot help the circumstance of our times. But we can be friends. Perhaps not openly. But we can be friends. We have—" She formed an arc with outstretched hand toward the meadow before them. "We have this," she said. "It is our meeting place. Our sanctuary. When we come here we come as equals. Women. Wives. Friends. We share the same dreams. The same hopes. We must not let others keep us enemies."

Louise reached down to take the mittened hand in her own bare one. "You are right," she said, brushing at tears with her free hand. "Henri says that it will never happen. Things will just go on, with worrisome rumblings from time to time. But nothing else. The British have been threatening for years." Louise paused, then added, "I don't mean you, of course."

Catherine's eyes clouded. "Andrew fears that this time might be different." Her words trailed off, and she bit her lip. "We must not think of it. It has not happened. Perhaps it never will. To dwell on it would be wrong. It makes me feel angry and frustrated inside. We live where we live. We can do nothing about that. So we must accept it."

"But we do not have to be shaped by it," Louise quietly agreed.

"We do not have to become like them," Catherine said. "We do not have to be enemies."

"Never enemies," Louise agreed. "Never at war. God would not wish it to be so."

They fell into silence, each busy with her own thoughts.

At last Catherine spoke. "What do you know of God?" she asked softly.

Louise moved to sit down beside her once again. "I know He is Father, Son, and Holy Spirit. The way. The truth. The life."

"He is all that to you?"

"No, perhaps not if I answer truthfully from my heart. I know that Scripture declares Him to be so, but I confess I do not fully understand it. But with the rumors of war"—Louise placed a hand over her heart—"I have . . . stirrings. I feel I want to know more about Him."

"I feel that way, too."

"You do?"

Catherine nodded. "I never really cared that much before. I never wanted to seek God. My father had the Bible in his hand each time I looked his direction. In the evenings by the fire while I stitched. In the mornings before he went about his daily duties. At the noon meal he read a portion. He insisted that I read the Scriptures, too. Memorize verses. I saw it as duty. But since Andrew—"

"Marriage has made a big difference," Louise offered solemnly.

"Oh yes. Andrew and I have been reading the Scriptures together. I have found a whole new purpose. A whole new attitude. We've been searching for truth. And when Andrew is away, I read almost from morning to night on some dreary days. I can't wait to discover something more. To have it to talk about with Andrew when he comes home. It's been exciting."

"And you understand?"

"No, not everything. But some things gradually are becoming more clear. It's like . . . like mining for gold. You find one nugget, then another and another."

"Do you suppose," Louise said, the yearning in her heart making her voice unsteady, "that when you find a . . . a nugget, you could tell me and I can take it home to Henri?"

"You mean . . ."

"Yes. There is so much that I do not understand. I ask Henri, but it puzzles him also. Henri is not so taken with reading and study. Or with such questions as this. 'Live a good life,' he says. 'That is what counts.' And he lives a good life. He is a good man. Always devoted to duty. To others." Louise's features turned wistful. "But if I myself were able to understand. To be able to show him such gems."

Catherine's face reflected her uncertainty. "But there is so much I still don't know and can't understand."

"Then perhaps we can find some nuggets together."

Catherine nodded slowly. "It is true. The two of us can seek what I do not understand alone. That would be wonderful."

Louise's thoughts raced onward. This would also mean regular meetings with Catherine. She found herself looking forward to the days ahead with new anticipation. She looked at Catherine and thought she could see the same anticipation reflected back.

CHAPTER TWELVE

Andrew returned from the summer's first sortie, and he had to stifle a groan at the sight of the seagoing vessel anchored in Cobequid Bay. He and his men were dirty and stiff and worn from seven long days in the saddle. He did not need unexpected official visitors at such a time. He yearned for home and Catherine. But the fort's sentries stood with uncommon stiffness, weapons etched sharply against the afternoon sky, and Andrew knew that he would not get home anytime soon. Andrew accepted the sentry's salute, spotted the official marching toward him, and felt himself tense up as well.

"Ah, Harrow, there you are." Captain Randolf Stevenage's drawl rang through the still air. "How gentlemanly of you to deign to join me."

"My apologies, sir." He found himself adopting the same manner as the guards, formal and absolutely correct. A private assigned stable duty hastened over and took the reins of his weary steed. "Had I realized you were coming, I would have been here personally to greet you."

"Yes, of course." Stevenage turned away on polished thigh boots, slapping his riding gloves upon his leg. "Well, I must take that to mean the Indians have intercepted my messenger. Or the Frenchies."

"That would be uncommonly strange, sir, begging your pardon." With any other officer, Andrew's normal demeanor would have been respectfully direct. But Stevenage was a full-fledged captain, while Andrew's own promotion was still as an acting commandant, and Stevenage was assigned to headquarters, while Andrew was relegated to a small backwater fort. And there was something about this man's manner which shouted peril. "But we have not had a single attack on the trails we guard in over a year," he explained, his tone matter-of-fact.

Stevenage wheeled around and stared up at him. "Are you questioning my judgment here, Harrow?"

"Far from it, Captain. I only meant that a lone man traveling fast would hardly be the likely target of an attack. Particularly when we have known such a long stretch of peace and—"

"Because I do not take kindly to having *subordinate* officers show such liberties. Not kindly at all."

Overcoming his fatigue and inner frustration, Andrew drew himself to parade-ground attention. "I humbly apologize for any slight, sir, however unintended."

"That's all well and good. Even so, we can't permit such a breach in discipline." Either Stevenage did not see the hostile glances being shot his way from the men currying Andrew's horse or he chose to pay them no mind. "How am I to know you did not choose to ignore my messenger and send him on ahead to his next rendezvous?"

"I must respectfully assure you, sir, that I did no such thing. You may check with the men who accompanied—"

"I may well do that, Harrow," Stevenage interrupted. "But of course you could have already bought their silence." His expression reminded Andrew of a cat playing with a mouse. "So this really comes down to your word against mine, doesn't it?" the man finished, with another slap of his glove against his leg.

Before Andrew could think of a reply, the stable hand closest to the fortress doors craned and shouted, "Rider coming fast, sir!"

"Thank you, soldier." Andrew gave a stiff bow and said as he walked past Stevenage, "Permit me to see what this is about."

A stranger came pounding through the outer gates, his horse blowing hard and steaming in the late June sun. He pulled to a dusty halt and saluted toward Stevenage as he stood glowering. "Begging your pardon, sir! My horse threw a shoe this side of Annapolis Royal. Had to proceed on foot a full day and a half before I found a village with a smithy and a forge."

"You—" Captain Stevenage obviously was biting down hard on his ire, for all the fort's eyes were upon him. He turned to where Andrew was standing and shouted, "Draw your men up for inspection!"

"Certainly, sir." Andrew was most gratified to find his aide-de-camp waiting nearby. "Carry on, Sergeant Major."

"Sir!" He stomped a polished boot as he wheeled about and roared, "Fall in for inspection!"

Clearly his sergeant major had spent the time since Stevenage's arrival preparing the troops, for Andrew could scarcely recall ever having seen the fort's soldiers looking so well fitted. Brass and boots and belts all were polished until they shone, muskets gleamed, hats and coats mended, and all the men properly attired. "Troop, atten-*shun*!"

Andrew stood front and center to the group, amazed to find that even the ones who had traveled with him had been quickly brushed up and brought to a fairly reputable state by the sergeant major. They stood alongside the others of his meager regiment, appearing more appropriate for the Halifax parade ground than the dusty courtyard of a frontier fort.

Captain Stevenage seemed taken aback both by their dress and how swiftly the troops were brought to order. He passed down their ranks with a glassy eye, leaving Andrew to wonder if the man had traveled all this distance just to find something to criticize. Andrew walked alongside him, as proud of his men and his fort as he had ever been. No matter that his command and his rank were both temporary. For this moment, for this point in his life, the fort belonged to Andrew Harrow. And his men had done him proud.

Stevenage reached the end of the rows obviously disgruntled. He wheeled about and marched to stand beneath the flagpole. Unbuttoning his pocket, he drew out a document with its watermark and ribbon of royal rank.

All was brought into crystal clarity as soon as Stevenage began to read. "It is recognized that Lieutenant Andrew Harrow has performed duties related to the running of Fort Edward in an exemplary fashion, accepting command for an entire winter while his commandant remained ill." Stevenage's voice sounded slightly strangled as he continued. "Andrew Harrow, you are hereby confirmed as captain in the King's Own Regiment of His Majesty's Service." The hand holding the document fell in defeat to Stevenage's side. "Congratulations." He would not look at Andrew as the mumbled word left his lips.

The sergeant major filled the sudden silence with a roared, "Three cheers for Captain Harrow!"

As the troops began their lusty cheer, Randolf Stevenage turned and started for the fort's main gates. "Walk with me, Harrow," he barked.

"Certainly." Andrew allowed the visitor to travel a few paces ahead so that he could murmur as he passed, "Well done, Sergeant Major."

"Knew he was up to no good, the way he came in here and started sniffing about," the older man muttered. "Congratulations, sir."

Andrew passed through the gates and stood alongside Stevenage. The officer pointed westward, across the sparkling ribbon of the Minas River. "Any trouble from your crop of Frenchies?" he sneered.

"None." Now that they were again of equal rank he could permit himself a clipped tone. "Not from them, not from anyone in our district. We have found the best policy to take is one of peaceful—"

"Governor Lawrence is hereby ordering you to draw up a plan of defense."

Andrew stared at Stevenage. "Against whom?"

"The Frenchies, of course. That is the purpose of my visit. I am assigned to carry the new orders to all the forts around the Bay of Fundy. You are aware they have once again refused to sign the king's order."

Only because the officials in Halifax insist on including in the document that the French must bear arms. But Andrew kept his retort to himself. "No doubt Governor Lawrence is aware that we are at peace."

"Governor Lawrence is *most certainly* aware of the larger picture, something which has obviously escaped you here in your little colonial outpost!" Stevenage's shout was loud enough to silence the quiet chatter back in the fort. "War has come to our homeland. Which of course is where our first allegiance lies, doesn't it, Captain Harrow?"

"Of course," Andrew quietly agreed.

"The officials in Halifax, those who are aware of the *true* course of events, have a new name for your Frenchie neighbors. They have been dubbed the 'Unreliables,' for there is great doubt as to which way they will go when conflict arises. And believe me,

Harrow. Conflict will arise."

Stevenage flipped his right hand and the gloves they held in a barely perceptible salute. "I must be off, Harrow. The lieutenant has informed me that the boat sails with the tide."

"Very well." Andrew did not offer to see him to the ship. As he watched the stiff, retreating back, his relief at the man's departure was overcome by deep sorrow. Not even his new promotion could wipe away the sense of being caught up in the sweep of a powerful and invisible tide.

Andrew could tell that Catherine was making a valiant effort to give him the sort of welcome he had come to expect. After seven days scouting the hinterland, the warmth of her love eased even the greatest burden of fatigue. Yet he could sense a shadow over her welcome, despite the smile and the hug as soon as he crossed the threshold. He pulled her to arm's length and asked, "How are you, my love? Is everything all right?"

"Why shouldn't all be well with me this day? You are home!" But the coquettishness looked as forced as her smile. "My husband is back home safe and sound, and the summer is as splendid as the winter was hard."

Andrew drew her to the little table where they dined and pulled her gently into a chair. He seated himself beside her and said, more quietly still, "Tell me."

She tried to hold to her smile. "You still have the dust of the trail upon you. Let me heat water for a bath. Everything else can wait."

"How can I relax when I know something is distressing you?"

Her smile faded. "It is nothing. I am being a silly woman, and I . . . I so wanted to make you welcome."

"You cannot help but make me feel at home." He squeezed her hands, feeling that somehow he already knew what it was, sensing the news before he even heard the words. "Tell me. Please."

"Priscilla Stevenage was here. She accompanied her husband on the boat." Her face crumpled. "Why does she hate me, Andrew?"

"It's not you. It's me. Randolf sees me as a threat."

"But why?" At the pain in her voice, Andrew squeezed her hands more tightly and sighed. There were times like now when he

173

regretted Catherine's desire to know about his work and all the related affairs.

But he had decided in their marriage's early days that if she truly wanted to know, he should tell her. As with so much else, he could not rely on tradition. It was tradition that had estranged him from his beloved father and barred him from being there at the old man's deathbed. No. If Catherine wanted to know, then he would tell her. "You know that I paid brief court to Priscilla," he began slowly.

"I know."

He sighed again, hating to say these things, but wanting to have it out and done with. "I fear she did not take well to my declining interest. But it is not just this. Randolf Stevenage is a man of mediocre talents. The two times he has been in the field were potential disasters, averted only at the last moment, and by the actions of underlings and not himself."

"How do you know these things?"

"My last visit to Annapolis Royal brought me into contact with a man who had been posted to Halifax. He begged me to find a place for him here. When I asked why, he confided that he had served under Stevenage once and never would again." He wondered at the ease with which he spoke of such things to her. But there was such intelligence in Catherine's gaze, such a hunger to understand and share his world, he did not even feel a need to remind her how private these discussions had to remain. "Randolf Stevenage used his father's connections to secure the posting in Halifax. He loves power and craves a higher rank. He knows the senior officers have their eye upon me. As a matter of fact, he arrived today to inform me that my promotion has been formalized."

"Oh, Andrew, that's wonderful!"

He accepted her hug and waited until she had resumed her seat before continuing. "Randolf came hoping to find something to criticize, something to take back with him from the field that might undermine the way his own superiors view me."

Catherine nodded, her composure as somber as he had ever known it. "Priscilla demanded to know where I kept disappearing to for such long afternoons away from the village."

Despite the day's warmth, Andrew felt a sudden chill. "You didn't tell her."

"Of course not. But I was so frightened. How did she know?"

"There is someone in the village who is spying for her—for them. It can be nothing else."

Catherine's distress mounted. "Why would anyone hate me like that?"

"They don't hate you, my darling. They are simply trying to curry favor with the powers in Halifax. Almost anyone here in Edward could be tempted. Someone seeking a permit for selling at market, or rights to transport goods for the army . . ." A dozen different possibilities sprang to mind, but he pushed them away. "It would do us no good to wonder. All it would make us do is question our neighbors."

She could not keep the tremor from her voice. "Do you want me to stop seeing Louise?"

He was sorely tempted to say yes. As spring had grown into summer the frequency of Catherine's visits up the hillside had increased, as had the length of her stays. But she was finding such joy up in the meadow, such purpose and peace.

And there was something else. Something Andrew could not precisely put his finger on. As though a still, quiet voice at the very center of his heart was whispering to him, urging him not to do what his more logical mind was suggesting.

And this quiet inner voice could not be denied. "No." The word was murmured, quiet as the birdsong beyond their open window. "I cannot ask that of you."

Any reservations he might have had over his decision were erased at the light which sprang to her eyes. "Oh, thank you. I wouldn't defy your decision if you had said I should stop. But it is so wonderful being up there with her, I wish I could explain. . . ." She turned, and her shining eyes fell upon the Bible lying open upon their dining table. "We have such a wonderful time reading the Bible together. She does not have a Bible of her own. There have been no French ships since the blockade, and books in the French villages are ten times what they cost us. She brings a church prayer book, and once she brought her parents' family Bible. But that was too precious, too large and difficult to bring again. It has five generations listed in the family tree at the beginning." Her words tumbled upon one another. "It has been so wonderful, the two of us sitting in the sunshine, the Book open on our laps. I read passages from our English Bible and translate, and then we discuss them together. The last time, Louise brought a French Bible that the vicar had loaned to her. Oh, I wish I could describe to you how it feels."

Andrew's own gaze turned to the Book. It remained open to the Gospel of Luke, which they had just started perusing before his departure.

A change seemed to overtake his vision, as though the whisper of his heart began to take on form before his eyes. Andrew saw not the open page but rather his beloved wife, seated at the edge of a meadow he had never visited and knew only through her. Alongside her was seated another woman, a stranger of darker hair and complexion, who laughed and talked in a language he did not understand. A total stranger, yet one who was bound to his wife by the Bible in her lap. The holy Book opened and discussed in different languages and held by different hands. So close, yet divided by centuries of war and hardship and conflict. So close.

Andrew drew the room back into focus and said, "Just be careful. That is all I ask. In your going and in your coming and in the time you spend with this Frenchwoman, take every possible care."

CHAPTER THIRTEEN

Henri Robichaud walked around to the back of his house and entered the shed where he kept his tools. This was the place where he felt closest to his father, where the heritage which had almost been lost was clearest to his mind and heart.

His father, a taciturn man, had measured out his words with the care of a miser weighing purest gold. But he had been a good man, good with his hands and better with his son. It was through work that his father had communicated best, showing by example the bonds that tied the Robichaud family to their God, to this home and this piece of earth. He had bound his son deeply to the place and the community, so deeply that even when he was plucked too soon from this earth, still his son strove to keep the fragile flame of heritage alive.

All his father's tools were still there. Even when they had long outlived their usefulness, Henri refused to let go of this part of his bond. Instead he had mounted the pieces high upon the walls on wooden pegs, so that everywhere he looked he was confronted with the imprint of that grand old man. Henri found himself staring at the wooden hay fork with the middle tooth broken off, the handle darkened almost black with his father's sweat. Next to it hung the poke used at lambing time, a collar to immobilize the sheep. Henri's gaze ran on around the shed's walls, taking in the ancient winnower and crop-cradle and flat-hammer and hardy and adze and broadax and auger—all vital components of his memories, his heritage.

He reached into the corner and pulled out his own eel spear. The shaft was as thick as his upper arm and carved from the trunk of an ash, one of the most hard woods to be found. Imbedded at the crown was a razor-sharp trident, each blade twice the length of his middle finger.

Henri took down his father's grist stone and spat into its center. Carefully he ground the trident's three fingers in slow circles, refining the points until they shone in the light streaming through the shed's open door. Finally satisfied, he reached back into the corner for a second more slender pole. He stepped outside, balanced the spear on one shoulder and the pole on the other, and started off.

As he rounded the corner of the house, Louise appeared in the doorway. His heart lurched at the sight of her. She was such a lovely one, this darkly beautiful queen of his home and his heart. From beneath her starched bonnet streamed hair long and lustrous as a raven waterfall, a shining river that he loved to run through his fingers. They had been married almost a year, and still he marveled at that simple movement. His fingers were so stubby, his hands so hard and rough, when twined through her long tresses. Gentle as he might try to be at those times, he could scarcely believe that she would permit him such a liberty, much less mean it when she said that she truly loved his touch.

But her normally dancing eyes were somber now, her usually shining face shadowed and turned down at every plane. Henri longed to set down his burdens, walk over, take her in his arms there on the stoop, and let the entire village know just how precious she was to him. But not this morning, not this day. Instead he willed himself to smile, though it was only his mouth that carried the movement. Louise answered with a smile of her own, one which did nothing to erase the sadness blanketing her features.

There was none of their normal banter, none of the promise to take care and be back before the setting sun. Today there was only a heavy silence, filled with all that remained unspoken between them.

Henri took the long path down the terraced earth to the bayside. He arrived at the correct moment, when the tide was beginning to flow out and pulling strong. He walked to the bushes where he had last moored his flat-bottomed canoe, and set down his tools. Normally two men were required to pull such a boat across the bank and into the water. Henri was one of the village's few men who could do so alone. His father had been another, but whenever he and Henri had come down to the water's edge together, his father had pretended that he could not manage the burden by himself. "Come help me," his father would say, "give me your young strength." And Henri would pull with all his might, dragging the rough-hewn boat down to the water's edge, feeling like the man he hoped one day to become.

Since his marriage, Henri some days imagined what it would be like to have a youngster there beside him, one whom he loved so much that he would willingly play the weakling and give his son the right to know a strength of his own.

But this morning he did not dream of times to come. Instead he felt only relief that he had a day of solitude before him, confined not by his own efforts but by the much stronger tides. He pulled the boat down to the water's edge and stepped deftly into its stable center. Two strong pushes upon the skiff pole and he felt the ebbing current grab hold. He reversed his hold on the pole and began pushing against the tide, keeping the boat to the edge of the retreating waters.

Searching the tidal ponds was only possible from a boat. The mud was so glutinous and deep that a man could not stand, much less walk. Just that spring a neighbor's prized cow had escaped the corral and stumbled into the low-tide flats. Before men could be gathered and a noose fitted, the bellowing cow had sunk out of sight and drowned. A dugout canoe with a flat bottom was the only conveyance of use in these circumstances, one whose outer shell had been hardened by a slow-burning fire. The thick skin bobbed like an unstable cork and drew only a few inches of water. It was a hard vessel to steer and harder yet to hold stable when fighting an eel.

Eel fishing was a very precise practice, one which required extreme care and attention, and therefore suited him perfectly this day. For Henri had not come out here to think. He only wanted to hold the world at arm's length. Henri had found that answers to the hardest questions came when he was able to forget about them entirely. Otherwise he found his thoughts becoming a storm, and nothing was solved, nothing accomplished. If he could only manage to put the problem aside for a few hours, more often than not he found the answer appearing all by itself.

The bay was empty today, which he took as a good sign. The grand English ship had unfurled its sails and left at sunset the previous day. He poled against the tide, carefully searching each of the gullies he passed. Henri had heard that Cobequid Bay held to the highest tidal surges in the world. He had seen it rise and fall as much as eighteen feet in each direction. As the tide continued to drop, more and more mud flats became exposed, the mucky black surface pocked and cratered. These ponds sometimes trapped and held huge ocean eels, which the women of his village salted and pickled. A barrel of pickled eel from Minas was a delicacy known as far away as France.

The morning was hushed and warm, the air so breathless each tidal pool became a mirror. Henri searched and poled, the sweat dripping freely from his brow. In the quiet solitude he found himself recalling the previous evening's events, ones which had robbed his night of sleep and stolen peace from his morning. Despite his desire not to think at all, the memory and its troubling mystery insisted on coming back time and again.

Yesterday Louise had invited her entire family to join them for the evening meal. These were occasions for great laughter and jollity, as Henri cared deeply for all the Belleveaux. Louise's two younger brothers, Eli and Philippe, considered Henri a perfect brother-in-law, for he seldom spoke and rewarded every story and most comments with his rich laugh. Henri loved the brothers' company and felt honored by the comfortable kinship shown to him by Louise's parents. He hungered for the sense of belonging to such a family.

Yes, Louise's mother was a bit of a scold. Marie Belleveau was known throughout the village as a woman more comfortable with a frown than a smile, and most times when she opened her mouth it was to nag. But she approved of Henri. He knew that even when she arrived full of criticism for his front garden.

"How you can show your face about the village with such a jungle for a garden I will never understand," were the woman's first words.

"You are right, of course, Mama Marie." Henri adopted his most soothing tone and bowed her into their little living room.

"And the state of your roof, I believe you have more moss up there than slate." She huffed herself down by the fire, for the setting sun had brought a north wind and with it an uncommon chill for late June. "And your shutters, the paint peeling so, never have I seen such a—"

"Here, Mama." Louise's arm swooped down with a cup of steaming cider. "Let's see if this will take the edge off your tongue."

Henri was not certain who of the family was more surprised at Louise's words. She rarely showed anything but patience and calm in the face of her mother's tirades. On the infrequent occasions when something did unravel her control, it was normally at the end of a harangue, not the beginning. Henri's eyes quickly scouted the room, and he found surprise on every face, including Marie Belleveau's.

So he did what he was best at, which was to warm the room with his most infectious smile. He turned to Eli to say, "Word has it you had a good day at market."

"Ah, let me tell you, you don't know the half of it." Young Eli considered himself to be the best trader in the village, and took it as a personal affront when anyone claimed to have made a better deal. "Took a load of our cheese down to Cobequid Town. The road was wet and the horses angry, but it was well worth the journey."

The adults settled themselves about the room and offered jests and jibes to punctuate Eli's bragging. All but Marie, who seemed to be studying her daughter with a pensive squint. Louise scurried about the kitchen, refusing offers of help from Philippe's new wife. Her back remained stiffly erect with an emotion Henri could not fathom. After all, it was she herself who had called for this family meal together.

The gathering remained in good cheer throughout the meal, warmed by a hearty stew and good cider and the prospect of a fine crop this year. Henri noted that Louise did not join in, remaining distant and reflective. Twice he slipped his hand into hers, masking his concern with a smile and warm compliments over the meal. She nodded to his words, but her gaze was unfocused and her hand cold.

As she was serving a steaming peach cobbler, there came a knock on the door, and the vicar let himself in. "I could smell the aroma of your cooking halfway across the village, Wife Robichaud."

The formal way of addressing a young woman was one from the distant days of yesteryear, but Henri felt pride and even affirmation of himself as he stood to greet the vicar. *Wife Robichaud.* "You honor us with your coming, Jean Ricard."

"I thank you for the invitation. No, thank you, Louise, I will take no stew. I supped with the Widow Lambre, whose son and granddaughter are up from Cobequid

Town. A lovely child, lovely. And bright as the sun. Yes, thank you, a piece of that sweet-smelling cobbler will be perfect."

Louise settled the bowl in front of the vicar, her eyes watching him eat and talk and laugh with the others, following the path of his spoon as it rose and fell. Marie observed them both, her own face gravely unreadable. Henri could only watch and wonder.

When the vicar had finished and pushed the bowl aside, Louise walked to the head of the table. "I have something to tell you."

The earnestness of her expression stilled them all. Clearly she had been waiting for the vicar to arrive before speaking. Henri saw Jacques Belleveau look a question at his wife, and another at the vicar. Neither showed any more awareness of what was about to come than Henri had. Louise's father said, "Well, out with it, child."

"There's something eating at your craw," her mother quietly agreed. "We've seen that this night."

"Yes. You're right." Louise twisted her hands into a knot so tight the knuckles stood out white.

Jacques pushed out the chair next to his own. "Sit yourself down here and speak with us. You haven't been off your feet all night."

She paused, then lowered herself to the

chair and forced a long breath. "I have made a new woman friend."

Henri fought down a sudden laugh. Not that Louise's words were humorous. But he could have made a joke, his way of dealing with almost any problem. Yet a single warning glance from Louise's mother halted the words before they were formed.

Louise gave no sign of having noticed the silent exchange. Her hands twisted harder together, and she said carefully, "She is English."

The room's sudden silence seemed as loud as a thunder clap. Then chairs creaked about the table as people adjusted to the news and cast glances at their neighbors.

"We met last year," Louise went on. "The day before our wedding. I had gone up to the high meadow to gather wild flowers. She . . . her name is Catherine. Catherine Harrow. She was married on the same day as Henri and I." She turned to look at him, and he was the first to break eye contact. He stared at the table, his troubled thoughts swirling his emotions into turmoil.

Gradually the glances about the table centered upon two men, Louise's father and the vicar. It was their place to speak first. Jacques Belleveau cleared his throat and asked quietly, "You have seen her again?"

"Yes." It was no longer enough to hold her hands together. Louise bunched up the apron, twisting and turning the starched material. "Yes. Last autumn and then again this spring. And summer."

Henri had been around enough Belleveau clan meetings to recognize the calm face and tone as Jacques's chosen manner in dealing with all troubling issues. "So you have met her several times, then."

"Yes. More . . . more than several. Many times." Another breath. "Almost once a week in May and June."

A sigh of surprise surfaced around the room, more telling than any words. Jacques shot a warning glance to the others, then turned back and held to the experienced calm of a clan elder. "And what do you talk about?"

"Everything." A single tear squeezed from one eye. "Families and marriage and winter and crops. Everything. We trade recipes. We talk about our homes." Louise's lips trembled along with her voice.

"Every week you meet with an English lady. And only now you decide it is time to speak with us, your family. Did you not think it should have been brought to us before now?"

"Of course I did." Another tear escaped.

Louise did not seem to even realize she was crying. "I was afraid. I was afraid you wouldn't understand, that you would tell me not to see her. That's what you're going to do, isn't it?"

"We're not saying anything just yet, child." The responsibilities of father, of clan leader, were evident on his face as he said, "First I would like to know a little more about these discussions of yours."

"We have talked about everything, just as I . . ." She took a shaky breath and cast a fearful glance at the vicar. "We have been reading the Bible together."

"The Bible." Gradually the vicar raised himself erect, his eyes showing surprise. "So that is why you asked to borrow one."

"We started with Matthew. Now we are in Luke." Another tear came, and this time she raised the edge of her apron and wiped her eye. "We pray together. For our future and for our families."

The vicar glanced at Jacques, then said to Louise, "What do you find in the Gospels, child?"

"Love." And for some reason this one word was enough to bring further trembling to her mouth. "She is like a sister to me. Please do not say I must stay away."

Henri, heart pounding, saw Jacques Belleveau return the vicar's glance, give his head a tiny shake. The table was a frozen tableau of surprise and concern, the tension as strong a force as the meal's lingering aromas. Eyes on the vicar, Jacques asked his daughter, "Why did you decide to tell us now?"

"Because yesterday she told me who her husband is." A tremor escaped from the stiffness with which she held herself. One which was echoed in her voice as she declared, "Catherine is married to Captain Andrew Harrow, the commandant of Fort Edward and the English forces of Cobequid Bay."

A slight breeze traced its way across the water, rippling the surface of the next pond and making it difficult to inspect its depths. Sometimes a big eel would become trapped in a small bit of water, chasing after food with such avaricious fury that it disregarded the lowering tide. Other times a smaller breed would simply not notice the water's swift decline until it was too late. The mud flats were a black plain now, broader than the remaining waters of Cobequid Bay. The sun was high and glaring down, making the stench of drying mud and seaweed very strong. Henri did not mind. He had farmed this very same mud all his life, up above the first range of dikes. This was the richest farmland ever harvested—his father had said those words so often he could remember them still.

He poled down to where the next pond was forming, ignoring the flapping drumbeat caused by the tails of the five eels he had already caught. Three eels was a solid catch by anyone's standards, but Henri enjoyed his reputation as the best eeler in the village. All five were of a size, as the local women said, meaning they were the length of his arm. Yet he would still look, still hunt, still work at pushing aside all the worries that kept him from feeling the first hint of hunger, though it was now well past noon and he could almost taste the cheese and fruit Louise had packed for his lunch. *Louise.* What was he to do about this quandary? And to make things far worse, Jacques Belleveau's decision that night had astonished everyone in the room. Everyone, that is, except the vicar.

Louise's father had remained thoughtfully silent for a long time after his daughter had finished speaking. Finally he had risen to his feet and said simply, "Louise is now the wife of Henri Robichaud, first and foremost. I feel it is right to make no decision until I have heard from him. Vicar?"

"I agree," the pastor had said, rising to his feet with alacrity. "And it is time I make my way homeward."

"Time for all of us." Jacques hurried his wife and sons toward the door, waving them forward with uncommon dispatch. "Henri, you will come and see me on the morrow, yes? Good. Until then, I bid you both a good night."

The house had emptied before Henri could come up with words to protest. He did not like decisions. Especially ones where his own heart seemed set against the wishes of his beloved wife.

But he could not help it, not even here and now as he poled down the black murky shoreline, not even when the waterfowl and the wind and the sun were all there in summer finery. He was very confused. He disliked this intensely, especially now that the vicar's earlier conversation with him seemed to overlay this issue. He thought back to the winter day when Jean Ricard had suggested that he was to be the next clan elder. Why not Eli or Philippe? He did not want the honor, no, nor the responsibility. Give it to them.

The wind caught the surface of the pond

into which he peered, and suddenly he was staring at a totally different image. One which came not from the water but from his memory. It was of the warm evenings when Louise had taken to bringing the Bible outside, the one she had been given by the vicar. She would read as he sat beside her and worked at one chore or another, retying his nets or carving a bit of wood, small and slow motions to keep his hands busy at the end of a tiring day. And from time to time she would read a passage aloud, words that had so moved her he could hear the music of her heart. More often than not he ignored the words, registering more the sound of her voice than what she was saying. Her speaking was enough to draw a new peace from his own soul. One he had never known before, except perhaps in the few moments of Sunday worship when he found himself able to set all distractions aside.

Henri stopped his poling and straightened to wipe his brow. There was his answer, there in the sunlight splashing upon the dark sparkling mirrors of a thousand tiny pools. He would not do as he was inclined, as his mind said was the logical conclusion. He would not ask Louise to stop her friendship with this woman. No. Instead, he would make it a clan decision.

There was to be the summer gathering in a week's time, the same kind of gathering where last spring he had announced their engagement. Let Louise invite this English-woman. Let this Catherine show herself. If she accepted, then all would have a chance to decide for themselves. If she did not, then perhaps the decision would be taken for them. After all, what English soldier—a commandant no less—would permit his wife to attend a French village fête?

Relief flooded his entire being. Here was a way of restoring peace within his house, a way of offering his wife the confidence he felt, and not reacting from fear over this strange contact. Yet even more strong than the relief was the sense that here and now, surrounded by the heat and the smell of the rich black mud, he felt a peace slipping into his soul. It was the same feeling he had known while sitting of an evening beside his wife. It was a mystery, this feeling, one which left him sensing that he had done something good. Something beyond himself and his own comfortable habits.

His attention was caught by a rolling motion in the pond just up ahead. His breath was trapped in a throat suddenly tight and dry.

With stealthy motions he poled over,

careful not to make more of a stir upon the water than necessary. This was a large pond, and it was connected on the far side to yet another. If it was an eel, and it sensed his coming, it could quickly move out beyond the reach of his spear.

The water's surface rolled again, and he felt a shiver of anticipation race up his spine. The boat was moving steadily now, the motion enough to carry him forward on its own. Quietly, silently, he set down his pole and reached for the spear, his heart racing. The thickness and the strength and the weight had been made not for the type of eel he had caught before, nor for the normal day's catch, but rather for just such a moment as this.

The water rolled a third time, almost within reach, almost there. He raised the spear as high as he could, stretching himself fully, arching his back, readying himself for the plunge. He felt as though all his life as a fisherman had prepared him for this single instant. His father's quiet counsel was all there, powering him now as he stabbed a two-fisted surging plunge into the black waters.

The waters erupted.

The eel writhed up and out of the water with such vicious fury it almost toppled him over. It was longer than Henri was tall, longer than the boat itself. The muscular body, black and strong, was almost as thick as his thigh. The tail wrapped itself up and around the spear, reaching back until it could strike at Henri's arm, raising great red welts to his elbow. The mouth was open and snapping, the teeth long as his fingers and needle sharp. Henri rammed the spear down upon the boat's flooring and held the eel in place with both hands. He ignored the eel's writhing attack, the slaps upon his arms and shoulders and face. Slowly, slowly the eel's strength ebbed away. Finally Henri felt safe to ease his weight from the shaft and take the first true breath since plunging the spear into the depths.

It was a prize, the largest eel he had ever caught. The largest he had ever *seen*. Almost as if in recognition of his feat, the tide began to flow back into the bay.

Henri dropped to his knees, his strength so drained from the battle he could scarcely pick up his pole. With small tentative pushes, he guided the boat back inland, following the water's gradual rise. He wanted to shout, to laugh, to call to the people of Cobequid Bay. He was coming home with an eel so large it would make a feast for the entire village.

Louise would be so pleased.

CHAPTER FOURTEEN

The basin Louise carried splashed salty water over the brim, not because it was too full but because Louise could not keep her hands from shaking. It had been one thing for her husband to come home with his trademark smile and the largest eel anyone had ever seen, ever recalled seeing, one so large the tail dragged in the dust as Henri made his weary way up the hill to their home. Coming in as he did, dumping the eel in the front garden as though it were nothing more than a load of vegetables, and announcing that he had the perfect solution. Paying the grand prize no mind, not even as people were trailing behind him, calling out to neighbors and friends to come and see this incredible catch. Then reaching out his arms to her, the sparkle back in his dark eyes, showing her that the love and the joy were there once more. Louise had laughed and shied away, both because all the village was watching and because Henri's entire body was dripping with slime and scales. The village had watched and laughed with them, and even before she had heard his solution to the dilemma, she had known in her heart of hearts that everything truly would be all right.

Only today it was an entirely different matter. At the waist-high fence which ran around her mother's herb garden, Louise paused to shift the heavy basin to her other hip and to marshal the arguments that she had thought of in the night. Henri had gone up alone last evening to pass on his idea to her parents, and had come back subdued. Which meant that there was still some convincing to do. But Louise was certain that his plan was the right one. Catherine was not a threat to the family, not at all. The best way to show this was for the villagers to see her for themselves.

Catherine was the first new adult friend Louise had made. Everyone else in her world she had known since childhood, even her husband. Every day now, the feeling grew in her heart that this friendship was something important, something *vital*.

"Are you intending to stand there all day?" Her mother pushed the shutter open wide and stared out at her daughter. "What are you doing standing out there in the sun? Your skin will be as dark as an Indian's."

There was nothing to be done for it. She had to go in, she had to speak, she had to make this happen. "Good morning, Mama."

Her mother met her at the door, took one look at the basin in her hands, and called, "Jacques, come here and see."

Her burly father walked over, his morning pipe sending wreaths of smoke curling up. "What do you have there, child?"

"Eel," her mother said, poking one finger into the heavily salted brine used for pickling. "And it is just as big as they have been saying."

Jacques held his pipe to one side, peered down, and gave a low whistle. "It's as thick as my leg."

"Thicker." Marie gave the contents another poke. "How much more is there?"

"We gave a piece like this to Eli, another to Philippe, and Henri took down another bit to the Duprey farm this morning. We then filled a barrel, and have enough left over to give us all a plateful at the summer celebration."

"Such an eel. Never in my life have I even heard of such a beast being brought out of the deep," was her father's conclusion.

"And by one man in a flat-bottomed canoe." Her mother shook her head. "Your husband is the strongest man in Minas."

That such a compliment would cross her mother's lips caused father and daughter to look at each other in amazement. Jacques stepped away from the doorstep, taking the basin from Louise's hands. "Come in, child, sit with us a moment."

Louise wished there were some way to release the band gripping her chest. She knew there would never be a better time than now. "I want to know what you think of Henri's idea," she said without preamble.

Jacques and Marie both paused in unison, then moved with careful, deliberate motions. Louise stood in the doorway and watched her father slowly pass the basin to Marie, then take his time selecting a chair, drawing it out and sitting down. He leaned forward, selected a taper from the fireplace, and began the long process of relighting his pipe.

Marie carried the basin to the kitchen shelf, put it down where the sun would strike it to aid with the pickling, then took a clean cloth and wet it from the bucket. "Come here, daughter. I must clean the brine from your sleeves before they dry."

"I asked you a question." But Louise did as she was told.

Still, the silence held so long in their front room that the sound of her mother wiping at her sleeves grated upon raw nerves. When her mother finally spoke, it was in a tone she seldom used, thoughtful and musing. "You have never looked happier than you have these past few months. For a time I thought perhaps you were with child."

Her father did not turn from his inspection of the fire. "Are you, daughter?"

Louise found herself blushing. "No. Not that I know."

"I know part of this joy is because you have such a good man," her mother went on. "As good as any I have known, and I have been blessed with a good husband myself, and raised two fine sons."

"Thank you, Marie," Jacques said, puffing hard on his pipe, watching the fireplace flames with studied calm. "I have tried hard to deserve you."

Louise looked from one to the other. She could scarcely believe her ears. This open warmth and lack of tension could mean only one thing.

"You are going to let Catherine come?" she blurted.

Neither parent answered her directly. Instead, Jacques asked the flames and her, "Did your husband tell you what your mother said to him last night?"

"No. He told me nothing. All I know is he came in very subdued."

Jacques turned from his inspection of the fire, but it was to look at his wife, not his daughter. He asked Marie, "You are not worried?"

"Of course I am worried. Here, daughter, let me have your other sleeve. How can I not be worried? Who in their right mind could live in such a time and not know worries?"

"True," Jacques murmured. "Very true."

"But you have yourself said for months that we know too little. Perhaps this is as the vicar suggested."

Louise felt as though she were a little girl again, and her parents were speaking about her, rather than to her. "You talked with the vicar?"

"Last night, and again this morning." But Jacques continued to watch his wife's face. "He said that in his opinion, nothing but good could come from two young women who draw together by drawing closer to God."

"I agree," Marie said, her voice moving with her brisk motions on Louise's sleeve. "Though my heart quakes at all the unknowns ahead, I agree."

"We are constantly saying we wish we knew more," Jacques said, almost to himself. "Not more rumors, but facts. Certitudes, upon which we can make rightful judgments. Perhaps this friendship will help."

Marie looked up then, her eyes searching. "Would your Catherine tell us?"

Louise found her legs weak with relief. "I can but ask."

"We will ask her together," Jacques said, and his eyes crinkled at the edges, along with the corners of his mouth. "And now, wife, tell your daughter what concerned her husband so."

"I said," Marie responded, rubbing the sleeve with furious speed, "I said your husband is the clan's next elder in all but name."

The candle sputtered noisily, the flame jumping and sparking and scenting the home with its tallow smoke. Andrew shifted in his chair, trying to concentrate on Catherine's voice reading the passage aloud. But his senses were almost overwhelmed by conflicting impressions. He felt such a sense of marvel at her willingness to abide by his decision. Though he had an inkling of how important it was for her to go to this celebration in the French village, she still was willing to turn it over to him. But if she did go . . .

"You're not paying attention," Catherine said, looking up from the Bible in her lap.

"I'm trying."

She smiled at that. "The pastor said something about that on Sunday. That trying was not enough to earn a place in heaven. Only believing."

Andrew had to smile in return. "I fear I was not paying any more attention then either."

"Do you want to stop for the evening?"

"No." He hesitated, then confessed, "I'm just wondering at how you are willing to place this decision in my hands."

"Have you decided?" Her voice was tense.

"No." The word was a sigh, one fueled by the concern in her eyes. He could marshal a dozen reasons why she should not go to Minas. A hundred reasons. But none would be enough to ease her disappointment. "Catherine, this could be very dangerous," he began.

"You mean, for us here."

"Yes. There is peace between our two villages. But so many in power would see this as a perilous act, especially given my position."

Andrew could see how she struggled to hold back her arguments. "What is it?" he pressed.

"Nothing." Catherine hung her head,

her golden brown tresses falling about her face. "It's nothing."

Andrew reached over and gently lifted her chin. "Tell me." Her eyes seemed to open so that he was staring directly into her heart.

"I prayed about this all morning and afternoon. And the only sense of an answer I had was that I should not argue with you," she said, her voice low.

Here was another wonder, how she could speak of prayer in such easy terms, as though it came as natural as life itself. "You are different, Catherine. You have a new depth, a settledness."

She did not deny it. "I wish you could let me go. You know I'll take great care."

He hesitated long enough to hear the evening fire crackle and sing and whisper sweet mysteries of home. "And if I refuse?"

She was instantly stricken, her face creased with disappointment. But all she said was, "I suppose . . . I can't go. No. I won't go against your wishes."

How much this means to her. How close she has come to this Frenchwoman. It is not wise. But to deny her . . . Andrew looked away from the sorrow and turned his gaze back to the Book.

They were nearing the end of the ninth

chapter of Luke, but Andrew found his attention caught by a verse in the next chapter. One which seemed to reach up from the page and speak to his heart with such clarity the breath caught in his throat.

"Andrew, what is it?"

He did not speak. Silently he read the verse and felt it resound within him. "Go your ways: behold, I send you forth as lambs among wolves." Then his gaze was drawn forward, as though a hand were tracing its way across the page, taking him further, pointing the way. And he read, "And into whatsoever house ye enter, first say, Peace be to this house. And if the son of peace be there, your peace shall rest upon it: if not, it shall turn to you again. And in the same house remain, eating and drinking such things as they give."

"Andrew?"

"A moment," he managed. His mind was thinking back over the nights of that previous winter. Hours spent seated beside his beloved wife, learning to cherish her more as she spoke with quiet awe over all the new truths she was discovering in her readings. Messages of promise and hope and love. Messages of mercy. *Mercy.* He had never thought much about the word. It was so alien to his life as a soldier. *Mercy.* But she was right. He could see it here, could feel the message in his heart. What was mercy but love given, an act through which love showed itself? And what else was he called to do, over and over by these words that had never really spoken to him before?

Or perhaps they had. Perhaps all those nights had been preparing him for just such a moment as this, when his entire vision seemed to shift, to open so that he could look anew at his circumstances, at the decision now before him, fueled by the challenge nestled deep within one small word. *Mercy,* so clear it was almost audible.

He looked up from the page and met her gaze with his own. "What would you say," he asked quietly, "if I were to resign my commission?"

She drew back but without the shock he had half expected. "You mean, leave the army?"

"I am bound by my oath for another two years, but yes. At that point. Leave the regiment."

The words seemed to hang there between them. "I think a part of me has known for quite some time this might be coming," Catherine replied slowly. "But I felt it was something you needed to decide for yourself."

Andrew shook his head back and forth, without taking his gaze from Catherine. "What of all the importance and security granted an officer's wife?"

"It is a wonderful thing to walk through this village as the wife of Captain Harrow," she confessed. "But I married you, not the army. And after this winter and the time with you and the Word . . ." She stopped, inspecting him. "Does that surprise you?"

"It does indeed," he replied softly. "It surprises me very much."

"You are a good man, Andrew Harrow." She stroked his hand, then raised her fingers to trace their way down the side of his face. "A very good man indeed. Whatever you set your mind to, I am confident you will make a success of it."

He nodded acceptance, not just of her words, but of the message intended for him that night. He turned his head slightly to kiss the fingers, then spoke softly, "Be sure to give my greetings to the people of Minas."

Chapter Fifteen

The path Louise led Catherine down was different from the one on which she had arrived at the meadow that morning. Only then did she grasp the enormity of what they wanted to do. Catherine slowed so that she walked a pace behind her friend, and she prayed as fervently as ever she had. She prayed for herself, for Andrew, for her community, and for the little village of Minas.

The closer they came to the French village, the more uncertain Catherine became. Everything was so alien. She had not been away from her own village at the fort since her marriage, not even to the Chelmsford markets. Yet here she was, walking down an unknown trail which broadened into a foreign village lane, cloaked from head to toe in a French outer garment supplied by Louise. Passing the first village house, she noted exotic stone foundations and wooden walls and a roof unlike anything she had ever seen before.

The eaves draped long over the house, great arms intended to shelter the home from the strongest winds and harshest winters. Little dormer windows peaked from the shingles, each nestled within its own alcove and each possessing its own steep roof. The result was strangely logical and quaint. Everything she looked at spoke of permanence and history. Even the newer houses were dressed in the ancient way, and Catherine realized just how much time these people and their village had seen, here upon the bay she called her own.

Louise glanced back at that moment, and Catherine saw upon her friend's features the same tension and anxiety she felt in her own heart. They traded nervous smiles. So much was at stake here. Why had she come? Why take such a risk for herself and her husband? Why force herself to be disguised and secretive around the friends she had known all her life? And whatever would happen if her father found out about this clandestine visit? She didn't dare even imagine such a thing.

A child came scampering down a side lane, laughing and calling to someone they could not see. The little girl skipped into sight, wearing a starched cap and matching lace beneath a sky blue dress, a miniature replica of Louise's own attire. When she spotted the two ladies walking toward her, she stopped in her tracks. She stared up at Catherine with great round eyes and a mouth forming an "O" of surprise.

It was the most natural thing in the world for Catherine to bend down beside the stock-still little girl and ask in carefully enunciated French, "What is your name, child?"

The mouth shut, a finger raised to nestle there in one corner. "Marie."

"This is my cousin's youngest," Louise explained, putting an arm around the child.

"He named her after my mother, his father's sister and his own godmother."

"Marie is such a lovely name," Catherine said. "Almost as lovely as the dress you have on."

The child overcame her shyness enough for her to raise the hem of her skirt, showing the petticoats and the pretty, colorful stockings. "My aunt Louise made it for me."

"Your aunt Louise is a very skilled seamstress."

The hand holding the skirt rose back to offer her mouth a finger's comfort. "Why are you wearing a long cape on a warm day?"

"Oh, I didn't want to spatter my dress with trail dust." Which was partly true. Catherine had decided Louise was wise to provide a covering for her English-style frock, and thus protect her from prying eyes.

Catherine rose and untied the long cloak. "There. Is that better?" she asked, sweeping the garment off.

"Ooooh, look, Aunt Louise, look! Her dress, it's *beautiful*. Can I touch it?"

"Of course you can." Catherine did as the little girl had done, lifting up one edge of the hem and offering it for her to touch. The dress was three shades of gray, like the sky of a departing storm, rising from dark to light in careful layers. "It's called satin. The material comes from England. Have you ever heard of England?"

"Yes. It's across the sea." She watched Catherine as she fondled the dress. "Why do you talk like that?"

"Like how?"

"I don't know. Different."

"Ah." Catherine gave Louise the first relaxed look she had managed since starting down the trail. "I suppose it is because French is not my first language."

Louise added, "But she speaks it wonderfully, don't you think, Marie?"

"Yes." She eyed Catherine, her gaze gradually losing all remaining vestiges of shyness. "You speak a different language at home?"

"Yes."

"Which language?"

Louise said, "Our little Marie will smother you with questions if you let her."

"I don't mind." And to the little girl, she said, "English. We speak English at home."

"Say something for me in English, please, please."

Catherine thought back to an earlier day on the hillside, when a dark-haired lady had opened the door to a strange and thrilling world with the words, "No, no, the eggs, they are two shillings a dozen." She spoke the words with exaggerated English correctness.

Louise gave a great laugh, and suddenly Catherine knew why she had come, as much as she could know anything in these confusing times. She laughed along with her friend, because suddenly the day was a good day, full of the fresh scents of summer and welcoming warmth.

The little girl laughed along with them, then turned and raced down the lane, calling as she went, "Papa! Papa! Come see the lady who speaks the English! And she is just as Louise says, with a smile as bright as the sun! Come look, Papa!"

The two young women looked at each other, laughed again, linked arms, and followed the small figure. And that was how the clan first saw them, walking arm in arm toward the Belleveau home and smiling in the sunlight.

Not even the sight of all the strangers coming around the corner of the fenced front yard could erase either her smile or her feeling of rightness, for there in the sunlight Catherine knew she was not alone. Not here, not anywhere, not ever.

The men wore baggy dark trousers, suspenders, and starched white shirts with high collars that rose up their necks. The older men wore matching coats, ones which reached long to the backs of their knees. They all wore strange round hats with wide brims, which they grasped and almost in unison swept from their heads in greeting.

The women stood together at one side, eyeing her with open curiosity. They wore dresses and small caps similar to Louise's, the colors a variety of pastels, like a gathering of rich spring flowers. A few of the faces were clearly questioning, even hostile, but not many. Every yard she could see had trees filled with ripening apples, and the air was sweetly scented. Beyond the home they approached, the field was given over to row after orderly row of a vast orchard.

Louise drew Catherine toward a tall, stocky man. "Father, may I present my friend, Catherine Harrow. Catherine, this is my father and the elder of the clan, Jacques Belleveau."

She looked into the face of the man with graying hair and white whiskers, curtsied, and said, "Your village is perfumed by the finest apple orchard I have ever seen in my life, m'sieur. It is as though I am smelling the fields of heaven itself."

The entire gathering seemed to expel a single great breath, and somehow mirrored upon almost all the faces was the knowledge that she had done something quite right.

But before anyone else could speak, the little girl's voice piped, "See, Papa! What did I say! She talks so funny!"

And the entire gathering joined in laughter, dispelling both nervousness and concern. So when Louise pulled Catherine about to where the women stood and said, "And this is my mother, Marie Belleveau," she had the courage to rise from another curtsy, take the woman's work-worn hand, and say, "You have raised the finest daughter on God's earth, madame. It is an honor to call her friend."

Louise's mother had the slightly pinched expression Catherine had come to associate with women more comfortable with criticism than praise. Yet this day, Marie Belleveau was able to respond with genuine warmth. "You are indeed as lovely as my daughter has described."

There came another tug upon her arm, and Catherine found herself facing a man not much taller than herself. Yet there was an air of immense strength about this man, with his cleft chin and ruddy features and dark hair. His compact body seemed ready to spring with barely contained power, a force which was mirrored in his black eyes. Louise said quietly, "And this is my husband,

Henri."

"Your servant, m'sieur," Catherine said, curtsying a third time. "It is an honor to have come to know your lovely wife."

"She is that, Madame 'Arrow. My Louise is lovely indeed." And the flashing smile broke through with all the force of this powerful man. "And I have not been honored with a curtsy from such a one as you, not in all my born days."

The good-natured surge of people pressed in on all sides, talking and gesturing and bowing over Catherine's hand. A few hung back, and she caught sight of occasional dark glances exchanged from those on the outskirts. But most were both friendly and eager. She allowed herself to be swept first in one direction, then another, until she was some distance from the only person she knew in this press of humanity. Yet it did not matter. Despite the fact that she understood only a portion of the hurried speech coming at her from all sides, she had the assurance that she was truly among friends.

Calm finally reigned when Jacques Belleveau shouldered his way forward and handed Catherine a pewter mug. "It is our custom to toast the season's crop with the first taste of last year's cider. You would do us great honor to make the toast yourself,

218

madame."

"Oh, but . . ." Catherine blushed but found the protest dying in the presence of so many smiles. She raised her mug, and stumbling slightly over the words, she said, "May this crop be as fine as the people of this village."

A quiet murmur greeted her words with an exchange of many glances among the ruddy faces surrounding her. And Catherine found herself filled with the sense that she had again done something very right.

She hid her shyness at all the attention by lifting the pewter mug to her lips. It was unlike any pressed apple juice she had ever tasted. There was the slightest hint of cinnamon, and a tiny sense of effervescence upon her tongue. No bite, no acid, no sugary trail left in her mouth. "It's . . . this is the most wonderful thing I have ever tasted!"

She was brought to yet another shy blush by the cheer which greeted her words. Jacques Belleveau raised his voice above the others and shouted, "To our guest!"

"Our guest!" And a flurry of voices urged her to turn and walk among the clan, around the house, and down to the orchard. There beneath the gnarled and ancient boughs were spread a dozen tables. They formed a semicircle around a well-banked fire and a roasting pit and the fragrant scents of apples and the coming meal. Catherine was seated at a table and swiftly joined by people introduced in a rush of names. Eli and Philippe and so many village children she could not even count, much less remember them all. Louise and Henri sat across from her, Jacques Belleveau to one side, his wife Marie to the other. Faces leaned in from the table's length to explain in words she could scarcely catch how the apple was taken at the last moment before the frost and pressed in great stone vats, then tightly sealed in oak casks. Sealed without air, kept without fermentation so that the juice would stay fresh and safe for even the children to drink. The oak softened the juice, and spice from distant islands preserved and added a hint of new flavor over time.

Catherine strained to hear and understand, looking at this gathering both from within and without. Her struggle with the rapid-fire French granted her the chance to be both a part of the tableau and see it from a distance. And it struck her with sudden force that this truly was a *clan* in every sense of the term. It was startling to look about her and realize that everyone here—all the adults and the children and the laughter and the voices and the chatter—all were *one family*.

Marie broke in with a question of her own. "Tell us about yourself. Who are your parents?"

"My father is the village notary."

"Ah. *Le notaire.*" Clearly the title meant a certain function here as well. There were impressed nods about the table. "And your mother?"

"She died the week after my second birthday."

A moment's respect for the departed and sympathy for the bereaved. "You were raised by aunts, then."

"No. My father is the only kin I have. His family are all still in England."

A shocked silence. Too concerned for the questions to carry any hint of rebuke, Marie asked, "But who raised you, child? Who prepared you for womanhood? Who told you of marriage?"

"My father had a series of housekeepers. I learned to call them aunties." There in the gathering of this clan, Catherine was suddenly reminded of a lifetime of loneliness. Who *had* prepared her for womanhood? Who? She had not understood the full impact of just what it meant to be motherless, not until she was surrounded by *one family.*

The tears came, catching her as much by surprise as the others. Loneliness had been so much a part of her life that she had never given it much thought. Now she realized more fully what she had missed.

Hands reached across the table, strong women's hands. While Louise reached for her, Louise's mother wrapped her in another pair of arms, and murmurs of care and concern came from all around. She struggled to free a hand to hide her weeping, but Louise's grip was as firm as it was gentle. Catherine tried to catch her breath and stammered, "Please excuse me . . . I'm so sorry."

"Shah, child, shah, there is no need for shame among friends." Marie Belleveau showed only kindness. "It is I who must apologize for questions I had no right to ask."

"No, no . . . I just, well, I've never seen a family like this."

"No, and you never will again!" Henri called from the end of the table. "Two families like this, and the earth would sink away in bewilderment and confusion!"

The laugh was welcome and shared by all the table. Catherine finally managed to raise her napkin and wipe at her eyes. Marie's hug became the companionable welcome of an older woman to a younger. And Louise gave her a look filled with such love and friendship it squeezed Catherine's heart anew.

Henri pointed at another table and some unseen person. "This clan is filled with a hundred years' worth of tangles! Take that strange bloke down there, the one who looks like he sprang up from the middle of his own rhubarb patch."

"Who are you jousting with now, Henri?" a man shouted back.

"Why, he is his own first cousin twice removed, if truth be known. His mother's sister's great-uncle was his father's brother's stepson's great-granddaughter!"

Over the shouts of protest from two tables away, Henri raised his voice to continue, "And that woman there, why, her aunt's second cousin once removed was also her grandmother's niece's wife's own stepbrother by marriage!"

The laugh carried away the last vestige of her sorrow, a gift rewarded by all at their table with comments reaching across to her, apologizing for Henri—he was nothing but trouble from the day he was born—but spoken with the smiles of people who cared for one another and for her as well.

"The vicar! Here comes Jean Ricard!"

Catherine found herself being invited to her feet once again. She turned to greet a tall, slender man. The newcomer wore a long black coat, almost like a robe, which buttoned up the front with what looked like a hundred small cloth buttons. He wore the same round hat as the other men, only his brim was wider. He walked up to her and lifted the hat from his head with one hand while offering her the other. "Jean Ricard, at your service, Madame Harrow," he said, bowing low.

"It is an honor to meet you, m'sieur," she said, curtsying deeply.

Henri cried, "There! Did I not say it! Does she not curtsy like a queen?"

A woman's voice called, "No, you have said nothing but nonsense all day, Henri Robichaud."

Another voice agreed, "Why should this day be different from any other?"

The vicar's smile shared the clan's jovial repartee, but his eyes remained fastened upon Catherine. "Louise tells me you are reading the Bible together."

"Yes, M'sieur Vicar, but I confess I understand far less than I would like to."

That brought a different smile, one which sparked deep in his dark eyes, the same flashing depths shared by all the gazes about the tables. "Then you and I have far more in common than we might expect. Tell me, Madame Harrow, what is it that has led you to read the holy Word?"

Catherine wondered if she should mention her father's legalistic attitude that had kept her from the Book in the past, and all the newness she had found for herself since discovering it as something alive and relevant. But she did not want to show disrespect, and so searched for something she had not expressed before. And she found herself saying, "I want to be a . . . a handmaiden of the Lord."

The vicar possessed striking features, with a great beak of a nose and piercing eyes and the high cheekbones of a hunter, a quester for truth. "Yes?" His query invited more.

"If I truly am the Lord's, I will be the wife to Andrew that I should be." And though she blushed at the heart's exposure these words revealed, still she pressed on, "And the mother for the children we hope to have."

The vicar bowed a second time, lower than the first. "You have honored us with your presence, Madame Catherine. May your worthy example help teach our own young maidens how to value the eternal lessons."

But Catherine did not stop there. "I have learned from the Scriptures that there is no way I am able to accomplish this. Not of my own doing. No matter how strongly I desire it. It is only through what our crucified Christ has done that I can be a worthy wife or mother. I must depend on Him—for all of life."

The vicar nodded slowly, his eyes growing thoughtful, then turned to Jacques Belleveau and said, "Perhaps it is time we join together in prayer."

"Aye, Vicar, your timing is right as always." The elder's cheeks were ruddy with delight. "The meal is ready, and so are our appetites."

Catherine stood with the others and listened to familiar petitions spoken in an alien tongue. And one not alien. She found herself not only listening to the vicar's prayer but to her heart as well, marveling at how easily she had spoken and the words she had chosen to say. Not in character for her, even in her mother tongue. Why now, in a language that was not her own? She did not know. All she could say for certain, as she stood with bowed head and heard the prayer, was that here in this foreign village and among a people who were not her own, she had indeed found herself at home.

CHAPTER SIXTEEN

Catherine raised a slender hand to push back her tangled hair, and peeked through a corner of the bedroom window curtain. It was not yet dawn, yet in spite of great weariness she was unable to sleep. She lay back, not wanting to disturb her husband. If she could not sleep, at least she should try to rest.

But it was not to be. Her entire body felt agitated and her stomach upset. At length she gave up and raised herself to a sitting position. Silently she pushed her feet into the woolen slippers by the bed and eased herself upward, her eyes still on Andrew. When he did not stir, Catherine breathed a relieved sigh and stole from the room.

The fire had gone out, but the front room was not chilled. In fact, Catherine felt too warm. As she reached for kindling she fretted that she might be coming down with the influenza.

She lowered herself to the rocking chair as a wave of nausea passed through her. This was the third day she had felt so sick to her stomach. The feeling had gradually passed as she had moved about her duties, but it had been difficult to prepare Andrew's breakfasts. Already she dreaded the thought of standing over a hot stove stirring the morning porridge.

But Andrew would not be up for another hour. She had some time to get herself in hand. Perhaps by the time she needed to begin breakfast she would be feeling better. She reached for her Bible and tried to settle herself into a more comfortable position.

But she found it difficult to concentrate on the passage. Her nausea came in swells, much like the tides of the Fundy. They swept over her, totally absorbing her entire body, making her fear she might vomit, wishing that she *could* vomit. Then at least the awful spasms might recede.

She laid aside the beloved Book and leaned her head against the back of the rocker. She dared not rock. Even the slight gentle movement seemed to increase her discomfort. She sat perfectly still, almost holding her breath in her desire to keep herself in control.

"Are you ill?"

The words from Andrew made her jerk upright. Another wave of nausea passed over her. She fought to regain her composure.

"I think it's just a bit of upset stomach," she managed to answer, trying hard to smile as she spoke.

"Perhaps you need to take some of the restorative from the cupboard."

Something deep within Catherine resisted. Not just that the potion provided to Andrew for his men was bitter in taste, but there was some inner warning that she should be very careful about any self-cures.

"I'm sure it will pass," Catherine answered. "As before."

"You've had this before?" Andrew moved toward her, rubbing his hand through untidy locks. His eyes held concern.

Catherine stirred restlessly in the chair. She had disclosed too much. But she could not retract the statement. "A bit," she answered, hoping that Andrew would accept the offhand reply and not question her further.

"Why haven't you said something? I had no idea you were ill."

"Not ill . . . really . . . just . . ."

But she was ill. She could not deny it. She felt terrible. "It will pass," she finally managed.

But when another wave of nausea passed over her, Catherine knew that this time she would vomit. With one quick movement she leaned over the ash bucket. Andrew's movement was just as quick. He was there to support her, to hold her head, as the first spasms racked her body.

"You must get back to bed," he said

when it seemed to be over.

Catherine shook her head. "I think I'll be all right now." She leaned weakly against the high back of the chair, beads of perspiration dampening her brow.

"But you must rest. And you must have some—"

"No, Andrew," Catherine interrupted. "That is much too harsh. I don't think—"

"Well, if not the restorative, then at least some tonic. I have worried about you lately. You seem to lack energy. And you've lost your color."

"I haven't been resting well, that's all."

"Is something troubling you that you haven't spoken of?"

Catherine was quick to shake her head. "Of course not."

"Then—"

Catherine spoke again. "It could be just a bit of upset. I'm sure it's nothing to concern us."

Andrew still looked doubtful. "I think I should ask Mrs. Dwyer to stop by. She knows about herbs and medicines—"

"Please, Andrew, no." His words had brought Catherine upright in her chair. She had no desire to be called upon by Matty Dwyer.

At the look of bewilderment on his face

she changed her tack. "At least . . . not yet. There is no reason to make a fuss about nothing. If it persists, then . . ."

Inwardly, Catherine fervently hoped that she might escape a visit from the tongue-wagging, eye-piercing Matty Dwyer. The wife of the village drover was a nag and a scold. Though Matty always seemed available, always seemed to be in the meeting hall whenever Catherine arrived, always was ready to stop by for a visit, Catherine had never felt comfortable around the prying woman.

Andrew seemed to detect her anxiety. "We'll give it a couple of days, then. But if it persists we'll have to do something."

Catherine nodded. How she hoped that it would not come to that.

"Let me help you back to bed."

"I'm sure that I can make it on my own. I feel some better already."

Catherine cast a glance at the used ash bucket. Andrew said, "Never mind that. I'll take care of it."

The very sight made Catherine's stomach heave again. She hated leaving the mess to Andrew, but she knew that in her present state she would never be able to clean it up herself. She managed a weak nod and accepted Andrew's outstretched hand. Perhaps she would feel better if she lay down for a while.

Louise smiled softly as she ran one finger over the handmade calendar that Henri had posted on the wall. She must be right. The calendar assured her. Yet she had never felt better. More alive and energetic. But it was too early for her to share her secret with her husband. What if she was mistaken? He would be so disappointed. He had spoken of a son more often lately. No, she must wait until she was sure.

She stepped back and untied the bow of her starched apron. She had some time before beginning the evening meal. She would walk over to visit her mother. A chat over a hot cup of tea would be her excuse, but if the opportunity presented itself, the discussion could lead to some personal questions. Her mother would know.

With long, easy strides she made her way through the grove that provided a shortcut. It was cooler there and not as dusty as going by the main road.

Soon she was tapping on the familiar door before admitting herself and calling softly, "Bonjour."

"Louise." Marie made her way from an inner room to the kitchen, wiping her face with her apron as she came. "Come in."

Louise smiled. "I am in already, Mama."

"So I see. So I see and welcome you are, too. But it is a warm day. Too warm for the kitchen. Come. Let's sit in the shade."

"But I came for tea," teased Louise.

"Tea? No, it is too hot for tea. I was shelling peas in the coolness of the sitting room. Apple cider, then?"

Louise could not suppress a soft laugh. "Apple cider, then, Mama. Apple cider and maybe some of your ginger cake."

"Ginger cake? But I have made no ginger cake today. Henri stopped by and ate the last of it two days ago."

Louise was surprised at her own disappointment. Once the idea of ginger cake had popped to her mind, she discovered that she truly did desire it. When she saw the look on her mother's face, she hastened to say, "No mind, Mama. We shall have whatever is in your pantry."

Her mother's keen eyes held hers. "But you wished for ginger cake?"

"I did—but no matter."

"We could have ginger tea."

Louise brightened. It would not be like

having the tangy ginger cake, but it did appeal to her taste of the moment. "Ginger tea. Yes, that is good. Let's have ginger tea."

Her mother's eyes still seemed to study her. "I will stir up the fire and put on the kettle," she muttered almost absentmindedly, shaking her head as she moved toward the stove and again mopped her brow.

"No," decided Louise. "No. That is foolish. The day is as hot for ginger tea as it is for plain tea. Let's have the cider."

Marie's hand stopped as it reached for the kettle. "You are having a hard time making up your mind," she scolded gently.

"Apple cider," said Louise firmly. "We will have the cider."

Marie stepped to the trapdoor that led to the cellar. "I will bring up some cold."

It would not be cold, but it would be much cooler than anything left exposed to the warmth of the summer day. "Here. Let me take the steps," Louise offered.

But Marie held out a hand to detain her, her eyes searching her daughter's face. "I will take the steps," she said firmly. "You find a seat in the shade."

Louise hesitated. Her mother did not usually turn down offers to run errands. "In the shade," her mother repeated, and Louise obediently turned to go, then swung back.

"Mama," she said, voicing the thought that would not go away. "Could you stir just a bit of ginger into the apple cider?"

Her mother rolled her eyes, then smiled and nodded before she disappeared into the coolness of the cellar.

Why this sudden desire for a taste of ginger? Louise shrugged her shoulders and lifted the heavy flow of hair from her neck. The day was indeed warm but beautiful. Overhead a bird called from its nest and another answered from a nearby apple tree. Louise smiled, then grew serious. Was she being foolish? Was it too early to be talking to her mother? How would she approach the subject? What were the right words to express her questions? Were her dreams really about to come true? Louise chafed in impatience as she waited for her mother to join her.

But she did not have to wait long. Marie soon reappeared, bearing a wooden tray shaped by the hands of Henri as a Christmas gift. On the tray were two tall glasses. Louise could smell the ginger. A small plate of biscuits, bountifully spread with apple butter completed the repast. This too was sprinkled with ginger.

Her mother put down the tray, tucked a stray strand of hair behind her ear, and lowered herself to the chair across from her daughter. Again Louise felt the sharp eyes bore into her own. "So," she said as she lifted her apron to flap at a fly that sought out the biscuits, "you are to tell me what I have dreamed to hear. You are to make me a grandmother."

Louise could not hide her surprise. "Why do you say that?" she asked.

"I see it. I see it in your eyes. Your face."

"But, Mama, I'm not sure, yet. I came to ask you if—"

"It's sure," her mother answered with a nod of her head. "And how have you been?"

"Fine. Just fine. I do not feel one bit sickish. Just . . . just happy."

"You look happy," responded Marie with another nod. "That is what gives you away."

"But—"

"And some other things. I have seen it before, you know. Many times."

"But it's so early. I have not even dared to speak of it to Henri."

"Speak of it."

"But he will be so disappointed if—"

"Do not worry about the *if*. Henri must be the first to know."

"But you know."

"Well . . . yes. But you did not tell me."

Still Louise felt a bit hesitant. "You are

sure I won't be leading Henri to a big disappointment if it is not so?"

"If you take care of yourself, there will be
no such thing. But you must start soon on
the tonic I will prepare."

Suddenly Louise felt her heart overflow
with uncontrolled joy. With one movement
she left her seat and gathered her mother
close in an embrace. Tears spilled down her
cheeks, but they were tears of joy. "I am so
happy I want to . . . to sing and dance," she
exclaimed. It was then that she noticed that
her mother, too, was weeping.

"And I join in your happiness," the older
woman answered as she returned her daughter's tight hug. "I, too, am happy. But it's too
hot to dance."

They both laughed as Louise stepped
back and wiped at her tears. It was the first
time she had felt the warm bond of womanhood with her own mother. Yet still she felt
the tug of being the child—the daughter. It
was so good to be able to share this special
event with another woman. With the woman
whom she called Mama.

The days did not get easier for Catherine. On rising from her bed, she went through the same miserable routine, feeling ill and weak. Andrew would have carried through with calling in Matty Dwyer, but the woman was down with gout. Silently, Catherine breathed a prayer of thankfulness.

But Catherine herself was beginning to be concerned. It wasn't normal, the way she was feeling, and she had no other woman with whom to discuss her strange malady.

Andrew was right. She *was* pale. And she had lost weight. She could see it in her face. Could tell it by the waistbands of her skirts. She now had to lap them over and pin them to make them fit. And she was so tired. It was all she could do to make herself face the household chores. And cooking was nearly beyond her. She longed to have someone to talk to. Someone who might know what was going on in her body.

Her thoughts turned to Louise. It had been weeks since she'd had the strength to climb the hill to the meadow. She was sure Louise was wondering what had happened to her. But she didn't dare attempt to send a message.

Yet as the days slipped past Catherine felt more and more determined to meet with her friend. She had no other woman to whom she could express her feelings—her concerns.

And then her opportunity came. Andrew was to be gone on a five-day patrol. Though she knew he probably wouldn't approve of the trek in her weakened condition, Catherine waited for the extreme nausea of early morning to pass, then slipped from the cottage and up the hill toward the hidden meadow. The fall flowers were in full bloom, and in spite of the way she felt, Catherine could not help but feel renewed and invigorated by the outing. She slipped a short note into the secret place where she and Louise had exchanged messages in the past and turned to make her way back down the hill, picking a few meadow flowers as she went.

"Now if only Louise comes to the meadow and finds my note in time," Catherine murmured to herself. Her note had asked simply for a meeting. Thursday. She dared not wait beyond Thursday. Andrew was due home on Friday.

Even as the thought came to her, Catherine felt her cheeks warm. It was not right, what she was doing. She should not be sneaking around behind Andrew's back. Doing what she knew he would not want her to do. No matter how deep her need for another woman's understanding and help.

Catherine turned back and retrieved her bit of paper from its hiding place. She could not do it. Make these secret plans. It was not right. She crumpled the paper in trembling fingers and shoved it into her apron pocket. Tears sprang to her eyes and rolled freely down her cheeks. If only, if only she had someone to talk to!

"Bonjour," a voice called merrily, and Catherine whirled about to see Louise hurrying into the clearing. She could not even reply but stood with a fresh burst of tears flowing down her cheeks.

"I have not seen you in ages," Louise called as she came toward her, arms outstretched. "I have been worried that you have been ill."

She was almost to Catherine when the welcoming smile left her face and she stopped short. "You *have* been ill. You look all done in."

Catherine wiped at the tears and nodded. Then she managed a wobbly smile, though she felt more like weeping. But that would not do. She took a deep breath and said, "I'm *so* glad to see you, Louise."

Louise took both Catherine's hands in hers, deep concern showing in her dark eyes. "I have been to the meadow every other day for the last weeks," she said. "I left countless notes—which I later gathered up for fear someone else might discover them. I have found no note from you. No indication that you have been here. I have been very worried."

She turned Catherine and guided her toward their favorite log and the shade.

"Sit down. Before you fall from your feet. Tell me what is ailing you."

"I've not been . . . been feeling myself," Catherine said with a sigh.

"Yes, I can see that," replied Louise with another searching look.

"I thought I would return to normal health long before now," Catherine continued, "but it has not been so."

"Please pardon my bluntness—but are you with child?"

Catherine felt her cheeks burn. "I . . . I think I must be," she stammered, "but I am not sure."

A few more direct questions by her young friend convinced Catherine that she was indeed expecting her first child. Hers and Andrew's. Amid the joy of knowledge was still the concern about how she was feeling. Was her nausea and fatigue a danger to the child she carried? How long must she endure this illness? Was it normal? What could she do to improve her condition?

"Mama has an herbal remedy. I have seen it work wonders with many of our village women in the past. We will have you feeling yourself in no time," Louise promised.

"Oh, if only that could be so," responded Catherine, new hope in her heart. "I have been quite beside myself wondering what to do. It is all that I can manage to make it through another day."

Louise reached over to pat her arm. "You poor dear," she said with sympathy. "I cannot imagine what it would be like to be so sick—especially at such a happy time. I have never felt better. Mama says that I have bloomed."

Catherine's eyes opened wide. "You—"

"Yes," Louise said, obviously trying to keep her demeanor subdued in light of Catherine's suffering. "Henri and I are to be parents also."

"Oh, Louise," exclaimed Catherine. "That is such good news!" For the first time Catherine took a good look at her friend. "And you do look wonderful. Radiant," she continued.

"And we shall have you looking radiant as well, you will see. Now, you sit right here and I will run down to Mama and get you some of the remedy."

"But you can't—"

"Oh yes, I can. We will not have you climbing this hill again until you are feeling better. I will be back soon. But you must rest. Just sit here—on the ground if you will—and relax and enjoy the smell of the flowers and the songs of the birds. The fresh air will do you good. I will hurry. But you may as well sit down and have a rest. Even with my hurrying, I will not be back for some time. It is a bit of a walk."

"Don't hurry too fast. It might not be good for the baby."

"Nonsense. I have never felt better, I tell you. I feel I could run uphill. Jump fallen logs. Leap the creek," Louise answered with a merry laugh.

"Well, even so. Please don't try any of those things."

"I will use good sense. I promise. No running uphill," she tossed over her shoulder as she quickly moved across the meadow with a swish of her skirts.

Catherine settled herself in the meadow grass, her back to a tree. It was so peaceful there. So serene. And she was so thankful. Thankful to have found some answers. To have someone with whom she could talk. That in itself relieved most of her concerns. She was to be a mother. A mother. Just think of it. Andrew would be a father as he longed to be. It was almost more joy than she could hold. And the herbs would soon have her feeling better.

And Louise—she too was to be a mother. They would share the same experiences of watching a baby grow and develop. They could bring the two little ones to the meadow and show them the wild flowers, let them listen to the songs of the birds. Teach them which berries were safe and delicious.

Catherine wound her arms about her frail body. She could hardly wait for the months to pass by. She had so much to look forward to.

"I climbed to the meadow the other day," Catherine said as she and Andrew lay side by side in the darkness. She felt him stir beside her and knew that his face no doubt showed disapproval. He said nothing.

"I had to see Louise," she went on.

Again silence. Catherine swallowed. She wished he would speak.

"I needed another woman to talk to."

"Wasn't it risky to venture so far when you have not been well?"

Catherine nodded in the darkness. "It probably was," she admitted.

Silence again.

"So, did you see her?"

"Yes," Catherine answered quickly. "I intended to leave her a note to arrange to meet me. But I felt bad about having gone there when I knew you would not approve. I know I certainly shouldn't climb the hill again without your agreement. I was just leaving when she came."

"That was convenient," said Andrew, but his voice sounded strained.

"Yes. I think it was an answer to my prayer."

Andrew made no reply.

"Louise brought me an herbal potion, Andrew. Her mother prepared it."

"Brought it? But how did she know you needed it?"

"She didn't. Not until she saw me. Then she insisted that she run home and get it."

"And you waited there in the meadow? What if you had gotten a chill?"

"It was a warm day. And the fresh air did me good."

"So you have this . . . potion?"

"I have been taking it for the past three days."

Andrew was silent. Catherine knew he

was wondering if it was safe for his wife to take medication made by a Frenchwoman.

"I've been much better," continued Catherine. "I even had some poached eggs for breakfast. And I kept them down."

Andrew stirred then, reaching for Catherine in the darkness. "You've been able to eat again?" he asked, drawing her close.

"I have. I am sure that soon . . . soon I will be feeling like myself again."

"Oh, to see the color back in your cheeks. To see you put on some weight again. I have prayed for that."

Catherine smiled softly as she nestled closer, her cheek brushing against his hard-muscled shoulder. "Yes," she said. "Undoubtedly I will be putting on weight."

Andrew made no comment, but she felt the shift of his body.

"We are to be parents," Catherine whispered and felt Andrew's body tense. His hand moved in the darkness to turn her face toward him, though he would not have been able to see her eyes in the dim light.

"Catherine, is this true?"

"Indeed it is. You are to be a father."

Andrew's arms pulled her close.

"Oh, Catherine," he said into her hair.

CHAPTER SEVENTEEN

Captain Andrew Harrow walked from the fort to his house. He tipped his hat to Widow Riley but did not stop. The latest dispatches from his regiment's home fortress in Windsor offered official congratulations for his promotion, but that was the only good news from England.

He paused at the point where his cottage path turned off from the main lane and looked out over the bay. The waters sparkled like burnished pewter beneath a cloud-flecked sky. He could hear calls of several boats but could not determine the language. He was struck by the fact that out there upon the waters, French fished alongside British, yet did not speak nor acknowledge the other. With no borders out there upon the bay, there was no way to define which patch of water might be English and which French. Andrew sighed. If only it were that simple to forget boundaries and histories and conflicting claims.

Reluctant to turn away from the lovely sight below, he thought about the golden days of summer and how aptly they described this Acadian season. So brief, these days of warmth and light, yet so packed with goodness and life. For a too-brief period each year, the entire world exploded in a frenzy of recreative power. The bay was packed with fish. Sometimes the boats coming back were so full with the day's catch that water sloshed over both gunnels at once. The village farmers were predicting another bountiful harvest, the seventh in a row. Game almost jumped into the pot. Andrew himself had shot a wild turkey in his back garden just three days earlier. There was so much beauty to this golden land, so much offered to all who called it home. If only—

"Ah, Andrew, good to see you. Were you waiting for me?"

Andrew turned to greet Catherine's father coming up the lane. "In a manner of speaking, yes. How are you, sir?"

"Passable. Bit of the grippe . . . hits me every year about this time." The older man was indeed limping more heavily. "Always say I know the coming of winter long before anyone else in this land."

"Indeed, sir."

"Good of you and Catherine to have me over for dinner tonight." John Price began making his way up the path. "My empty house seems to echo most loudly after sunset."

Andrew did not know what to say. John Price was not a man given to speaking of his own internal state. The older man filled the silence with, "Can't say how good it was to hear that Catherine is with child. A little one about the place will do us all a world of good. How is my girl holding up?"

"She was a bit under the weather at first, but she seems to be doing fine now." Andrew did not mention the days and nights of horrid sickness, leaving her so weak she could hardly stand. Nor was there any need to mention the fact that the cure had come from Minas. "The midwife seems most pleased with her progress."

"Good to hear. Of course, I wouldn't expect anything else from my Catherine. She always was one for getting on with things. I'd imagine the pregnancy hasn't slowed her down a whit."

"I wish it would," Andrew chuckled, then turned serious. "She does far too much for a woman in her condition."

"Nonsense. You mustn't worry so, man. Catherine has always been hardy." Price limped onto the stoop, then said, "I suppose the dispatches confirmed your appointment as fort commander."

"Yes, they did." Andrew did not ask how Catherine's father had come to hear of the dispatches' confidential contents. As the controller of Fort Edward's supplies, John

Price wielded considerable influence, both within the fort and the town. He had sources that preceded Andrew's tenure by some years.

"Then accept my congratulations."

"Thank you, sir."

John Price halted outside their door. "The rest of the news, it affirms what we long suspected?"

"Yes." The word was almost a groan, its burden of worry was so great. "The king has ordered that we attack France upon all fronts."

"That's as it should be, then." John Price stared out over the forested hills rising on the fort's other side, beyond the river, which sparkled as it fell into Cobequid Bay, out to where ribbons of smoke rose from the unseen village of Minas. He thumped his fist upon the doorpost and muttered, "We must teach those Frenchies a lesson they will never forget. Never."

Andrew bit back his angry response. Arguing with John Price would not change the man's way of thinking one jot. Which was as sad in its own way as the dispatches themselves, for John Price represented the attitudes of Andrew's superiors in Halifax and Annapolis Royal, almost to a man. He waited until the possible outburst was safely stowed back down deep, where it would not disturb his wife's welcome or the evening repast. But he could do nothing for the sense of futile helplessness, which left him so weary he felt his words carried little more strength than the evening breeze. "Shall we go inside?"

Captain Andrew Harrow led his troop along the mountain trail but did not make the turning at the fork. Instead he continued straight down from the watcher's knob. He heard the guard corporal spur his horse forward and readied his response. The man reined in alongside Andrew and said, "Begging your pardon, sir, but did you mean to take this trail?"

"I did indeed, Corporal."

"But, sir," the young man hesitated. He knew his captain was approachable, but no doubt was uncertain how far he should press it. "If I'm not mistaken, this leads down to the Frenchie village."

"Correct." Andrew kept his voice calm, though his heart was racing far ahead of their steady pace. "Tell me, have you ever seen the French village?"

"Me, sir? Why, the only Frenchies I've ever seen, face-to-face like, are the traders that come into Cobequid and Annapolis Royal." The corporal gave a nervous glance down the trail. "They've their ways, we've ours, and never the twain shall meet. Least, that's my way of thinking, sir."

"Indeed. But if we are to engage the . . ." But he could not even say the word "enemy," could not include it as part of the ruse. "It may do us good to have a look at their own preparations."

"If you say so, sir."

"Right. Go back, make sure the line is dressed and the men are fitted properly for a visit. And order the standard unfurled."

"Yes, sir." The corporal wheeled his horse about. Andrew did not turn to make sure his orders were carried out. His thoughts remained locked upon what lay ahead. The corporal's sharp commands to one private to button up his tunic and straighten his braces came and went without conscious acknowledgment. Finally the corporal returned to say, "Requesting the captain's permission to carry the standard."

"Granted." The regimental standard was a colorful flag, triangular in shape, sewn in gold and red and russet hues of finest silk, with tassels to catch and snap in the breeze.

It was always carried in a saddlebag whenever the commandant or adjutant were leading a troop. The corporal moved his horse to a half pace behind Andrew's, the standard strapped to a pike riding high upon his pommel.

The village of Minas was silent, as would be normal in the middle of a workaday afternoon. The first person to catch sight of their arrival was a young girl, not more than five or six, dressed in a starched white cap and a sky blue dress. The little one turned, caught sight of the company of riders, and stood as if transformed to stone.

Andrew winced at the look of stricken terror on the young face. It reminded him of the expression in Catherine's eyes the night before when her father was staring into the fire and spouting forth about the coming conflict. The uncertainties and tragedies of war for women and children were all too clear, and he felt anew his own helplessness.

Catherine had told him last night, when they were alone, of Louise's request. During their last meeting upon the meadow, Louise had spoken of how the village wished they could have some solid sense of the world's events, not just rumors and bits of gossip picked up on market day. It would so help them in making decisions for their future.

Andrew had heard Catherine out, knowing from the first instant exactly what was to be done, asking when she was finished only if she knew which of the villagers might speak English.

His thoughts snapped back to the present when the little girl found her voice and gave a shriek that seemed to go on forever, too high even for the birds to imitate. She turned to flee, only to fall headlong into the dirt. She did not seem to even notice, did not halt her shrieking for an instant. Finally she regained her legs and raced away, screaming as she fled. Andrew's face blanched. She was but a child.

"Troop, slow walk," he called, reining his horse back and patting its neck to calm it. He did not know exactly where he was going, or how he would ask for the vicar.

A woman's frantic face appeared in a window. He called out, "Where is your priest?" He was answered with yet another shriek and a slamming of the shutters. Andrew led his troop onward, to where their lane intersected a broader way. He breathed a sigh of relief when up to his right he spotted a steeple. "Troop, right face!"

The village itself seemed to unfurl away on either side like a scroll. Andrew's mind was so captured by the risk he was taking and the need that squeezed his heart that he rode almost to the church courtyard before his first impression of Minas actually registered. That notion was of *history*. Every house he saw here in the center of the village spoke of an age more in tune with what he recalled in England than anything in Edward or the other English settlements. The church itself was lime washed in an ancient style, built of stone and wood and roofed with silver birch bark. The effect was stunning, a stately crown set upon the green of the village.

A black-robed figure appeared in the church doorway. Andrew slid from his horse's back and walked to meet the man, carrying the reins. But not too far. Not too quickly. He did not want to alarm the vicar, and he could not afford for his men *not* to hear what he was about to say. The vicar hesitated a long moment, then walked toward him. To Andrew's vast relief, the man called out, "You are English?"

"We are that, sir. My name is Captain Andrew Harrow."

"Ah." Relief softened the man's features, but only for an instant, for Andrew frowned mightily and gave his head the tiniest shake. Immediately comprehension lit the cleric's eyes. "And why are you here?" he demanded.

"I was hoping that a man of learning might know English, for alas, my French is nonexistent."

"Slowly, my son." He kept his tone low. "Slowly and I can understand, though it is many years since I studied your tongue." The vicar gave a stiff little bow, ignoring all the soldiers but Andrew. "Jean Ricard, vicar of Minas, at your service," he acknowledged, raising his voice to a stern level.

"Honored, sir." Andrew took a breath and said what he had planned, what would go over well if any of the men were to speak at Fort Edward of what transpired here. Which they were bound to do. He also raised his voice. "I am here to respectfully request that you convince the others of your village to sign the Oath of Allegiance to His Royal Highness the King of England."

"I am only the vicar, Captain. Such things are decided by our clan elder. He acts as—how you say—the mayor? Yes. The village mayor."

"Does this elder speak English?"

"Alas, no."

"Then I must deal with you, sir." Andrew continued to pitch his voice so that the troops could hear him clearly. "Time is growing short, sir. Very short indeed."

"Sir." The corporal sounded tensely nervous. "Behind us."

Andrew turned, drawing the priest with him to where they were no longer shielded by the horses, and saw a group of men bearing pitchforks approaching warily.

The vicar called out something in French. Answered in the same tongue, he spoke more sharply. Reluctantly the men began to disperse.

The vicar turned back to him. "You have news, then? From England?"

"Indeed I do, sir. And it is my sad duty to inform you that the conflict in Europe is worsening with every passing day."

"Oh, this is bad, this is very bad indeed." The vicar held his hands tightly in front of him. "You are certain?"

Andrew kept his voice carefully neutral. "Sir, I assure you I did not ride here to deal in rumors."

"No, no, of course not, forgive me." The vicar drew himself erect. "Sadly, Captain, I am afraid I must tell you that the people will refuse to sign your oath."

"Even with the *fact* of imminent conflict?"

"Please, what means imminent?"

"Definite. It is coming. The conflict has already started in Europe. It is certain to arrive here."

"Ah." The vicar nodded his head, acknowledging with a single glance that he understood. It was for this Andrew had come, to confirm the rumors, not to request once more what he knew would be denied. "The conflict, it will arrive this year?"

"No. The last ships of the year have already arrived from Europe."

The vicar smiled only with his eyes. "Then for once we must give thanks for the winter storms, yes?"

Andrew willed the man to see beyond his harsh tone, hoping against hope the vicar would understand just how much the news hurt him as well. "It is hard to say exactly what will happen with the spring, since such conflicts have risen and fallen within a season before. But your entire village is at risk unless—"

"Impossible, Captain." The vicar held to form with his response. "They have refused to take up arms for the king of their home country. This is—how you say—their very nature. How could they be expected to do such for the English king? You ask from my people what they cannot give."

"Not I, Vicar. But my superiors in Halifax and Annapolis Royal are unanimous in their opinion that such a document must be signed."

"Yes. So the rumors say."

"These are not rumors."

"Some of our young people . . ." The vicar hesitated, clearly uncertain how far he should go. "Some are thinking that it would be better to move north. Start over in a distant outpost, beyond Tatamagouche or farther still."

"It will make no difference. All the land east of Quebec Province is now under the dominion of the same man, Governor Lawrence in Halifax."

"All land not controlled by the French forts," the vicar corrected.

"Sir, not a single French ship has managed to land and service the remaining forts this entire summer. You yourself must know this, as you have not seen a French ship in Cobequid Bay for four years. I hope you will understand me when I say that soon *all* Acadian land will be under British dominion."

The vicar's brow furrowed, his frustration obvious. He finally noted in a tentative tone, "We have heard rumors of battles to the west of us, even at the gates of Quebec itself."

"These rumors are true."

The vicar stiffened. "Then Quebec has fallen?"

It was Andrew's turn to hesitate. In an instant's flight of reason and thought, he decided this was important enough to risk. "Sir, I have received dispatches which state a regimental force gathered from the southern American colonies was soundly defeated by the defending French garrison. I tell you this only because I am *certain* that such a loss will only harden the resolve of the government in Halifax."

"But why!" The vicar's cry startled several of the horses, causing them to back and snort. One of the troopers reined in sharply with an oath, which caused Andrew to shoot him a furious look. When the man muttered an apology and Andrew turned back, the vicar continued, "Why must the mighty British kingdom see a village of poor peasant farmers a threat?"

"Because, sir, because you are not just *one* village." He dropped his voice discreetly. "The number of French settlers is a *hundred* times greater than the troops at Governor Lawrence's disposal. Were you to take up arms against His Majesty—"

"But we will not! What can we do to convince you of this?"

"Sign the oath of allegiance. There is no other way."

The vicar's shoulders slumped. "This we

cannot do. We cannot."

"Then I must bid you good day, sir." Andrew snapped off a salute and turned away, sick at heart.

To his surprise, the vicar followed him around his horse. When the tall steed sheltered them from the gazes of the others, Jean Ricard murmured, "You are still studying the Gospel of Luke, m'sieur?"

"Every chance I have," Andrew softly replied. He could risk no more. He fitted his boot into the stirrup and swung himself onto the horse.

The vicar looked up at him. "You have perhaps heard the story of the Good Samaritan, Captain?"

"I have."

The vicar nodded, a slow motion of approval, then raised his right hand and made the sign of the cross in the air between them. "Go with God, m'sieur."

CHAPTER EIGHTEEN

Catherine was very glad the trail had become so familiar. She climbed slowly, pausing often for breath. The autumn sky was heavy with its clouds in a hundred shades of gray. The bay, a sheet of metal, lay breathless beneath, waiting for the winter just beyond the hills.

When the trail turned sharply, in a manner she now knew so well, she entered the sheltering boughs of the highland firs. Their scent was fresh and strong as their arms joined overhead to form a fragrant tunnel. *Like a hall leading to their meeting place,* she thought as she paused and leaned against the nearest trunk. *Like an entrance hall to a highland chapel.*

As soon as she saw Louise in the meadow, she could no longer contain the tears that had threatened all day. The two women rushed together, holding each other closely against their growing abdomens. The bit of awkwardness made them giggle through the tears as they backed away and in unconscious imitation traced a free hand over their unborn.

"Look at us," Louise laughed. "Like a pair of old women."

"Winter has never looked to be as long as this coming one," Catherine replied.

"Do you remember last autumn? We came up and discovered we had been married on the same day."

"It snowed that day," Catherine recalled. "The first snowfall of the year. I thought I had never seen a more beautiful sight."

"Nor I. But for me the beautiful sight

was of your smile."

"You remember my smile?"

"You smiled like the sun emerging from a winter shadow. You cast a new spring light over my world." Louise brushed at one tendril of hair. "I will never forget that smile, not as long as I live."

Arm in arm they walked over to the fallen log which had become their pew, their place of sanctuary, of studying the Scriptures, and talk. The breeze chose that moment to turn and come straight from the north. Slight though it was, the wind now held the whisper of winter. The two women shivered and pulled shawls closer around them.

"Shall we begin our lesson?" Catherine asked as they settled on their log.

"Yes, let's do that," Louise agreed. But when her hand dipped into the basket, it was not a Bible she brought out. Instead, she handed over a bundle bound with twine, saying shyly, "This is for you."

"What is it?"

"A gift. For the baby."

Catherine could not help but thrill at the word. *The baby*. Said so matter-of-factly, yet so full of promise. Carefully she unbound the twine. "Oh, Louise!"

"Henri made it for you. It is silver fox. He hunted them and cured them and sewed the furs, all himself."

Catherine stroked the surface. "It's the softest thing I have ever felt! But the value, I can't . . ."

"Please take it, Catherine. It would make him so happy. I only wish he could see your face right now."

Catherine held up the fur stitched into a careful square, four feet to a side. The stitching was so tight, and the furs matched so well, she could scarcely tell where they were joined. "It's so beautiful, Louise."

"We have a tradition of lining the baby's crib with fur its first winter. We also use it as a blanket on the bench by the fire, for it protects the infant from drafts."

Catherine raised the fur and stroked it across her cheek. "Tell Henri I will think of you both every time I see it."

"This will make him very happy." Louise sobered. "The entire village is speaking of your husband's visit."

Catherine let the fur drop to her lap. "I could hardly believe my ears when he told me about it."

"The vicar called him an honorable man. He said . . ." Louise stopped and bit her lip. "Jean Ricard said that your coming to this meadow, and our becoming friends, was an act ordained by God."

Tears rolled down both faces as the two women stared into each other's eyes.

"I don't know how I am going to make it through this winter without you," Catherine whispered.

"Nor I." Impatiently Louise wiped her face, clearly not wishing to give the season's last visit over to sadness at the long separation to come. "Have you decided on names yet?"

"We are still talking. And you?"

"If it is a boy, no. I want to name it after Henri's father, and he after mine. But if it is a girl, we have agreed on Antoinette."

"That is a lovely name," Catherine said, reaching into her own basket for a parcel bound in brown paper. "This is for you. Well, for the baby."

Louise unwrapped the gift, then sat wiping tears as she stared at the gift. "Oh, Catherine," was all she could say.

"It came from England on the last ship. I wanted one for my own child, and I was fortunate to be able to obtain two."

The ring was flat and silver and as broad as Louise's palm. She lifted it by the round ivory handle and heard the musical chime. "Oh, listen! It sings!"

"It's called a teething ring. It is strong and safe for the baby to bite—see, there are no sharp angles anywhere."

Louise shook the ring once more. "Oh, Catherine, it sounds like the tiny bells of angels! Thank you."

"I'm glad you like it."

Louise settled the ring back into the paper. "You are more than a friend. You are the sister I never had."

Catherine tried to keep the tremble from her voice. "I have thought that exact thing. Many, many times."

Andrew paused at the trail's fork, dropped the load of game to the snow, and leaned heavily against his musket as he looked up the hill. He had thought long and hard of this next approach and decided the safest way to accomplish it would be upon returning from a hunting expedition. Searching for game was one of the few reasons he could leave the village alone and not raise suspicions.

Though the snows had been even heavier than the year before, this year there had been strong thaws interspersed, so the white ground cover was not so deep. Nor was it so bitterly cold. It was the middle of January, and he had seen signs of everything from fox to bear to deer.

The trail was empty of all save snow and tracks. Tree limbs were bowed under heavy white capes. Andrew found the trail just as Catherine had described. His snowshoes clumped flat and solid upon the upward-wending path. As he entered the final thicket the snow became littered with needles from the surrounding firs, their scent as strong as incense.

He passed through the final veil of trees and moved into the opening, now covered in white. The meadow floated high above the surrounding countryside, and the winter setting made it even more breathtaking. The north face dropped so sharply that only the peaks of tall firs rose above the ledge.

The surrounding trees created three walls from nature's finest hues, even in winter. The fourth vista was more splendid than any stained-glass window he had ever seen in England. Andrew's eyes drank in the sight of Cobequid Bay and the slow rise of smoke from many chimneys. From this height, it was easy to blur the boundaries between British and French enclaves. He turned, taking in the forest and snow-capped hills behind. It was as Catherine had described. Her meeting place with the Frenchwoman was indeed inspired, holy ground.

A slight motion from the meadow's western side spun him about. A man stepped from the trees, his stocky girth made broader by his winter coat. Black hair was almost hidden by the coonskin cap, and the equally dark eyes flashed as he stared at Andrew.

Andrew did not need to even think about his next move. He tossed his gun from him and stood with arms outstretched and empty. The action was rewarded with a broad grin, and Andrew knew instantly it was the man Catherine had described.

"Henri?"

"*Oui, c'est moi.*" The burly man stepped forward, and offered Andrew his hand. "*Et vous êtes Andrew, n'est-ce pas?*"

"Andrew. Yes." It was the first time he had shaken a Frenchman's hand in years. Henri's grip was strong as iron.

Reluctant to release the handshake, the two men studied each other. Finally Henri flashed another great grin and circled his arms in a barrel-shaped girth before his belly. "*Louise—elle est trop grande.*"

Andrew had to laugh. Henri joined with him, their laughter echoing back and forth about the hills.

Henri reached inside his coat and drew out a leather-bound satchel. He opened it, showed Andrew some pages of writing, and beneath it a tightly bound packet of dried herbs. He made a nest in his arms and symbolized rocking the baby to come. Andrew's smile and nod reflected the anticipation in his heart. Henri smiled in return and said, "*Pour Cat'rine. Après la naissance, pour la santé.*"

"You want Catherine to drink this after the baby has come. I understand." Andrew loosened his belt, reached inside his own coat and extracted a tightly wrapped bundle. He handed over the letter Catherine had been writing almost since the first snow, a diary of her winter. Then he untied layer after layer to reveal Catherine's little gift and offered it to Henri.

His eyes wide with surprise, Henri accepted the present with both hands. Andrew said, "We know your ships have not arrived this year. Catherine still remembers your wonderful feast and all the flavors. She thought you might be needing pepper and cinnamon and other spices."

Henri held the tiny packages up close to his nose and drew in one fragrant aroma after another. Andrew had never seen a man take such pleasure from simple seasonings before, but on this strong man it seemed perfectly natural. Reluctantly, Andrew pointed at the setting sun and the trail behind him. "I must be off."

Henri folded the letter and the gift and stowed them away, then grabbed his hand a second time. Andrew nodded his understanding and thanks, then walked over, picked up his musket, and started for the trees. At the beginning of the trail, he turned back. Henri waved, then made a single fist and pressed it firmly over his heart.

Andrew nodded agreement and turned away. Henri's final message warmed his way down through the shadows of the descending trail. *Friend.*

CHAPTER NINETEEN

Henri carried the Bible with him out into the dawn. Here it was late March, and already they had experienced two solid thaws. He stood and breathed in air caught between the freezing blade of winter and the first hint of coming life. The wind rising from Cobequid Bay carried enough of a bite to make him draw the sheepskin coat up tighter around his neck as he walked down to the barn. But he did not enter. He sat on the bench by the east-facing wall and, sheltered from the wind, looked out over the steel gray waters and the hills and the land.

His orchard raised gnarled black arms in silent greeting to him and the day. The sun lanced through the clouds and blazed a path across the fields, turning the patchy snow into burnished shields and the bay a brilliant mirror. He took a heady breath, clasping the Book in his work-worn hands.

He opened it and tried to concentrate, but anticipation fought with nervousness, joy with apprehension, and the words swam in and out of focus. He did not mind. The power and clarity he had found that winter within its pages brought the same sense of peace he had come to know and love. For many winter nights he had sat with Louise by the fire, listening more and more carefully as she read to him, occasionally speaking up with thoughts of his own. The parable of the planter and the seeds falling upon three types of soil had touched him deeply. He had sensed a seed being planted deep within his own soul, taking root and growing strong. He desperately wanted the seeds planted within him to thrive.

A familiar voice called to him, and he rose to shout, "Over here!" He stood and watched Jacques Belleveau approach with his rolling gait. His father-in-law said, "No man should be alone on such a day as this. How goes things?"

"The midwife and Mama Marie, they said nothing except to go away." For once Henri's famous smile failed him. "I came here to be away from Louise's moans. They tore at my heart."

"Aye, I still have nightmares of hearing my Marie the night before Louise was born. The women, they say it is forgotten as soon as the baby is laid upon them, but not I." Jacques pointed at Henri's hands. "What is that you hold?"

"Louise's Bible. Come, sit here with me in the sunshine."

Jacques eased himself slowly down onto the bench beside Henri. He had suffered through a long and lingering illness that winter, one which even now was not yet gone. The wasting cough was finally easing, but the slow recovery had cost him much in energy and well-being. Jacques remained a burly man, but his age was showing. "She has you reading it now as well?"

"I tell you, Papa Jacques, it is my greatest source of strength."

Jacques Belleveau wheezed a laugh. "Of all the men in all the world, you are the last I would have thought needed more strength than you already have."

"I am not even sure I understand well enough to say the words. But one thing I do know." It felt good to talk, to have something weighty enough to draw his mind away from all that was going on inside their little farm home. "There are things which I cannot face alone. I have feared these things all my life long. Ever since the day you found me in the fields, I have been terrified of . . . of defeat." He grimaced an apology at the older man. "I am sorry. I do not say these things well."

"On the contrary." Jacques Belleveau crossed his arms over his chest and leaned back against the barn. "You say them as clearly as I have ever heard."

"The nights my wife and I study the Word together, I find myself looking at what I have always run away from. And I know it is because I am strengthened by something which is not my own. My heart and my mind, they can look into the terrors of my night, and they are at peace."

Jacques stared out over the strengthening day. From the barn behind him came the sound of cattle shifting into wakefulness, wanting to be milked and fed. "Always before I have thought these ideas to be the realm of the vicar."

"I as well. But now"—in the air before him, Henri fashioned a thought with his hands—"now I feel as though some of the words I read were written for my heart alone.

Some nights I talk over a passage from the Book with Louise, and I feel as though the wisdom I have never known has been laid open there before me, the mysteries revealed."

Jacques Belleveau stared out toward the horizon a long moment, his breath rasping hard in the quiet air. Finally he said, "Perhaps my wife was right in what she said."

Before Henri could ask what he meant by those words, another set of footsteps hurried around the barn. "Henri!"

"Here! I am here!" When he saw it was his mother-in-law, the air became trapped in his chest such that he could scarcely manage, "Louise, is she . . ."

"Louise is fine." Marie Belleveau gave a flushed and weary smile. "You may come and meet your daughter now."

Andrew always looked forward to the annual spring journey to Annapolis Royal. The first ships over from England arrived with papers and journals less than four months old. Along with the news, he replenished both his supplies and his troops, arguing with all the other garrison commandants for whatever able-bodied soldiers had been transported over to Acadia from England. He reviewed the winter with his fellow officers and traded information. Most of all, there was the sense of liberation after winter's confines.

But this year there was a special significance to the journey. He breathed the fresh sea air, different here on the Bay of Fundy, more heavily laced with salt and distant climes. The wind was stronger, the town less sheltered than around their beloved Cobequid Bay. Annapolis Royal itself had a solid, patrician air, as it well should. Only Halifax was a larger establishment, and it still held to the raw-plank odor of a brand-new city. In this older town many of the houses were built of fine Acadian stone, solid as the seaside cliffs. The fort was a massive affair as well, with great towers supporting thirty-pound cannons aimed both seaward and inland toward the forests. The sea-born wind snapped countless flags and pennants, and everywhere there was the sound of drilling soldiers and shouted orders and troops on parade.

Yet not even the signs of renewed military preparedness could displace Andrew's deep-seated joy. He entered shop after shop, working down the almost endless list Catherine had given him. Even as he had mounted his horse for the departure from Edward, she had continued to add more items. And he could refuse her nothing, not when she had stood there in the doorway of their house holding little Elspeth.

Elspeth Anne Harrow was named after Catherine's mother, a decision that had brought tears even to stern John Price's eyes. Andrew carried the sound of that little child and the joy of her gaze with him through the entire four-day journey. He smiled as he watched the shop mistress measure out a yard of blue silk ribbon.

"Ah, look here, now. The gallant captain must see this already dressing the lovely lady's hair," the matronly shopkeeper said with a soft Scottish burr.

"Indeed I do. Her hair and gown both. You're sure this is the finest ribbon you have?"

"The finest this side of London, good sir." She lowered her eyelashes. "And you'll be hearing that again when your lady-friend lays eyes on it, you mark my words."

"I doubt that seriously, ma'am. Seeing as how the lady who has captured my heart is scarcely six weeks old."

"Oh, for your daughter now, is it? And sure it must be your firstborn, seeing the light there in your eyes."

"It is indeed. The ribbon is for her christening gown."

"And a lovely day that will be. Where would you be coming from, then?"

"Fort Edward."

"Hard it must be, having to journey so far away from the little one."

"Yes. And from her mother."

"Gallant, handsome, an officer, and a good husband as well." The shopkeeper shook her head as she rolled the ribbon and tied it with string. "Where would you be when my daughter was looking to wed?"

Andrew paid for the merchandise, returned to his heavily laden horse, mounted, and rode up toward the fort. He entered the main gates and saluted the sentry just as the clock struck three, the time of his appointment.

It was hard to confine his joy and his impatience to return home, now that his errands were completed. But the brisk tension within the fort left little room for the homey emotions which came most naturally these days. Andrew walked to where his sergeant major was surveying the final wagonload. "That the lot?" he queried.

"It is, sir. Only there's been a certain bushy-tailed captain out here looking for you, must be five times now."

"Stevenage is here?" Andrew felt a chill in his gut. "I thought the man was stationed in Halifax."

"Must have traveled over with the general," the sergeant major said, then looked over Andrew's shoulder and stiffened in a salute. "Ten-shun!"

"Ah, Harrow, back from your little gallivanting I see. Good. Come along, then. The general would have a word with you."

Andrew stifled the sudden rush of irritation, his usual reaction to Captain Randolf Stevenage. He did not bother with small talk, merely followed the man back to the commandant's quarters. Once through the door, Stevenage announced loudly, "I managed to locate Harrow for you, sir."

"Good, good. Afternoon, Harrow."

"General." Andrew snapped off a sharp salute. When it was returned he went into parade-ground rest. The general was seated behind the fort commandant's desk, a red greatcoat tossed over the back of a nearby chair, medals gleaming in the light. Andrew had always liked the man. "I was not expecting to find you here, sir. Otherwise—"

"Say nothing of it. I just arrived on the morning tide, a snap inspection, on my way up to Beausejour."

"The French fort? Has there been trouble?"

The great mutton chops bristled as General Whetlock's chin jutted aggressively. "No, and we are going to take it before they have an occasion to offer any."

Andrew hid behind a calm mask, but inwardly he was rocked with emotion. "Sir?"

"I don't suppose you've heard about our forays in the Ohio Valley."

"No, sir. I just arrived myself this morning."

"Absolute shambles. We were outgunned and outmanned. Lost a great parcel of land west of Pennsylvania. Oh, we'll get it back. But for the time being we must be sure there's no such trouble here in the north."

"Sir," Andrew said struggling to make sense of it all, "my region has been at peace for years."

"Yes, and we intend to keep it so. But under *British* control."

"It's under British control now. There haven't been any French troops in our area for almost five years."

"I told you, sir," Randolf Stevenage muttered at his side. "He's gone soft over the enemy."

"Sir, I protest."

"That will do, Stevenage." To Andrew,

279

the general went on, "What's this I hear of a foray into the French village, what was the name?"

"Minas, sir," Stevenage offered quickly.

Andrew managed to keep the shock from his voice as he answered, "Sir, I urged them to reconsider signing the king's loyalty oath."

"And?"

"I'm afraid I failed in that mission, sir. They say they cannot agree to take up arms against their own countrymen, particularly when they will not take up arms *with* them. But if the governor could see fit to take out that one stipulation, I am sure—"

"Nonsense!" The general slammed his fist down upon the table. "Harrow, you as commandant of an outpost garrison must see how that simply will not do!"

"But, sir, we have lived in peace—"

"A peace which remains a myth, so long as our backs are watched by a force a dozen times the size of our own! Have you any idea how many able-bodied French settlers there are within this region?"

"No, sir, but—"

"Fifteen thousand! Do you know how many troops I have under me for all of Acadia? Twelve hundred! Can you imagine what would happen if they chose to take up arms against us?"

Andrew knew he risked his commission by saying more, but he could not remain silent. He could not. "Sir, their own reluctance to fight for *anyone* could not be more clear."

The general went on as though Andrew had not even spoken. "I'll tell you what it would be. It would be an absolute debacle, the likes of which the British army has never witnessed. Why, we could be eradicated, our towns and villages lost, wiped out to the last man, woman, and child!"

The general's face had gone bright red with the exertion of his arguments. He observed Andrew with a hard gaze. "Stevenage here has asserted that you do not have what it takes to carry out my orders."

"Sir, I am yours to command. But I cannot bring myself to fire upon people who are not my enemy. Nor upon unarmed women and children. I certainly do not believe you could either, sir."

"The *men* are armed. Every one of them possesses a veritable arsenal. And they are potentially our enemy unless they sign the king's declaration!" His gaze blazed with his words. "You are aware, are you not, that refusing to obey a direct command in a time of war is a crime punishable by hanging?"

"Yes, sir," Andrew confirmed, dismayed that his commanding officer felt it necessary to warn him so. And made more miserable still by the knowledge that such fate awaited him, were he to attempt to resign from the regiment during a time of conflict. "I am."

"Very well. Go back to your post, Harrow. And remember that any man who is not for you is against you. Especially now." General Whetlock turned away, clearly disgusted with the exchange. "You are dismissed, sir."

Andrew turned to the door, far too apprehensive to more than glance at Stevenage's smirk as he opened the door and ushered Andrew from the room.

CHAPTER TWENTY

"Shah, child, hush now, it's all right." Louise rocked the tiny form back and forth, the words a constant litany spoken as much to her own heart as to the baby.

She sat where she could look out the door, waiting for her husband to return from the highland meadow. Henri had offered to make the delivery, though the morning had threatened rain and there was so much for him to do around the farm. Even with enough work to keep a dozen men busy, still he bound up her letter in oilskin and carried it up to leave it where she and Catherine had agreed—tucked beneath the fallen log they had used as a bench.

Oh, for those days to come again! Louise looked down at her child, her own sweet baby. The infant's tiny face was screwed up in pain, and she gave off a weak mewling sound, half whimper and half cry. "Oh, my sweet one, I would give anything to make you better. I would give you my life itself."

Almost as though in reply, the little eyes opened, and the crying stopped. One tiny hand unfurled to accept Louise's finger, and then the eyes closed and the face relaxed into slumber. Two months and two days old now, little Antoinette had not slept a single night through since birth. Whenever the pain eased she slipped instantly into a sleep so deep sometimes Louise could not help but worry if she would ever awaken again.

The baby was not doing well. Louise had tried every herb and medicine the village midwife and her own mother could suggest. Together they had worked through the meager store of local remedies available to them: Calomel was a favorite for infants' complaints, but it had shown no effect upon Antoinette. Physic nuts brought from some distant isle had been ground and fed to the fussing child along with cassia, but they had come right back up again. James' powders, the solution to so many problems, had helped not one whit. Asafoetida had been tried, along with minute quantities of belladonna. In desperation she had tried a thimbleful of her mother's laudanum, which had done nothing but send the baby into a sleep quiet as death and scared them all out of their wits.

The midwife had finally shrugged her confusion at this little baby who ate so little and cried so much, and said simply that she would outgrow it. But Antoinette's symptoms were not getting better. What was more, she was not growing. Her frame felt feather light, merely skin and bones beneath the blankets. Louise's heart squeezed tight with the fear of not knowing and of having nowhere else to turn.

The heavens opened, and the rain fell in great silver sheets. As she sat within the protection of her beloved home, Louise felt as though the sky was crying for her, weeping the tears of her frightened heart.

It seemed as though her world was being shaken by invisible hands. For not only her baby was sick, but her father as well. Jacques had never recovered from his winter cough; instead, he had become more quiet and subdued and then had begun to waste away. Over the past two months he had seemed to pass through stages of aging that should have taken years.

What was more, all the rumors drifting in with the early spring traders were bad. There were stories of war in Europe and conflicts closer to hand. The English governor had again issued a demand for all French settlers to sign the declaration of loyalty, this time warning of dire consequences if the French did not agree. Never had the troubles disturbed her as they did now.

Louise looked down at her beloved slumbering child, and wondered whether she would ever regain the recent inner peace she had discovered from her reading of the Book with Catherine, with Henri.

"Louise's baby is still sick."

The words seemed to drift through their cottage like unwanted shadows. Andrew looked up from the cradle to where Catherine stood by the kitchen worktable, upon which Louise's letter was spread. Her face mirrored the feeling of his own heart. "What is the matter?"

"Louise writes that she doesn't know. Antoinette won't eat as she should, and she cries all the time."

Elspeth gurgled, wiggling her entire body as she watched Andrew's dancing fingers. He turned back to his daughter. "I think she recognizes me," he noted fondly.

"Of course she does." Catherine walked over to stand by her husband and said to the baby, "You know your daddy, don't you? Such a smart baby."

Elspeth's little arms and legs jerked up and down, delight on her face as she looked at both of them together. Her little mouth opened wide with squeals of happiness and good health. Normally, watching his baby daughter was enough to wipe away the strain of whatever Andrew's day had brought. Yet tonight he could not shake off the concern over their friends' infant. *Friends.* Strange to feel such a bond, especially when he had never met Louise and had seen Henri only that one time. But he had grown close to them through Catherine's shared affections. And now as he bent over his happy daughter's bed, he worried for parents and child both.

"I wish there were something we could do for them," he murmured quietly.

"Oh, so do I, Andrew." Catherine bent over the cradle and touched the round little face. Elspeth crooned and waved and wiggled. Andrew leaned to place a kiss on a tiny waving hand, his eyes misting with the emotion that overtook him. Catherine went on. "Louise says the nearest French doctor is in Beausejour Fort. There or Port Royal."

"They might as well be in Paris, then." Beausejour and Port Royal were the two remaining French bastions in Acadia, and both required long journeys by ship. "The British navy has been blockading them since last April," he noted. "There is no way a French family could get passage."

Andrew felt his wife shiver at the news. "Things are bad, then."

"Things are terrible," Andrew replied gravely, knowing there was no point in trying to shield Catherine from the full truth. "And they are growing steadily worse."

She stood and placed a hand on his shoulder, drawing him up. Andrew did not object. He did not wish to speak of such things while so near to his daughter, as though the love and joy he felt there by her little form did not belong to the world in turmoil beyond their cottage door.

Catherine led him over to the table and stood as he settled into the chair from which he could watch her prepare their meal. She said, "You have received new dispatches?"

"Yesterday. I didn't want to tell you, what with the note from Louise."

She sat down beside him. "Tell me."

"It is not good."

"I want to know."

Others in the regiment would have considered him weak to unburden his soul to his wife. But he had known their relationship was strengthened by doing so. Now it seemed as natural as their praying together. Even when the news was bad.

"The dispatches from England all refer to the French as 'belligerents,' " he explained. "This is the word used to describe enemies in battle."

She paled but bit her lip and said nothing. Andrew continued. "All winter long there have been raids upon our western forts and outlying settlements. Some say it is by Indians, others by Indians and French together. There have been losses, but it is hard to gather how many. The numbers seem to increase with every telling." He took a breath and said what was most difficult of all. "There has been another defeat. Just last month it happened. The French of Quebec turned back an expeditionary force brought up from the colony of New York. Casualties were high."

Catherine swallowed. "But all this is so far away." Her words sounded forced out through a throat constricted with fear.

"Not anymore. I'm afraid the blockades of Beausejour and Port Royal are merely a foretaste of things to come."

The baby's happy gurgles seemed out of place now, a contrast to the heavy silence which gripped her parents. Finally Catherine said, "Then it is war?"

Andrew nodded slowly. "Soon, I fear." He turned in his chair and looked out at the gathering night. "I find this uncommon strange."

Catherine reached over for his hand. "What is that, dear?"

"At a time filled with such portents of dismal news," Andrew said to the darkness beyond his window, "I find myself most concerned about a family I don't even know, and a child only a few days different in age than our own."

Henri shook the rain from his oilskin and draped it over the Belleveaux's front porch railing. Before he could knock upon the door, however, it was opened. "Louise, I thought you were at home!"

"Well, I am here," she said with a smile that warmed his heart. Those smiles were scarce these days when her mother-heart yearned over their suffering child. "Hello, my love," she said, putting her arms around him.

He accepted her kiss and embrace, there upon the porch where the night sheltered them from eyes within and without. "What is this, now?"

"Only that I love you very much, Henri dearest." Her dark eyes shone as she looked up at him. "And that I am proud of you. So very proud."

Though her eyes were rimmed with sleeplessness and worry, though their life seemed shaken by so many forces at once, still she could look at him with a love that melted his heart. "I do not deserve you," he whispered into her hair. "Nor this welcome."

"Oh, but you do." She grasped his hand and pulled him inside. "Here he is," she announced to the room.

Henri's entrance was halted a second time by the sight of the crowd in Jacques and Marie's front room. Almost every one of the clan's graybeards was present, they and many wives as well. For some reason his heart began to hammer in his chest. "A good evening to you all," he finally managed.

"Come sit with us, Henri." Jacques Belleveau's voice was as strong and firm as

Henri had heard in months. "Will you take a hot cider?"

"I have never refused Mama Marie's good drink, and shall not now." When his smile was not reflected in the faces of those present, he slipped into the chair and wished himself a smaller figure. What on earth had he done to have caused all the clan leaders to gather? And looking so somber.

When Jacques spoke, it was with a cadence as solemn as the gathering. "Henri Robichaud, it has been with great honor that we have welcomed you into our family."

Henri accepted the pewter mug from Marie but found himself unable to drink. He sat grasping the mug, trying to formulate a response, possibly an apology, for whatever was to come.

As though she understood what her husband was thinking, Louise reached over and laid her hand on his shoulder. He glanced up and was rewarded with a comforting smile and a look of shining pride. He turned back to his father-in-law, more confused than ever.

"This old body of mine has chosen a bad time to fail me," Jacques went on. "Now, when so much needs attention, I find it will not serve me as it should."

"I told you not to talk like that," his wife

said crossly.

"It is something that needs saying and is nothing less than the truth," Jacques replied in his grave manner. "For five months now I have been feeling the winds of a different winter blow through my soul. With God's help I will renew my strength yet again. But I have rested here on my bed, and I have seen the approach of what must someday come to all."

Henri felt the hand that was holding his shoulder tremble, and the same chill coursed through his own body. He said, "May you know many more years of strength and good cheer, Papa Jacques."

A murmur of agreement ran about the room. When all were silent again, Jacques continued. "So do I hope as well. But I have lain here and felt all my world shaken. And I have come to realize that my strength is not up to the task ahead."

Henri's eyes opened wide with panic at what he sensed was coming. "Papa Jacques, please—"

"Let me have my say, Henri. I and the men gathered here have spoken long, and we are in agreement. It is unanimous. The clan needs a younger man at its head. One with the strength to meet whatever comes."

Henri sat in a silence so great the fire's

crackling sounded like musket shots in the room. He looked at his wife. How could he accept, when there was so much weakness in him? When thinking came so hard, when finding answers to life's questions seemed so elusive?

His gaze was drawn to where the vicar sat, there against the far corner, almost lost in shadows. The man's strong gaze held him fast, and Henri found himself recalling an earlier discussion. One where the vicar had told him to find strength and wisdom from Louise and from God. At the time, the words had seemed meaningless. Now it was as though the vicar had been preparing him for this moment all along.

Henri turned back to meet his father-in-law's gaze. As he did, a second thought struck him hard. Perhaps it was more true to say that *Another* had been preparing him.

"It is our clan's way to pass the position of elder to one man," Jacques Belleveau intoned, the words clearly spoken from rote. "For there are times when decisions must be made swiftly, and a gathering cannot be called. The elder is *asked* to seek the wisdom of all, but ultimately the decision is his and his alone."

Henri's heart was thudding so hard he was surprised no one else in the room seemed to notice.

Jacques went on. "Henri Robichaud, will you accept the clan's leadership?"

Henri felt his wife squeezing his shoulder tightly, communicating silently her belief in him. He took a breath, one that held time for him to feel his life shift to a new axis. Truly, it was Someone unseen who had been busy preparing *him*.

"I will," he replied. "With God's help, I will."

CHAPTER TWENTY-ONE

Catherine had brought her baby to show around to her quilting friends. She waited until the end of the afternoon gathering to approach the vicar's wife. Norma Patrick met her with a smile and eyes only for the infant. "Oh, isn't she growing up big and beautiful, yes, such a sweet baby. Look at that smile!"

Catherine handed over the bundle without being asked. "She likes you, Mrs. Patrick. Anyone can see that."

"Oh, she likes everybody, doesn't she? Yes, such a little angel." She chuckled as the baby cooed back to her. "I declare I don't think I have ever seen a happier baby."

Catherine felt herself warm with pleasure. "I was wondering if you might be willing to look after her for tomorrow afternoon."

"Why, of course—"

"Going for another of your long mysterious walks, are you, Catherine Harrow?"

The two women turned as one, startled by the snappish tone. Catherine found herself facing Matty Dwyer, the wife of the village drover. While she was called to many sick beds, he carted wagons back and forth to Chelmsford market for the farmers, transported some of the fort's incoming supplies, and did a bit of gardening upon land which always looked to be lost to weeds. The woman's chin and nose both pointed like accusing fingers as she said, "Uncommon strange how you're always off wandering about, isn't it?"

"It's not the least bit strange." The pastor's wife came swiftly to her defense. "Anyone who is housebound with a new baby needs to get away occasionally. It's only healthy."

Catherine smiled her gratitude to Norma Patrick, but nonetheless felt a sudden chill seep into the village's great room. There with the children and the laughter and the women and the talk, there among the friends she had known all her life, Catherine found herself caught by foreboding.

But her voice was steady as she said, "I love walking in the woods."

"Aye, and I say that's uncommon strange, how you come back after hours alone, your dress wet and your boots muddy."

"And I say you had best watch your tongue, Matty Dwyer." Kindly Norma Patrick was seldom seen to exhibit anger, but there was a dangerous spark now in her eyes. "It isn't so long ago that you were warned about your peevish nature."

The woman was all angles and sharp pointy edges, and she held her ground with, "There's not a thing wrong with asking a simple question. Especially in times like these, when the village needs to know we're safe and protected from the likes of Indians and Frenchies and turncoats." The accusing gaze returned to Catherine. "I say it's right for the village to know where she goes and who she talks with. For all we know, she could be spending her days nattering away with them Frenchies over Minas way. Who knows what she might be saying to them? Wonder what them soldiers up in Halifax would say if they heard news such as that, how the wife of their adored young officer is off consorting with the enemy."

Catherine felt as though a fist had clenched her middle and could only hope the alarm did not show on her face. Thankfully, Norma Patrick saved her from needing to answer. Gently the pastor's wife handed the wriggling bundle back to Catherine before drawing herself up to full height. "Now, you mind your speech, Matty, else you find yourself brought before the congregation and churched."

Catherine hid her anxiety by leaning over the baby. She had never known anyone churched since her childhood, seldom even heard it discussed. It was one of the village's worst punishments, as banishment from the congregation also meant being shut out from the great room and every social connection within their little community.

The warning was enough to back Matty Dwyer up a step. "I still say it's uncommon strange," she muttered, turning away.

"Be off with you, now," Norma Patrick responded. "And watch where you wag that tongue of yours."

The two women watched Matty leave the great room before Norma mused, "Now, I wonder what on earth has gotten into her?"

"She frightens me," Catherine admitted. She didn't explain that the sarcastic jibe about Andrew was the most frightening of all.

"Nonsense, child." The pastor's wife brought out the reassuring smile Catherine had known for so long. "There is nothing wrong with going for walks in the forest." Yet there was a new keenness to her gaze as she hesitated, then asked, "That's all you are doing, isn't it?"

"I gather flowers, and berries when they are in season." Catherine struggled to keep her voice light and steady. "And mushrooms after the rains. Andrew loves mushrooms."

"And you are a fine wife. You say you'd like me to keep the little one for you tomorrow?"

"Just for a while, if it's no trouble."

"How could such a little angel be any bother?" Norma's smile was full of warmth now. "Bring her by anytime after the midday meal."

Catherine said her good-byes around the room, trying to show no haste as she took her leave. Only when she was far down the lane toward her home did she permit herself to draw a shaky breath, and stop to allow the strength to flood back into her weakened legs. *Churched.* Her darkest nightmares had come to life in there. Would they church *her* if they knew she was visiting with a Frenchwoman? Perhaps. No, not perhaps. Most certainly. Not to mention what would happen to Andrew's military career. Catherine pressed the cooing bundle closer and hurried toward her home. How would she ever survive the shame, the isolation of being cut off from the village and all the people she knew and needed? Maybe she should not go.

And yet, and yet. She turned down the side lane, which meandered around the great old chestnut, now turning bright green with the season's fresh bounty of new leaves, and reflected that there was no way she could deny Louise. Not in her hour of need.

When she passed through the door into her own home a shiver passed through her entire body.

She settled the baby into the cradle by the fire, then went about preparing their evening meal. Her actions came almost by rote, as her mind whirled with the events of the afternoon and the accusation.

Through the open window she heard a familiar tread, and hastily Catherine patted her hair into place and wiped her hands upon her apron as she went to greet her husband.

When Andrew entered his doorway, he looked as weary as Catherine had ever seen him. More than weary. He looked defeated. She rushed to him and cried, "What is it?"

Andrew shook his head. "Just a long day."

She could look at him and see it was something else. But she held back from pressing for an answer. He needed comfort and rest. "Come sit by the fire."

He dropped into the chair by the baby's bed, and watched his daughter play with a rattle as Catherine helped him with his boots. "Thank you, my dear. You don't know what it means to have this home to come to, especially on such a day as this."

She let a hand trail lightly down the side of his face, wishing there was some way to erase all the questions and concerns she had of her own. "Are you ready to eat?"

"Food, yes. Then rest." He fumbled with the buttons to his summer coat. "I feel as though I could sleep for a century and still not rise with an easy heart."

She clasped her hands to herself. "Oh, Andrew, something dreadful has happened. I know it!"

For once her husband did not answer her directly. Instead, he turned his gaze toward the open window, staring out past the nearby shrubbery to where the hillside had been turned a burnished gold by the fading day. "Every day since my return from Annapolis Royal, I have felt as though I was waking from a dream—no, a nightmare."

Silently she lowered herself into a chair from which she could watch her husband without distracting him. His face looked stricken, an expression she had never known before. When he went on, it was to the diminishing light beyond their little home. "There has been such peace here. We have not even had an attack upon our trails in over four years. I hear of the perils and difficulties faced by some of our other settlements, and it seems as though I am listening to news from a different world. One which belongs more to England than to our land. Here there is only peace. Here there is only . . ."

He turned to her then, eyes shadowed with sorrow. In a voice as solemn as the tolling of a funeral bell, he said, "We have attacked and taken Fort Beausejour."

The entire village of Minas was held by stunned silence. The report was so bad, so difficult to accept, that everyone had retreated to shivering clusters, like newly bereaved seeking shelter.

Even Henri had no smile of greeting as he and Louise entered her parents' home.

Marie hurried to take the baby into her arms. Jacques sat by the kitchen table, a place where he was spending more and more time these days. Walking tired him so, and the weather had been too blustery most days for him to remain upon their porch. The chair by the kitchen table granted him the sense of being a part of the family and the home, while the cooking fire warmed him.

"The baby is asleep, then?" Jacques greeted them.

"Finally." Louise did not attempt to hide her weary concern. "After keeping us both up almost all the night."

Jacques nodded to the gray day outside, a pale noon sun struggling to break through the overcast. "Fort Beausejour has indeed fallen. A carter just came in from Cobequid Town this morning. They are calling it the Velvet Revolution, for scarcely a shot was fired on either side. The French soldiers were so demoralized from the long siege that when they saw the English gathering and priming their long guns, they surrendered."

"Jacques, please, such talk is not fit for the home," Marie said from her corner where she rocked the tiny form.

But he paid his wife no mind. "And now there is a rumor that half the remaining forces at Port Royal have been called westward to help defend Quebec against the expected British attack."

Louise watched as her husband lowered himself into the chair opposite Jacques. Though Henri now carried the title of village elder, he bore a lifetime's habit of following Jacques's lead. The older man held strong ties to the outside world, and many of the village's allies still preferred to speak first with him. With any other new elder, all this might mean trouble. Between Henri and Jacques, it came as naturally as breathing. Henri's brow furrowed with the effort to understand, and he showed no reluctance to ask for guidance. "What does that mean?"

"It means," Jacques replied quietly, "that we are defenseless. Not just Minas. All of Acadia is now under British control."

Louise stood by the doorway, feeling utterly apart both from the news and the discussion. Her entire world was held by concern for her ailing baby. There was room for nothing else but Antoinette. When the silence lingered long enough for her to feel she could change the subject, she said, "Catherine and I have arranged to meet this afternoon. I want to go."

Jacques stared at Henri. Marie looked up from the baby and stared as well. When no one spoke, Louise implored, "I need to know if there is anything she can do to help us. I have to see her, Papa." She looked to Henri for support.

When Jacques's eyes remained fixed on Henri, he said quietly, "The baby . . . she is not doing well."

"I have to try," Louise begged again.

Jacques turned to look at Louise. The gray light from beyond the window gave his face deep hollows and folds. The skin hung from his chin and neck. Only his voice retained the calm tone of an elder. "You know it is likely that with all this new risk, Captain Harrow will not allow her to come."

"And if she does? I must be there."

"Yes." Jacques nodded once.

Marie broke in. "But what can the Englishwoman do? There is no doctor in Edward!"

Jacques stared at his wife and asked, "Do you have the heart to tell your daughter not to go?"

Marie opened her mouth to speak, but her gaze turned back to the sleeping little form in her arms. She looked up at Louise, and the desperation in her daughter's face reflected in her own. Marie sighed and shook her head.

It was all the accord Louise needed. "Then I must fly. If the baby wakens before

I return . . . I will hurry."

CHAPTER TWENTY-TWO

Louise raced up the hillside, chased by a whirlwind of doubts and fears. The sky was filled with great sheets of scudding gray clouds shredded by the rising wind. The trees about her waved and called—whether urging her on or warning her back, she did not know. All she could think clearly was, *What if Catherine does not come?*

Her mind knew that her mother had spoken the truth. There was no doctor in Edward, not even one in Chelmsford. All the villages of Cobequid Bay, English or French, were limited to the liniments of traveling traders, the herbal lore of generations, and a barber to set the occasional broken bone. But her heart would not listen. Louise could not afford to rely on the facts. Her baby was suffering. In the light of each new dawn, when hope burned strongest and the love welling from her heart made her almost able to *will* her baby to get better, even then she was coming to see that her beloved Antoinette was losing ground.

If only there would be *something* Catherine could do. Some remedy she might recall, passed down in the English village that she had forgotten to mention, something from the dim recesses of the English past that might give her baby strength, and give herself hope.

The wind in the forest now seemed to echo her own inner litany of woe. *What if Catherine does not come?*

But when Louise rushed through the final thicket into the meadow, there was Catherine. Her long brown tresses were tossed about by the wind, and her face held a look as stricken and distressed as Louise's own heart.

The dam of Louise's emotions—all the fears and pains and weariness of too many nights spent walking the front room, cradling her fretting baby—all of it came crashing through in a burst of tears and choking sobs as the two women clung together. Louise's heart poured out in her words and her tears, only to be tossed and tumbled about by the same winds that tore at their skirts.

Louise felt the storm was personally attacking her as she returned down the trail. Her skirt snapped about, trapping her legs, hindering her from going where she knew she must. She felt herself to be in a waking nightmare, one in which she struggled to run in a morass intent on sucking her under.

The grass in the field surrounding the little Minas church was shivering and flattened low. She gripped her bonnet with one hand and as much of her dress as she could hold with the other, pinning her shawl in place by keeping the edges under her arm. Louise felt a rush of relief as the vicar appeared in the doorway. His first words were carried off by the wind. As she drew closer he called, "What in heaven's name are you doing out in this storm?"

"I went to see Catherine about the baby," she gasped out as she rushed through the door and into the alcove's relative calm. She flung off her bonnet and her shawl, crying, "Oh, Vicar, what am I going to do?"

"You are going to come up front with me and sit down and warm yourself and drink a cup of good hot cinnamon tea." He took her arm in a surprisingly strong grip and led her down the central aisle. "Now, sit yourself right there and tell me what is happening," he said as he stoked up the wood stove that heated the little chapel for Sunday services.

"Nothing new. Nothing you don't already know. You have heard it from me and from my mother and probably from every other woman in the village." She watched as he broke a long cinnamon stick in two, set the halves in a pair of cups, and with a fire-blackened cloth lifted the steaming pot from the top of the stove. She took the cup he offered, then stared blankly down at it.

"Now then." The vicar settled his lean form beside her. The steam from his mug rose and drifted in air untouched by the storm beyond the chapel walls. "Tell me what is on your heart."

Here and now, within the safety of these secure walls, his comforting presence, she gave voice to the fears which terrified her. "So many babies don't live beyond the first few months. I have known this all my life. I lost a little sister when I was eight. I haven't thought of it in years. Henri lost a brother. Here I've been married to the man for almost two years and only now do I learn that he once had a sibling."

She looked up then and saw in Jean Ricard's dark gaze the same answer she had tried not to face the night before. "He told me because he wanted to prepare me for what might come. But I couldn't live if I lose my Antoinette! I would rather die with her!"

Instead of the rebuke she expected, rather than chiding her for such thoughts,

Jean Ricard gave a solemn nod. "You have given your life to your child. How can you possibly go on if the baby is assigned to the grave?"

The gust of wind shivered the walls about them. Louise felt all the tears remaining in her heart come springing to her eyes. "Yes! How can I live? How is it possible to go on? I can't! My life would end with hers!"

"It is not yet time to speak of death." The sky beyond the chapel's tiny lead-paned windows had turned dark with twilight. The vicar's face seemed even more lean and craggy than ever. Only his eyes retained their same gentle light, a glow like the coals in the fire behind him. "You will know if such a time comes, and God will supply you with the answers only then. For now it is your fears speaking, and these too you must turn over to God. Rely on His strength. Not on yours. He will see you through. Remember this when you feel attacked in the night by all that is beyond your control. Rely on God's strength. It will come one day, one moment, at a time. Just when you need it."

They were words she had heard a hundred times before. A thousand. And they answered none of the questions which filled her mind with a storm's chaos. Yet here and now they granted her the stillness of genuine peace, enough so that her tears ceased and her voice quieted. "But what am I to do about my baby?"

The same calm, gentle peace she felt growing within her soul was there in the pastor's voice. "Whatever God shows you to do."

The storm continued long past dark, its force so great Andrew watched the fire flicker and dance from winds blown down the chimney. He lay in bed without moving, afraid he would disturb Catherine. She had looked rather worn lately. Though caring for him and the child was enough to exhaust anyone, still she insisted upon hearing the growing tide of dire news. And she remained desperately worried over Louise's little Antoinette.

His eyes moved to where their own baby's cradle glowed ruddy and warm in the firelight. He longed to rise and walk over and stare down at his beloved child. Each time he held his daughter it was the first time all over again.

A soft voice said from beside him, "Do you wish to tell me what bothers you so?"

He rolled over in bed. "I thought you were asleep."

"As you should be." Catherine turned toward him. "Do you have to go out on patrol again tomorrow?"

"At dawn." Though their region of Cobequid Bay remained as calm and peaceful as ever, the troop had been on constant alert since the taking of Fort Beausejour.

"Then you should be asleep. You are not resting enough."

"I was just thinking the same about you." He stared into Catherine's brown eyes, her gaze softened by love and the fire's glow.

She stroked his face, her hand as soft and warm as her voice. "What is troubling you so?"

"It is so strange," he said, clasping her hand and drawing it into the space between them. "With all there is to occupy my mind, I cannot stop thinking about little Antoinette."

Catherine was silent a long moment, then said, "It is a problem of a size and form that we can work with."

Andrew drew back a fraction. "I don't understand."

"We are surrounded by forces beyond our control. There is nothing we can do about war in England."

"We cannot change the way the authorities feel about the French," Andrew agreed. "We cannot erase centuries of conflict and suspicion."

"But this baby, this tiny helpless child . . ." Catherine stopped and swallowed hard. "This one life has form and meaning."

"It is more than that," he discovered, his wife's words a mirror to what before had remained beyond reach within himself. "This one family's distress gives a very real face to what all the French must be feeling. I ache for them, for their uncertainty and despair."

"As do I," Catherine whispered. "I think of God's teachings, all that we have studied and learned, and I yearn to help, but I feel so helpless to do anything." Her eyes filled with tears. "I think of Louise and that little baby all the time."

"I too wish there was something we could do to help them," he quietly agreed.

"I know you do." She freed her hand and returned it to his face. "And it is one of the many things I love about you. But now, my beloved husband, you must sleep."

"Let us pray for the child first," Andrew replied.

Catherine's gaze flickered over to the quiet form in the cradle. She murmured, "And her mother."

"And father." Andrew lowered his head, and as he did so, he felt a growing sense of warmth and power within their little haven against the storm. There was Someone else who also cared.

CHAPTER TWENTY-THREE

Andrew knocked on the door to John Price's office. A muffled voice called from within, and he pushed it open and entered. "Afternoon, sir. You wished to see me?"

"Ah, Andrew, good of you to stop by. Will you take a coffee with me?"

"Thank you, but if you will excuse me, I must soon be on my way." Andrew hesitated to cross the floor with his boots, muddied almost to the hilt from the trail. "I have spent all day on patrol."

"Yes, yes, of course." John Price must have noticed Andrew's hesitation. "Come, come, man, sit yourself down. I am no stranger to the trail myself."

"Aye, sir, thank you." It was only when he settled into the chair that he realized how tired he was. His bones still seemed to vibrate from the horse's motion.

But Price appeared too caught up in his own thoughts to notice. "Sure you won't join me? The drover just arrived back from Annapolis Royal this morning, brought two sacks of fresh beans. Might be the last we see for quite a time."

"It does smell good, I must admit." Andrew watched him pour the tin mug full. "Much obliged, sir."

"Think nothing of it."

Andrew took a first sip, felt the bitter warmth down to his center. "Any word from headquarters?"

"As a matter of fact, there were a few things." Price's features were even more ruddy than customary. Against the white of his sweeping sideburns, his complexion held to an alarming shade. "Nothing of great importance to you, of course. But I have been called to Halifax."

Despite his bone-weariness, a faint chime seemed to sound within Andrew's mind. "Indeed, sir?"

"Yes. It seems that the governor himself wishes to discuss the findings of my recent survey."

Andrew gazed about the cramped office. The wall opposite the door was made up of floor-to-ceiling cubbyholes, almost every one of which was stuffed with papers and invoices and forms. A massive black safe, squat and formidable, sat behind his father-in-law's desk. The two windows were flanked by shelves crammed with more papers and survey scrolls. The air smelled of dust and drying ink. Andrew wondered what it was that he was not seeing, something that seemed just beyond his grasp.

"As you know, I have been busy assessing the surrounding country."

"Indeed," Andrew murmured again. "We have all noticed you riding out more than usual."

"Yes, the orders I had were to survey everything from here to the far boundaries of the Minas River."

Minas. Andrew sat upright at the word, as though it prodded him to identify what he was not seeing clearly. "You have been to the French village?"

"Of course not, man, don't be daft. What on earth would I have to do with the Frenchies? No, I surveyed them from a distance. Saw all I needed to."

Andrew stared at the dark steaming liquid within his cup. No, it was not Minas. Something else, something . . .

The realization struck him with such force that he jerked to his feet. The coffee splashed over his hand as he reached forward and swiftly set it down on the side of the desk.

"Anything wrong, Harrow?"

"No, not at all, sir. I just recalled . . ." Andrew knew his hasty departure would cause comment, but he could not tarry. Something this important could not wait another instant. "You must please excuse me."

———— ❧ ————

But the closer he drew to his home, the slower his steps. The idea which had half formed in his mind there in John Price's office now seemed outlandish as he turned down the lane to his house. How could he suggest such a thing to Catherine? And yet, there was such a sense of rightness, no matter how illogical it might seem. Even now, as he sought reasons not to speak of it, he found himself filled with the sensation that the idea had not come from himself at all.

"Andrew! I wasn't expecting you for hours."

"Hello, my dear." He accepted her welcoming hug, then used the iron boot-horn imbedded in the stone by his front door to pry off his muddy boots. Now that he was there and facing his wife's shining eyes, he felt almost reticent. "What have you been doing today?"

"Oh, I've been busy as always. Dinner is

316

far from ready. Will you have a cup of tea?"

"No, I took coffee with your father." He entered the front room, slipped on the soft old shoes she kept for him by the fire, and bent over to croon at the baby. The sight of the happy young face brought a new light to his eyes. A smile to the drawn lips. But his eyes quickly darkened, and the smile left his mouth to be replaced with a look of deep sadness. He said with resigned firmness, "Your father has been called to Halifax."

Catherine was caught halfway back to the kitchen. "Halifax?"

"Yes. Something to do with survey work he was assigned." And there he stopped. He simply did not know how to continue.

It was then Catherine said, "Andrew, there is a doctor in Halifax."

Still he could not lift his eyes from the crib. "I know."

But when she did not say anything more, her silence forced him to turn and face her. The instant he looked into her eyes, he knew that she was thinking the same thing as he. "It could be dangerous, Catherine."

"Not," she said slowly, "if I take Antoinette as my own daughter."

Andrew exhaled and released the tension he had been holding ever since the possibility had struck him there in his father-in-law's office. Catherine's quiet yet assured words could not have been a clearer indication to him that the idea had come from beyond his own mind. "Yes," he quietly agreed. "That way, we should all be safe."

Henri carried a shovel and the pair of burlap sacks up the winding trail, feeling as though they were the heaviest burdens of his entire life.

The bundles clanked together as he climbed. It was not the weight of the load which tired him, but all the premonitions which he carried along as well. All the responsibilities. All the questions without answers.

That morning Jacques had insisted that Henri, the head of the clan, take control of the clan's secret wealth. Each family contributed a small share of the farm's income in every good year, and there had been many good years since the last time of hard need. Many years indeed. The resulting accumulation of coins was what he carried, an amount that had shocked him when Jacques had tallied it all up that morning. Enough to buy the entire village's land and have some left over.

Jacques had explained how he never spoke of the amounts. Only to take it in and save it, and have the others trust him and his good name. He and one other elder kept the books, honest and accounted for to the last farthing, nothing ever spent on themselves. All for the clan, just in case. Jacques had refused to accept Henri's protest that his health would improve. He had simply repeated those three dread words: *Just in case.*

Henri arrived at the last thicket before the meadow and dropped his burden to the ground. The afternoon was hot, feeling warmer still in contrast to how cold and wet the previous days had been. But even without much of a summer, just an occasional warm day, the crops were doing well. As though they had decided to ignore the weather and help prepare for uncertain times ahead.

The boughs of the surrounding firs leaned in close about him, sheltering him and his secret. Henri cleared the ground of its blanket of needles, the perfect disguise for his diggings. He looked carefully around to give anchoring points for the location, then his shovel bit deep into the soft earth. Soon he was standing inside the sodden hole in order to make it deeper still. His breath came in steady grunts of effort, for the soil was heavy with the dampness.

When the hole was waist deep, he stepped free and dropped the bags inside, one on top of the other. He covered in the hole, tramped down the earth, then scattered the pine needles back into place. He walked carefully around the spot, until he was certain that not even he could tell exactly where the hole had been dug without his sight markers.

Now he stepped into the meadow itself and took a deep breath of the sweet-scented air. The rain-drenched firs and the bright new wild flowers filled the meadow with honeyed perfume. Wiping his brow, Henri seated himself on the log Louise had described as their bench. His heart ached anew for her anguish and for their little girl. He would do anything, give all he had, to see Antoinette be well and strong. Anything at all. Yes, even his beloved land.

He found himself dropping to his knees, the action coming as naturally here as it did when he knelt beside his wife before entering their bed at night. He clasped his hands together and bowed his head. Such hard, powerful hands. His wrists were thicker than Louise's ankles. His fingers were black from digging, the shirt sticking to his chest from the recent effort. He closed his eyes, and he prayed. "My God, my God, I am such a simple, ignorant fellow. The world is so full of things I do not understand, and filling with more every day. Show me what to do. Give me the words. Give me the wisdom. Give me the strength." He paused, then added with a catch in his voice, "I give our little Antoinette into your hands."

As he knelt there, Henri remembered a passage Louise had read with him the previous winter, back before the times had become so confusing. And suddenly the peace he had known through those long winter evenings, when the fire in their hearth was enough to keep the night and the world at bay, such a peace was there with him now. A peace that filled his soul so completely that there was no longer room for worry, only for the final words to his prayer, ones from the passage and from the memory, *Give me a light for the darkness, a lamp for my path. Show me the way I am to go.*

Henri opened his eyes and grinned sheepishly at the little bird which had come to settle on the other end of the log bench. He noticed then that the small branch on which the bird had settled had begun to bud. A surprising occurrence, for the tree had lain there for several years. Even so, part of the roots had taken hold once more, and the branches were sprouting leaves. For some reason this gave him a great sense of confirming hope.

As he rose to his feet, he noticed the oilskin packet tucked there beneath the branch and its new green leaves.

Louise looked up from the letter and looked around at the three expectant faces watching hers. She was surprised at how calm she felt. It was more than simply the result of her constant fatigue, or because her nerves were worn down to passive acceptance. No. As she sat and read the letter, she knew Catherine's suggestion was the answer to her anxious prayers. She did not care that the plan was so brave as to be almost foolhardy. This felt *right*.

"Catherine wants to take my own baby and go to the doctor in Halifax. Her father is called there on official business. There will be a military escort and wagons, because they will bring back supplies. Catherine says the doctor is the best in all Acadia. He was trained in . . ." She looked down at the pages in her hands, the fragile leafs held without any trembling. She stumbled over the unfamiliar "Edinburgh."

Her mother stood there beside Jacques's chair holding Antoinette, who was quiet for a change. Marie looked first at her husband, then at Henri. When the two men remained silent, she asked, "But how will they convince the English doctor to look at a French baby?"

Louise glanced at her husband and father, and knew instantly that the men had been silent because they had already guessed the answer. "Catherine has offered," she quietly replied, "to exchange babies with me for the visit."

Marie's gasp was the only sound in the entire room. Louise waited for someone to object, but when the trio said nothing she went on. "She will tell her father that Elspeth has not been sleeping well and has started to fret, which is true, but she thinks it is merely the beginning of teething. She is certain her father will agree for them to come along. He has often invited her to come on one of his journeys. She refused in the past because she has never had any interest in visiting the distant towns."

Jacques turned to look at Henri. Louise took the opportunity to study her father. Jacques was not doing well. The afternoon sunlight had turned his eyes into caverns from which only the dimmest light seemed to glow. Jacques asked, "What do you think, Henri?"

"If we do nothing," Henri replied slowly, "I fear for our daughter's—for her life."

"As do I." Jacques looked at his hands upon the table. "My own illness has reminded me that death and danger lurk just beyond our immediate vision."

"Don't talk such nonsense," Marie scolded.

Jacques looked at his wife, a quiet glance without reproof, yet enough to draw tears to Marie's eyes. Jacques replied, "If we can help Antoinette in this way . . ."

Marie brushed impatiently at her eyes. She nodded and sniffed, "Such an offer, how could we refuse?"

"More than that," Henri added. "How could we ever repay her?"

Louise glanced down at the pages once more, relief swelling her heart and misting her gaze. Eventually she managed, "Catherine says she and her husband feel as though they are doing it as much for themselves as for us. This gift to us is the only answer they have found to these distressing times."

CHAPTER TWENTY-FOUR

Catherine clutched her baby so closely that Elspeth squirmed in protest. Reluctantly Catherine's arms relaxed. It was only for a few days. A few days and she would be back again, hopefully with an improving Antoinette. She shuddered at the thought of having her baby's life threatened by illness. Poor Louise. Her friend had suffered so over the past months. Never knowing from one day to the next if her baby would remain with her, or if there would be a tiny grave dug beyond the orchard.

Catherine lifted a corner of the blanket to take a peek at her daughter, then leaned to press a kiss to the smooth forehead. "I shall miss you," she whispered. "I will miss you more than you'll ever know. But we must do this. We must. We cannot let Antoinette die."

Catherine moved on. She was almost to the meadow. She prayed that the other mother would not keep her waiting, yet at the same time she hoped for more time with her own baby girl. Even so, each additional moment would just increase the difficulty of the parting.

Louise was there, pacing back and forth before the fallen log. Her eyes were red rimmed. The tiny bundle in her arms was clutched tightly to her heart.

"I may never see her again," Louise whispered.

"Nonsense," Catherine denied, her voice more confident than she felt. "It is only a few days until I will be back, and with Antoinette much improved. You'll see. God would not have planted this idea in Andrew's heart for it to come to naught."

"She has weakened further in the past few days," Louise said with trembling lips. "She might not survive the trip."

"I shall care for her as if she were my own," Catherine promised.

"How can I ever, ever repay you? To risk taking my baby to an English doctor, to leave your own baby behind."

"I know that you will care for *her* as if she were *your* own, as well," Catherine said, but her arms tightened around her now sleeping daughter.

"I will," nodded Louise. "I will. But—"

"No more arguments. We must do this. It is the only way to help Antoinette."

Louise drew the shreds of her composure about her like a cloak of strength. "Tell me about Elspeth. What does she like for comfort?"

Catherine looked lovingly at the baby that stirred in her arms. "Mostly her father," she said with a forced smile. "I'm afraid he spoils her some. She delights in having him lean over her crib and tickle her toes or talk silly baby talk." Her eyes threatened to spill over again, but she forced herself to continue. "She does like being bounced when she is fussy—she is working on some teeth now. And she likes to chew my finger. Or a bit of cloth wet with cold water. Or the silver ring, like the one I gave you."

Louise nodded. "I will remember."

"She also loves to hold a corner of that soft fur Henri made for her. Does Antoinette have one?"

Louise nodded with a wobbly smile.

"And Antoinette?"

"She has been far too ill to express preferences." Louise's hand lifted to stroke the fevered cheek with the back of her fingers. "Do you know, I still have not seen her smile."

Catherine could not imagine Louise's pain. No smiles. Why, Elspeth had been blessing their home with smiles and coos for months.

"She will soon be smiling," Catherine assured her. "You'll see."

Louise wiped at tears again. "We must hurry," she said, but with no indication of releasing her baby.

"Yes," agreed Catherine. "If we are found out . . ." But she would not say it. Would not even think it. They must not be discovered. For the sake of Antoinette. Catherine took a shaky breath and said, "We must pray."

Louise looked up. "Of course. We must pray."

They knelt together in the softness of the meadow grasses, each holding close the treasure they cherished the most. Each aware of their need of a God far greater, far more powerful, far wiser, far more in control of a world raging about them than either of them could ever be.

As they knelt, their trembling voices lifted in prayer, asking that God be with each of them in their hour of personal need. To be with their babies, each entrusted to the other. To be with the men whose lives they shared. Good men. Strong men—but men at the mercy of their times. To be with their countrymen, French and English alike, trembling on the brink of disaster.

When they arose, their faces shone with a fresh sense of strength. Of assurance. God had met with them. They felt His presence. Whatever lay before them, they felt confident that He would see them through.

Reluctantly, they each placed a final kiss

upon the brow of their own baby, then tucked each precious girl in the other's blanket. Catherine turned away with a lump in her throat, hoping to muffle her sobs until out of hearing of her friend.

"Oh—I almost forgot," said Louise fumbling in her pocket. "The vicar asks your husband to remember what he said when they met, something about the Good Samaritan. And Henri has written you and Andrew a letter."

Catherine accepted the single sheet, hardly able to see through the tears in her eyes.

It was written in a crude, childlike scrawl. Catherine needed to study it to make out the French words. It was plain that Henri did not spend much of his time writing.

Louise, looking over Catherine's shoulder, traced her finger along the letter's final line and read aloud, "When the world is not as God would have it, it is a double blessing to have friends such as you."

Catherine swallowed over the lump in her throat. Andrew, too, would be touched by the message. "Thank him from us both," she whispered.

Louise nodded. Without further word the two exchanged a one-arm embrace, careful of the two babies cradled between them.

Catherine could not resist reaching out a hand to Antoinette's blanket, the one which now covered her Elspeth. "Take care of my baby," she pleaded. "Take care of my Elspeth."

Then she turned and almost ran down the path leading from the meadow.

Louise stood transfixed, her eyes on Catherine's retreating figure. It was beyond her to understand such sacrificial devotion. She shifted Elspeth in her arms and was rewarded with a sleepy smile as the baby stirred.

"I will," she whispered. "With my very life if need be. I promise."

She lifted her eyes to see Catherine's form swallowed up by the tall dark pines. "And you . . . I know that you will care for my Antoinette. You would not have offered this if you would not."

Weeping, she turned toward her own trail home. She felt a tug as a small hand reached up to grasp the ribbons of her bonnet. Her tearful eyes turned to the baby she held. So healthy. So plump. So content in her arms. If only she could see her own Antoinette looking so. It would be a miracle, an answer to her most earnest prayers. "You are beautiful," she whispered to the child. "No wonder your mama loves you. I love you too. Almost as though you were my own." Elspeth answered with a cooing smile.

Due to leave at six in the morning, Catherine gladly would have left earlier. She had not slept well. Her heart was heavy with longing for her child. Antoinette did not ease the longing, even as Catherine held her close and tried to coax her to nurse. The baby just whimpered and turned away. Catherine endured added discomfort. Elspeth had always nursed so hungrily.

Andrew's sleep was also disturbed by the whimpering baby. She seemed too weak to cry lustily, but her mewing was enough to leave them both restless and wakeful. *What if she truly cannot survive the trip?* Catherine found herself thinking. She had promised Louise. Had she made that promise foolishly? The baby was so weak. So sickly. Watching the frail little one filled Catherine with deep concern. *Let's be going*, she wanted to call into the early dawn. *We have no time to waste. The baby needs help now.*

The two-wheeled conveyance carrying her father arrived promptly at six, as Catherine knew it would, along with two other carts and an armed troop.

Catherine clung to Andrew, wishing with all her heart that he was going with her. But when he put in his request to the general to make the journey, he had been turned down point-blank.

Andrew lifted her chin and looked into her eyes. "It will be all right," he whispered. "Just keep the blankets close about her face."

"But what if Father—?"

"He won't. You know what little interest he has shown in our child. Besides, he will be much too busy minding the team. And once you arrive in Halifax, his hours will be spent with his duties."

"But what if she . . ." Catherine could not say the word, but she knew Andrew understood.

"You mustn't even think of that," he said softly. "In just a few days you will have her safely in the doctor's care."

"And if the doctor isn't able to help?"

"He is said to be the best there is, as good as anyone in London. He must have something to help her."

A querulous voice startled them both. "Well, well, if it isn't the lady of the forest."

Catherine moved away from her husband's embrace to face Matty Dwyer, the sharp-faced drover's wife. Before she could think of how to respond, the woman said, "Been taking more of those walks of yours, have you? And this time with the baby."

Catherine felt the breath freeze in her throat. Fortunately, her father was busy with the drovers, including the woman's own husband, and not paying any mind to their conversation.

"Uncommon strange it is, how a mother would take a newborn up into the forest like that." Matty Dwyer's eyes seemed gripped by fever, the way they burned and probed. "Makes a body wonder, it does."

"There's nothing to wonder about," Andrew said, using as sharp a tone as Catherine had ever heard from him.

"Yes, wonder why a mother would risk her child like that," the woman said, ignoring Andrew. She turned away and tossed over her shoulder, "I imagine other folks might wonder who it is she's been in such an all-fired rush to speak with. And why."

Catherine stared after the woman, her heart squeezed by the sudden fright. Only when Matty Dwyer had moved behind her husband's wagon did Catherine bury her face against Andrew's jacket and cling to him. "What are we to do?" she whispered.

"Exactly as we are doing now," Andrew said. Anyone else would think the man remained utterly untouched by the confrontation. But Catherine could hear the trace of concern, even as he attempted to hide it from her. "We must remember our mission here."

"I'm so afraid."

"Be strong, for us, for Elspeth, for Antoinette. And hurry back," she heard him whisper. "I am going to be so lonely until I get my two girls back home again. I am almost glad I've been called off to Annapolis Royal."

"Annapolis Royal? But you've said nothing."

"Word came last eve, by dispatch." He glanced at the baby. "You have been so worried I was not sure whether I should tell you at all."

"No, no, you did right." But she could not help her feeling of distress, as though somehow he was abandoning them. "Must you go?"

"The general signed the orders. I am to leave at first light tomorrow." He ran a hand over Elspeth's blankets that now bundled Antoinette. "I shall miss you terribly."

"Did they say why?"

"The summons said nothing further, only that I am ordered to muster my troops and appear. But I'm quite sure to be home again before you."

Catherine held him tighter still. "Do be careful."

"It is you going on the perilous journey." He looked down at her with a grave smile. "I will be counting the days. I will miss you—both of you—so much."

Yes. Yes, it would be hard for Andrew. He would miss leaning over the small crib and watching his daughter respond with chortles and squeals of delight at seeing him. He would miss giving her rides on his polished boot. Letting her tug at his mustache, wrap tiny fingers in his hair. Yes, he would miss them both.

Catherine pushed herself back. Her father was anxious to be on the trail. They had a long way to go. She heard the horses of the accompanying soldiers stomping in impatience. She must go. She must. "Pray for me," she whispered.

Andrew nodded.

"And I will pray for you. Every day. Every mile of the way," Catherine promised and with one last look into his eyes she turned toward the clumsy cart.

They had fashioned a seat of pine boards, padded only by a heavy moose-hide throw. It would not help much with the sharp jolts and jars, but it was a place to sit and hold Antoinette as the heavy cart rumbled its way over the rugged bushland trail.

Andrew helped her to settle herself, spoke a quiet greeting to John Price, and squeezed her arm with one final good-bye. Catherine's father flicked the reins, and the conveyance jerked into motion. As they started up, Catherine turned from a final wave to Andrew to see Matty Dwyer standing on the trail's opposite side, her arms folded across her chest, watching intently as the wagons rolled off. Catherine turned. She had no time for the woman's prying ways. Not then. She fought to control her tears as her thoughts traveled to her infant daughter. Did Elspeth have the same feelings, sleeping in another cradle? Did she look about her at strange faces—the unfamiliar room—and wonder what had happened to her world?

Catherine forced the thoughts aside. God was with her baby, with all of them. There was a duty to be done. The baby in her arms needed medical attention. She would do her best to see that the little one got the help she needed—in time.

She lifted the infant to her shoulder and

brushed a kiss against the hot little face. *Please let us hurry. Please, let us get there with no delays*, she pleaded silently.

Her father stood stoutly before her, his legs braced wide against the roll and pitch of the cart. The driver of the lead wagon was not hurrying the team. Good sense demanded that they travel cautiously. But her father would make certain they would not dawdle. Catherine knew him well enough to be sure of that fact. Unless something totally unforeseen happened, they would arrive in Halifax precisely as planned. For Catherine, it could not be too soon.

"Look at her. She is a little pig," chuckled Louise as Elspeth nursed hungrily.

Henri smiled. "No wonder she is so round," he responded.

"And several pounds heavier than our Antoinette," Louise added.

"Our little girl will soon catch up. When she comes home—this one better be on her guard. Our Antoinette will soon make her look like the runt of the litter."

Louise smiled. It was exhilarating to think about Antoinette returning strong and

337

healthy. But she sighed when she thought of the long, long way to Halifax. Henri, who had once visited the market there, had drawn a crude map in the dust of the garden path to show which way their baby would travel. Louise tried not to fret as the time passed and the distance grew greater and greater between her and her child. Would Antoinette travel safely all the way there and all the way back? Thoughts she tried to shield against continued to stab her heart. What would happen if she did not endure the trip? Would her baby be buried beside the trail in some remote part of the forest? And if she were, what then? What would become of Henri and her? How would Catherine explain that she could lose a baby—yet still have a baby in her cradle? Would Catherine be *churched*, as she had once feared? What would happen to Andrew's career as a military man?

Louise again pushed all of the troubling thoughts aside as Elspeth pulled away from her nursing. Milk dribbled down one side of her mouth, and Louise couldn't help but laugh as she wiped it away with a corner of the blanket. A loud burp escaped the small child even before Louise could lift her to a shoulder. The young woman laughed again outright. Elspeth responded with a giggle of her own.

The soft sound brought tears to Louise's eyes. Was this what it was like to have a healthy child? Was this what she could one day enjoy? If Catherine brought her this gift of joy, of peace from troubled nights and long, anxious days, it would be far more than she would ever be able to repay. Louise closed her eyes, pretending for one moment that it was Antoinette who squirmed happily in her arms.

It was going to be so hard to wait.

CHAPTER TWENTY-FIVE

The thought that Catherine came back to again and again throughout the four long days of travel was *God's hand is on this journey*.

The little baby did surprisingly well. There were times when she whimpered and squirmed as the wagon bounced over boulders, or the team of horses slipped and struggled through muddy bogs. Though the baby was so fragile looking, with dark circles under her eyes, Antoinette seemed to be holding up well. Catherine checked often, feeling her forehead for fever, passing a finger lightly over the little head's soft spot to watch for dehydration, coaxing the child to nurse, if only a few drops of nourishing liquid. Antoinette's dark eyes seemed to study Catherine carefully, no doubt puzzled about the change of face bending over her.

Hour after hour the wagon jounced and pitched on the rough trail, climbing ever higher through great trees which stood like ghostly sentries above unseen cliffs. Catherine prayed over the little one, watching Antoinette and stroking the fine dark hair, the smooth cheek.

John Price seemed little concerned with the baby's presence. Having never paid the child much mind, here on the trail he seemed to have even less time for his granddaughter. He remained preoccupied with his papers, which he continually perused. Eventually growing impatient with their slow progress, he barked at the sergeant major, urging them to greater speed.

Throughout the third day of travel, the summer fog did not lift, but rather condensed and settled more firmly. That evening, as Catherine moved away from the fire and began to nurse the baby, she realized just how isolated she had become. God seemed very far away just then. All the growth and strength she had sensed within herself vanished in a cloud of fatigue and confusion.

She longed for her little Elspeth. The pain was so sharp she had to bite her lip to keep from crying. She searched the night but saw only drifting tendrils of silvery mist and trunks huge as temple pillars and shrouded by dark. *What am I doing here? How could I have ever thought to leave my baby behind and take to the road with someone else's child?* She heard the sentry's steady footsteps count a circle around their gathering, listened to the soldiers talking quietly by the fire, and turned her back to them all so they would not hear her weeping.

But the next morning, when she awoke before the others to a world of green and a sky of sweeping blue, she herself felt reborn. They had made camp upon a high knob, surrounded by stony peaks and forest valleys of emerald green. The night's fears seemed as distant as nightmares from her childhood. She looked down at the pale and silent Antoinette, and felt a sudden welling of love. It was not the same as for her own Elspeth. No, but it felt like God was using this journey to create new space in her heart, a space intended to hold even more love than before, a love for this needy little child.

Henri leaned over the crib and chuckled

as the little face immediately blossomed into a delighted laugh. "She is a cheerful one, isn't she?"

Louise moved over to stand beside her husband. "She is that."

He glanced at his wife. "This is hard for you, no? Seeing healthy Elspeth here, the one who is not your own."

"In a way, yes. I miss Antoinette so." Louise reached out and allowed the tiny waving fist to attach itself to one finger. "Yet I feel as though I am looking after my own sister's child."

Even so, as she reached down into the crib and bundled up the infant, Louise felt a hollow ache for the child who belonged there. *Please, dear Lord, make my baby well.* But all she said was, "Time for the little one's next feeding."

Henri reached up, and with a movement of surprising gentleness for all his strength, he brushed a lock from Louise's face. "You are a good woman. Better than I should ever deserve."

She made to laugh, though at the moment it would take some effort. "Do you see how she feeds? Never have I seen one as hungry as Elspeth."

But Henri's gaze was soft and open and only for his wife. "I do not know why the

Lord decided to bring us together," he murmured. "But I thank Him every day for the gift of you."

The longing of her heart gradually eased, as though she heard not just the words her husband spoke, but rather another voice speaking along with his. One so filled with love she could not help but accept the gift of peace. She settled the nursing baby more comfortably and asked, "Would you pray with me for our baby?"

Catherine had never known anything like the city of Halifax. Although it was less than five years old, already it was so large it could have swallowed a dozen Edwards and scarcely have noticed. The hills rising along three sides were all ugly and scarred where the forests had been felled for timber. The houses and the fort and the raised plank sidewalks all seemed to have *exploded* from the earth. There was such a frenetic energy it almost frightened her.

And the noise. The air was filled with banging and hammering and shouting. And dust. The streets were packed with regiments of soldiers marching and stamping and snapping their weapons to their shoulders and then pounding them back into the earth at their feet. They and the countless wagons and the horses and the mules all threw up so much dust she carried a handkerchief before her face and covered the baby's face with gauze as she hurried along the wooden sidewalks.

Neither the noise, nor the dust, nor the strangeness bothered little Antoinette at all. That first day the doctor had given Catherine an elixir that had seemed to ease the infant's distress almost instantly. Since then the child had spent most of her hours either eating or sleeping. Whenever she awoke, her expression seemed one of surprise at the freedom from pain. Catherine knew the baby could not remember such things, yet she could not help feeling that the child was not disturbed by the outer clamor simply because the greater internal suffering had finally been eased.

But the imprint of her earlier distress was still visible. The baby was far too small for her age. That very morning, the doctor had warned her as gently as he could that the child might not ever fully recover. She had suffered much, and her body might be permanently weakened, he had explained, urging Catherine to take special care and keep her sheltered. Catherine had stammered out her thanks, aching from the thought of having to convey this news to Louise. But at least the baby seemed genuinely to be on the mend, especially after this morning's second visit, when the doctor had expressed satisfaction with little Antoinette's immediate progress. It seemed that she had responded to the medicine he had given. It had been very startling to hear this man refer to this baby as her own. But as she had walked the sidewalk back toward their inn, Catherine found herself looking at the baby anew. As though somehow having the doctor call her *Elspeth* had drawn the two of them closer together. Wrapped another bond around them, tightening the cords which Catherine now believed would hold them together for life, no matter how far apart they might be, no matter how different Antoinette's future might be from that of her own child.

As she approached the inn's entrance, Catherine jumped at the sound of cannon booming in the distance. Either from the sound or from her reaction, the baby began to cry. Catherine cast a glance out to where the rock-lined harbor spread in the distance, so crammed with ships it was hard to even count their numbers. Those coming or going could not maneuver under their own sail. Instead, they were towed out by men bending over the oars of smaller gunboats.

Stepping inside, Catherine asked the inn's day-clerk, "Is it usual to see so many ships at anchor?"

"Oh no, ma'am. Especially not this late, not after the spring convoy arrives." The young man looked out the front window with a keen yearning to his pinched gaze. "No, there's something up, you mark my words. I'm thinking of joining the forces, make a name for myself in the fighting. Earn myself some good land, as they say."

Catherine's nervous smile of thanks was lost upon the young man, whose gaze remained fastened upon the harbor and the ships. She could not suppress a shiver of fear as she climbed the narrow stairs to her room. This place and its noise and its constant call of battle was certainly not for her. The sooner her father finished with his mysterious business and they could return to Edward, the better.

CHAPTER TWENTY-SIX

The fort of Annapolis Royal had never looked more foreboding.

Andrew stared at the numerous regimental standards flying from the towers and ramparts. The martial air was heightened by the cracking of muskets in target practice and the squadrons dressed for regimental inspection shining and sweating in the afternoon sun. A second line of sentries stationed out beyond the fort's main gates seemed like harbingers of the news he feared to find inside. Andrew found himself tense and worried long before the inner gates were reached.

Trumpets sounded within the fort. Andrew and his men were forced to step aside as a mounted troop galloped past. Andrew recognized the officer in charge, an outpost adjutant as he had once been himself. Andrew called out, "What news?"

The officer turned to him, gave a salute of recognition, and grinned with such fierceness Andrew felt his blood chill. The man shouted back, "War!"

Andrew gathered himself as best he could and signaled his men onward. He turned in his saddle as their horses clip-clopped across the wooden drawbridge. The men who followed were as dusty and weary as he. Still, he felt obliged to order, "Button your tunic, Corporal. You men, dress that line. All right, show some pride, the general's eyes are upon you."

The words were rote, a warning passed

through countless generations of colonial soldiers arriving at the main garrison. Only today it happened to be true. General Whetlock was indeed standing by the parade ground's flagpole, addressing a group of officers.

Andrew slipped from his horse, tossed the reins to the standard-bearer, and hurried across the dusty ground. The general noted his arrival with, "Ah, Harrow. You made it, then. Any trouble along the road?"

He snapped off his best salute. "No, sir. Why? Should there be?"

A murmur ran through the line of officers, not quite a chuckle. Yet Randolf Stevenage was not the only one to sneer in Andrew's direction. Andrew ignored them as best he could. He knew officers here at the main garrison were prone to consider soldiers stationed at outlying forts as scarcely better than colonials.

The general cut into his thoughts with, "You haven't heard the latest, then."

"We've been riding hard for two days, General. We haven't seen a soul on the road." Which in itself was exceptional for that time of year. Not a drover, not a cart, not a French trader, not a single person.

"Join me in my quarters." The general turned back to the gathering and continued,

"You men have your orders. Any questions?"

There was a chorus of "no sirs" in response. The general nodded. "Very well. Carry on."

Andrew went back and directed his men to decamp and see to their mounts. He then turned to follow the general indoors. He was initially glad to see Randolf Stevenage mount up and ride away at the head of another troop. But Stevenage paused by the main gates to shoot Andrew a look of pure triumph, a very disconcerting signal from the man at the best of times. Now, when the fort was full of shouting and trumpets and standards and dust and men, it caused Andrew the greatest of unease.

"Come in, Harrow, come in." From beneath his bushy white eyebrows, the general tossed Andrew a penetrating glance, one which whispered a warning to Andrew's heart. This was as disturbing as the fort's martial air, for the general had long been a friend of the Harrow family.

Andrew maintained a formal stance as the general unbuckled his belt and handed it to his aide. "We are still awaiting the regimental officers from Port St. John, and a few—"

A second aide knocked on the door.

"Begging your pardon, sir. Colonel Lewis and his men just rode in."

"Have them join us immediately." The general unfurled a large map of Acadia upon his desk as he waited. Andrew felt a pang of unspoken danger as he spotted regimental numbers scrawled along both shorelines of his beloved Cobequid Bay. The general studied the map as he asked, "What was the status of your region when you left, Harrow?"

"Peaceful, sir. May I ask—"

"All in due course. How many men did you leave at the fort?"

"Scarcely two dozen, ten of them on the sick list with influenza. But my orders were to report here with the strongest contingent possible. Sir—"

The clump of heavy boots cut him off, and he turned to greet six men in dusty uniforms. The senior officer led them in, saluted the general, and said, "Colonel Thomas Lewis reporting as ordered, sir."

"Excellent. Gentlemen, you know Captain Harrow, I presume." There were nods all around. "Right. I suppose you also have not heard the latest news. No, of course not. Well, not all of it is bad. Let us get the worst out of the way first. Gentlemen, I regret to inform you that General Braddock has been killed in action."

There was a murmur of disbelief about the room. General Braddock, a legend in his own time, was a man of great military bearing with a string of victorious battles to his credit. General Whetlock continued. "Ten days ago there was a battle at Monongahela. The general led an expeditionary force, some of the men seasoned troops from England, the rest colonials from the south, conscripted and rather ill-trained. They were met by eight hundred French regulars, reinforced by an uncounted number of Indians."

The number was staggering. Andrew's fort at full contingency held merely sixty men, and with that he was expected to cover a territory stretching four days' ride in every direction. Eight hundred regular soldiers was half as many as the British army had to control all of Acadia.

"The British goal was Fort Duquesne," the general continued. "I regret to say they never made it. They were forced to withdraw and took heavy losses. General Braddock fell while directing their retreat."

There was a moment's stunned silence before Colonel Lewis said, "Begging your pardon, sir. How heavy?"

"Our losses were—well, quite heavy indeed." The general's cheeks fluttered with his sigh. "We lost upward of five hundred men. The French lost twenty-three."

Surreptitiously, Andrew scanned the other faces in the room, noting a growing and bitter desire for revenge. He shook his head, only a fraction, wishing there were something he could say, something he could do to halt the momentum building toward catastrophe.

"The other news is better." General Whetlock attempted to gather himself and put on a more positive face. "A second force, this one of navy and marines out of Halifax, has attacked and successfully defeated Port Royal. Which means that the French no longer have sea access anywhere along the Bay of Fundy."

But which also meant that the army's defeat only looked worse in these officers' eyes, Andrew realized. Colonel Lewis's tone grated harshly as he said, "Your orders, General?"

"Yes. Quite right. On to the future." General Whetlock took in the map and the entire province of Acadia in one broad sweep of his hand. "Gentlemen, yesterday the senior officials of French Acadia were gathered in Halifax. They will not be allowed to leave."

Andrew gripped the windowsill behind him, forcing himself to remain steady, though he heard the words with mounting panic.

"Governor Lawrence has determined, with the accord of the senior army and navy officials in Acadia, that there is too great a risk of the French settlers using our current losses in the field as an opportunity to revolt."

Andrew cleared his throat. "Sir, excuse me, is there any evidence of this happening?"

"There have been stepped-up attacks on every road in Acadia, except your own." Whetlock's gesture waved the exception aside. "But that is beside the point. What we are dealing with here is the *threat*."

"Quite right," Lewis murmured, shooting Andrew a warning glance.

"The French have refused time and time again to take the oath of allegiance to the British Crown. They have been warned. They have flouted our warnings. They will now pay."

No. The cry of Andrew's heart was so strong he thought it was audible. He felt a sense of cold sickness sweep through his being. *It cannot be. They are not a threat. We live in peace.*

"We could march in and wipe out the enemy, of course," General Whetlock continued, "but Governor Lawrence has decided that since this particular lot has been peaceful in the past, we should follow some moderating course. Grant them a semblance of political freedom. Despite the fact that this direction puts us to a great deal of trouble—and expense." He straightened from his map and commanded, "All the French settlers of Acadia are to be gathered up forthwith and loaded onto His Majesty's vessels. They will be taken to the French provinces further south, or back to France itself."

"About time," muttered Lewis. "Ship them off to where they can do no harm."

Andrew protested, "They are doing no harm here."

"That will do, Harrow!" General Whetlock clearly was ready for such a comment from him. "Colonel Lewis, you and your men are to make a sweep southward, as far as Antoineville—you see it here on the map. Return with every French person of every village along this route. My aide has lists ready. Check them carefully. Ships are scheduled to arrive here the night after tomorrow. Which means you must move swiftly."

"Swift it shall be, sir."

"Men, women, children. Allow no one to escape. You have four villages to cover. Conscript whatever carts and wagons you require. Confiscate anything of value. All that the French leave behind is to become property of the Crown. Any questions?"

"None, sir."

"Very well. Make haste, sir. And be back on time."

Whetlock accepted the salutes and motioned for Andrew to remain where he was. When the room was cleared, he said, "Close the door, Harrow."

"Sir."

When Andrew had returned to stand before the general's desk, Whetlock snapped, "There is only one thing which keeps me from court-martialing you on charges of disobeying direct orders in the face of the enemy." Whetlock's gaze and words lashed with fiery rage. "Which, I remind you, carry a penalty of death by hanging. That one item, Harrow, is the respect I hold for your family. I had heard you were growing too fond of your French neighbors. That is why you were called out and another garrison sent in to take over."

Whetlock shook his head, the muscles in his neck cording like an aging bull. "Captain Stevenage has come upon some most disquieting news. Until now I tended not to believe him. But that comment in the face of Colonel Lewis, with us at war . . ."

"Might I ask what Stevenage has reported?"

"Mrs. Stevenage received word from someone in Edward that your wife has been seen consorting with the enemy."

"Impossible, sir." But Andrew's mind was trapped by the picture of Matty Dwyer, the drover's wife. "My wife has never in her entire life had contact with any enemy of England. I must protest in the strongest—"

Angrily Whetlock waved him to silence. "Harrow, you are hereby ordered to take your men and clear out the two French villages north of here. You will then report back here and surrender to me your resignation from His Majesty's forces."

This time Andrew was unable to mask his horror. "Sir—"

"Your alternative is to be drummed from the corps, your good name scarred with the brand of a dishonorable discharge." General Whetlock leaned across the desk, rage burning in his eyes and his voice. "Disobey me on this and I will see you sent back to England in irons! Is that perfectly clear?"

CHAPTER TWENTY-SEVEN

Louise was uncertain what woke her, the shouts of neighbors or the torchlight dancing upon her bedroom window. The noise seemed to ignite with the light as it pushed her eyelids open, echoing through some gentle dream into a nightmare of awakening.

When she sat up, Henri was already slipping into his trousers. "What is it?"

He turned to her, and there upon his strong features she saw something which left her feeling that he knew. No matter that all outside was confusion and clamor, her husband *knew*.

"Get dressed and prepare whatever it is you need," he said, his voice calm.

"But what—"

"I will go to Papa Jacques. If anyone knows the truth, he will."

But before he reached the front room, their door slammed open. "Henri!"

"Here."

Louise's brother Eli rushed in. "The English! The English are coming!"

"Sit. And calm yourself. We cannot know what to do until we know what is happening." Henri's strong arm forced the younger man into a chair by the table. Louise had never heard her husband speak thusly. In the place of a man who was most comfortable with laughter, a man who preferred to duck from problems and questions that could not be answered, stood a man who *commanded.* "Now tell me."

Eli must have heard the same strength in Henri's order, for he visibly forced himself to take a full breath. "They came to the house last night."

"Who did?"

"English soldiers. They had a roll book. They wanted Papa, but he was not well. You know how he's been slipping—even the soldier could see he should not go. So they took me. I tried to tell him you were the elder, but no one understood—"

"So they took you." Henri spoke more quietly now, pressing the younger man to focus upon what was important. "What then?"

"They took me to the English fort. There were dozens of us in all, five from Minas including the vicar. I recognized clans from villages all along the bay, even the other side."

Louise looked up and saw torches and worried faces crammed into the windows and doorway of her little home. Faces which once had belonged to friends, but now were so full of woe and worry that the flickering shadows turned them into strangers.

"An officer came in, one who spoke French. He read a proclamation. It said . . ." Eli stopped and gulped for more than breath. "The officer said because we had not signed the oath of allegiance, we were all to be deported!"

The shock on the faces crowding their windows and doors turned into cries. One voice shouted, "They can't do that!"

"Quiet!" It was more than Henri's order that silenced them. His voice held a force which demanded obedience. "Go on, Eli."

"We are to be deported," Eli repeated. "Tonight. The soldiers allowed only two of us to return to Minas. They are still holding the vicar! He and the others were kept as hostages. It was the same for all the other villages."

"Silence, I tell you!" Again Henri's order stopped them before the crowd's clamor gathered full force. "When are they coming, Eli?"

"Soon. Hours. Tonight. We will be loaded onboard the boats before dawn. We can take only what we can carry."

Louise could hold back no longer. "But what of Catherine? She could not—"

"I asked for Captain Harrow. I said that right, did I not? Captain Harrow."

"You said it correctly," Henri quietly replied, his expression telling that he already knew what was coming.

"The commandant gave me such a look of scorn, as though he had expected something and I had confirmed it. He spoke a little French. All he said was, 'That hole has been plugged.'"

"Then we know what we must do," Henri said, straightening and turning to the windows. "You have heard the message. Hurry home and prepare."

A man's voice Louise thought she recognized as belonging to Gerard Duprey shouted out, "But what about our animals?"

"Only what you can carry," Henri replied. His face looked so grim it could have belonged to some man other than her husband.

"They are not able to do this to us!"

Another voice shrilled, "This is our homeland! Eight generations we have lived and died here! They can't—"

"No discussion!" Henri barked out the words. "Not tonight. If they are coming we must be prepared, as best we can."

"And if all this is merely another threat?"

Henri shook his head. "They do not hold the vicar and the others hostages merely to make threats. Go and ready yourselves."

Louise felt the shivering of her frame spread until her legs threatened to collapse. "But my *baby*! What about—"

Henri moved with lightning speed across the room, gripped her with his strong hands, and said with a voice that did not require volume to carry its force, "Yes. Go and prepare your baby, Louise."

"But—"

"We must hurry," he said, his eyes shouting all that his voice did not. When she knew he was certain she would not speak again, he turned back without releasing her arms and repeated, "Go and prepare the best you can."

A woman's voice from the back of the throng cried, "Horses! I hear horses!"

"Hurry, all of you," Henri urged.

Swiftly the people scattered, and in the distance drumming hooves were answered by a rising tide of wails and cries.

The horror which gripped Louise turned her voice to a hoarse croak. "This can't be happening." She turned large eyes to her husband. "What will I do with Elspeth?"

"We must take her."

The words were spoken sharply, giving Louise the sense that there was no time or room for argument.

"Take her?" she echoed weakly. "But I

can't—"

"We cannot leave her," responded her husband. "Not alone—can we? They think she is French, remember? She could end up on the point of a bayonet."

"Oh, dear God" was all Louise could manage. No soldier could be that cruel.

"Dress her warmly. The sea air will be frigid." And Henri moved away to whip the blankets off their bed and bundle needed supplies for the unknown journey.

But the dismay would not free her feet to move. "Henri, my baby."

"I know, my love. I know." Still, he was turning away, moving and reaching and cramming things into a hold-all. "Pray as you move, but move you must. And fast."

Tell me, Lord, Andrew prayed as he rode at the head of the force. *Tell me what I am to do. Tell me now.*

The words became a litany whirling within his mind and in time to the pounding of the horses' hooves. His troops had been doubled in number by the addition of a squad from the garrison. Their lieutenant was a sharp-eyed younger man whose gaze remained hard and fast upon Andrew. Clearly he had been warned by a superior, possibly the general himself.

But Andrew was too alarmed and confused to concern himself over the lieutenant. Should he disobey a direct order? It would mean imprisonment in chains and a swift hanging once he was shipped back to England. What would happen to Catherine and the baby? *The baby. The baby.* The storm of emotions tossed the beacon of tragic pain up over and over within his mind. His baby— where was Elspeth now?

He slowed his horse, then stopped. Behind him the troops halted in a furious pelting of dust and loose stones. The lieutenant guided his horse up close, one hand upon his sword and the other tugging savagely upon his horse's reins.

Andrew did not speak. From the pandemonium of conflicting emotions and thoughts, one firm conviction had arisen. He could not pull innocent people from their homes. All the arguments and all the fears and all the conflicting loyalties did not stop this solid knowledge. It was the only clear direction he had received to his prayers. This and a sense of determined strength, an awareness so great that even the keening of his heart could not blind him to this truth.

Yet even as he reached the one decision he could take with any certainty on such a scarred and wounded night, still his heart shrieked with painful panic, *My Catherine. My baby.*

The lieutenant reined in next to his own mount and shouted, "Captain, we were ordered to make all haste!"

"I . . ." Andrew halted before the word was shaped and strained forward. "Quiet in the ranks!"

In the sudden silence he heard it more clearly, the creaking of wheels and the snorting of animals and the cries and moans.

A horseman came sweeping around the bend. "Who goes there?"

"Captain Harrow and troops from the Annapolis Royal garrison."

"Ah. Captain Falton here. Good to see you, Harrow. What word?"

"We were ordered to round up all citizens of the two French villages north of Annapolis Royal."

"You can turn around, then." Falton wheeled about and shouted, "Hurry up, you lot there!"

Andrew was uncertain he had heard correctly. "What?"

"We cleared that area out on our way back. The trail led right by them, and the colonel said we might as well do so if we had time. It's left us mighty strung out along this trail, I don't mind telling you."

Andrew's sudden relief felt ground together in his heart by the cries and calls in a language not his own, painful shouts of words that sounded like names. Captain Falton wiped his brow. "Horrid business, this."

"I suppose you could use more troops, then."

The officer brightened. "I should say so. You can spare some of yours?"

"You can take them all. Our only orders were to clear out villages you've already seen to." Andrew backed his horse away from the tightening throng. "I relinquish command to you, Falton. I must fly."

The lieutenant raised one gloved hand in protest. "But, Captain, the general—"

"Our orders are carried out!" Andrew wheeled his mount around and dug his spurs into the horse's sides. "There is a crisis with my child! I must fly!"

CHAPTER TWENTY-EIGHT

Henri appeared beside Louise as she packed, and struggled against a rising chaos of woe and panic. "You are ready?"

"I think . . . Y-yes, I have—"

"All right. Hurry now, take the baby, we must go and see to Jacques and Marie."

"But my home!" Louise wailed. "Henri, our baby, we can't leave until Catherine returns!"

Henri's grip upon her arm tightened. "Hush, you can hear the horses and the soldiers. The British are here, Louise. *They are here.*"

She saw the sorrow, the tense helplessness in his eyes. Beyond their window came the resonant sound of a trumpet, a signal both to the soldiers and to herself. "Yes." It was all the speech she was capable of. "Yes."

"All right." He shouldered the massive pack. "Give me the baby. Take the food. Good. We are off."

As they scurried up the lane toward her parents' home, there was time for one backward glance. Just one. A fleeting glimpse of all that was being torn from her life and her heart and her arms. Then a squad of five horsemen swept around the corner, the great beasts snorting and blowing and their sweat-streaked bodies cutting off her vision. She cried aloud, reaching back to what was there no longer.

Henri had no free hand. Instead he maneuvered behind her and shepherded her forward, saying simply, "We must help Papa

Jacques."

The horsemen shouted words she did not understand, but their meaning was clear enough. Torches and swords waved in the night, urging them to greater speed. The baby awoke with a start at the thundering hooves and shouting men, and added her frightened cry to the tumult.

"Jacques! Jacques! My home, my things, my life!" Her mother's voice cut through the hue and cry, the angry flow of harsh English commands, the tramping of frenzied horses. Marie's calm was gone, vanished like smoke in the rising night wind. She appeared on the porch, disheveled and screaming and waving her arms, "Henri! Henri! What am I to do? The soldiers, they are—"

Marie was silenced as Henri deposited the crying baby into her arms and rushed into the house. Marie turned a panicked, tear-streaked face toward her daughter. Her eyes were caught in the torchlight, two blazing orbs of alarm and dread. "Louise, what are we to do, the soldiers!"

"Calm yourself!" Louise's tone was sharp as her voice rose to be heard above the squalls of the terrified baby. "Don't frighten the child!"

Marie looked at her daughter with eyes that saw nothing but the soldiers and the night. Louise did as Henri had done, coming in close, looming over the shrieking baby, drawing in so tightly she could say in a hoarse whisper, "Be calm and see to the baby."

"Yes. The child . . . of course." Marie looked down at the bundle in her arms, and the action of rocking the baby calmed her before yet another thought of alarm. "But, Louise, the child . . . your Antoinette—"

Soldiers on horseback raced up, shouting down at them, then turning to call at troops marching up on foot, using pikes and muskets to spur the wailing crowd to greater speed. Louise shouted through the open door, "Henri!"

"All right, we must go." Henri appeared in the doorway with yet another bundle. Louise's brother Philippe appeared after him, Jacques leaning heavily on his arm.

Then another realization caused Marie to scream, "Eli! He's not back from warning the distant farms! How—"

"Let us hope he does not come back at all," Henri replied grimly, urging them forward and into the wailing throng. "Let us hope at least one of us has slipped through the English net and escaped into the forest."

"But my son," Marie wailed. "What—"

"Marie, enough." Jacques seemed to

straighten at the thought of what Henri had suggested, at least enough to give authority to these few words. "We need strength. We need calm."

There was little of either as they were herded from the village and across the Minas River ford. All around them rose the wails and cries of a great funeral march, but the soldiers paid them no heed. Louise's frantic glances were enough to show how all her world was being torn asunder, all her friends transformed into strangers by the night and the tempest.

She asked her husband, "Do you see Catherine's husband?"

"Nowhere." Henri shouted up at the nearest soldier, "Captain Harrow!"

He was answered with a harsh laugh. The horseman, an officer by the looks of glittering gold upon his shoulders, turned and called to a man at the fore. The other officer turned to glare at Henri and said in heavily accented French, "You are friend of Harrow?"

"Friend! Yes, friend!" Louise's heart felt squeezed to painful tightness by the look they gave her husband. But still Henri shouted, "Where is he?"

The two officers called back and forth over the tumult but only in their language.

Harrow's name came up, amidst looks of disdain and headshakes. But to Louise and Henri they offered nothing more.

More troops were gathered by the long pier. As they approached, Jacques groaned, "Why must they rush us so?"

"To keep us from fighting back," Henri said. Even he was puffing from the load and the haste. "And to catch the tide. Look there."

At the end of the long pier, lit by torches, waited more boats than Louise had ever seen. Narrow coastal barques awaited the people of Minas, they and all the others she could now see streaming down from adjoining trails. A long line of torchlit misery, pushed and prodded and herded toward the pier.

At the entrance to the pier Louise's panic surged like a great incoming wave. She turned and struggled against the flow, even as it tightened about her to begin the long march seaward.

"Louise!"

She flung herself against the people who had once been friends, screaming with an energy that seemed to tear her throat, "My baby!"

"Louise, no!"

A pike was shoved into her face, the

spear's point over a foot long and glinting angry yellow in the torchlight. She felt a sudden urge to fling herself upon the point, to halt the tide of sorrow.

"Louise, come, you must come with me. Please." Henri's voice shook with tremors of one who understood what was passing through her mind. "Please, my love, please, you are my life, come with me now."

She turned and sagged against him, suddenly so weak she could scarcely place one foot in front of the other. "Oh, Henri, they have my baby."

Together they joined the long line snaking toward the boats. At the pier's end Henri dropped his heavy burdens into the bottom of the next vessel, groaning as the weight dropped from his shoulders. Through the hollow ache of her sorrow, Louise realized it was the only protest her husband had made that entire night. But the thought was soon swallowed by the silent awareness that filled her being and left her shaking with dread. The boat filled and then pushed off, its place at the pier taken by yet another. There were cries and calls from up and down the pier, and over the water from all the boats. People shouted for loved ones and children and parents, the wails so mixed it was as though one great voice spoke for them all, calling and weeping for what was theirs no longer.

Shadowy skeletons took shape in the first dim light of dawn, and Louise realized they were being taken toward larger seagoing vessels. Their masts cut like giant spears up into the departing night. The oarsmen guided their vessel up close to the side, and those who could were pushed and prodded up the netting. Others were lifted in rope-slings. Louise took the baby from Marie. The baby was wailing still, a fact that had escaped her until that very moment. But as she heard the little one's strident cries, she knew that here was one who needed her desperately.

She found the strength to rock and calm the little one as she was slung into the bosun's chair. She held the rope with one hand and the baby with the other as she was raised to the ship's deck. Once there she allowed Henri to wrap his great strong arms around her and felt his head drop to her shoulder. She heard him murmur, the words swept away in the tumult surrounding them. Yet she knew he was praying. And though the words themselves were lost and gone, the message remained, that and the first fragile flickering of calm.

She looked shoreward and felt her heart rise up in a tide of woe and fear. *Her baby— her frail little Antoinette was still there. Left be-*

hind. Abandoned.

Gradually the deck went silent. In the first light of dawn there rose a faint tendril of smoke. Then another. And another still. Tiny lights in the distance fueled the gray spirals that steadily rose higher and thicker until all the sky seemed supported by great rising pillars pushing upward.

The smoke of their burning dwellings shouted a silent message to all the gathering. There would be no going back.

CHAPTER TWENTY-NINE

Andrew raced against the night and the wind. He rode as he had never ridden before, pursuing all the unseen forces that were tearing apart his world. The distance which had taken two days to cover at the head of his troops, Andrew now did in the space of one night. One long, dark, harrowing night.

He saw little more of the trail than a long silver streak of reflected moonlight. After an hour and more of spurring his horse and shouting encouragement into the steed's ear, the ribbon stretched out like an endless nightmare, taunting him with the threat that it would never end, that he would never reach his goal. And every thundering hoofbeat pounded in time to the name shouted over and over in his head. *Elspeth.*

Twice he passed French villages, or what remained of them. There was movement at neither, which only spurred him on to greater speed, as though the silence which met him as he looked down upon the dark landscape and shadow-houses only warned him of what he was yet to find at his journey's end. *Elspeth.*

Three times he stopped at waystations for new steeds, twice moving so fast that he had stripped off the blanket and gear from his lathered horse and saddled his new mount before the bleary-eyed keeper had roused himself. The third time, in the gray hour before the dawn, he moved more slowly, his arms and his legs so weary that the saddle threatened to bring him down. The keeper came, took one look at his state, and wordlessly pulled the saddle from his lifeless fingers. Andrew watched and drank pitcher after pitcher of cold rainwater drawn from the corner keg, feeling strength fill him with each draught. *Elspeth.*

He knew he had arrived long before he was able to see the village. The smell of charred cinders drifted in the chill morning mist, stronger and stronger until the stench tore a cry of dismay from his throat. The noise gripped the steed's heart, for the gallant animal thundered down the final slope, took the turning to Minas, and burst from the forest and into the first field—past the first blackened, smoldering house.

Andrew reined his horse, looking frantically about at the desolation and the ruin. It felt as though his own heart were being branded by the sight. He wheeled his horse around and dug his spurs into the animal's ribs. "Hyah!"

There was no sun that day. It dared not show its face upon the sight which greeted Andrew as he raced down the trail and came to the exodus gathered by the mouth of the pier. He felt as though his own worst nightmares, the ones so awful they could not be recalled in the morning's light, all had come to life in the tableau before him. The long pier of Fort Edward was lost beneath a wailing, shouting mass of humanity. At the end of the pier floated a longboat, with another waiting to take its place. A third was rowing out to a lone ship floating in Cobequid Bay. The mist drifted in and out, painting the scene a bleak gray, as though the day itself was shamed by what it saw and wished only to hide it from view. To wash it of substance, to cleanse it from memory.

"Get a move on there!" A lone officer stood waving his sword at the meager throng still standing at the pier's entrance. Andrew turned, and only with effort did he recognize Randolf Stevenage. The captain's voice was as hoarse as the call of morning crows from his long night of deplorable duty. "Sergeant, get those people moving! Use your pikes if you must, man! The ship must make the tide!"

"Aye, aye, sir! You lot, pick up your goods and move off, or you can swim to France!"

Andrew slid from his horse and sprawled in the well-churned mud. His legs simply gave way beneath him. He picked himself up without noticing that he had fallen. Then he spotted a familiar face amidst the final throng. "Vicar!"

"You, there! Harrow! Hold off, man, these Frenchies—"

"Vicar!" Andrew searched his exhausted brain and finally came up with the man's name. "Jean Ricard!"

Up ahead, a skeletal face redrawn by grief and terror turned toward him. With recognition came a shout torn from the pastor's throat. "They have taken all my people!"

"My baby!" Andrew gripped the man's cassock as much to keep from falling as to halt the man's progress. "Where is Elspeth?"

"My flock," the priest choked. "My children."

"My *child*," Andrew said the word a sob. "Where is Elspeth?"

Jean Ricard's eyes were unfocused, staring in terror. "They held some of us as hostages at the fort. Only when the last ship started boarding did they let us come forward."

"But my baby, Vicar, my child, where is she?"

Jean Ricard lifted a heavy, black-robed arm and pointed out toward the empty waters. "There. With all my flock, all my children. Gone."

Andrew's hands went so numb he could no longer hold the vicar's cassock. He staggered back in horror, slamming into a soldier, and would have gone down had the man not caught him. It took Andrew a long moment to turn and recognize the insignia upon the man's uniform. "Sergeant, where has the other ship gone?" he gasped out.

"Which one, sir? There's twelve out there gone upon the tide, and this lot here's soon to join 'em."

"But where, man? Tell me where!"

The sergeant stared at him with consternation. "Sir, my orders—"

"Sergeant! Get that last lot down the pier

or you'll be sailing with them." Stevenage's officer chopped at his horse's reins, making the weary animal snort and dance in Andrew's face, pushing him back. "Stand easy there, you!"

Andrew drew himself up. "Sergeant—"

Stevenage's voice came out a hoarse snarl. "My wife knows all about you and your precious Catherine and your consorting with the enemy!"

"I command—"

"Soon enough you'll be commanding nothing at all! *My* orders come from General Whetlock, and his from Governor Lawrence himself. I told them all along you weren't to be trusted!" But the night had taken a savage toll upon Stevenage. There was no satisfaction in his features, nothing save the scarring remnants of a living nightmare. Another savage chop to the reins. "Move that lot out, Sergeant!"

Andrew stepped around the horse and grabbed the sergeant's stirrup. "Where have the other ships gone?"

"Have you missed the entire night, sir? Each ship is dispatched to a different location. Boston, Washington, Louisiana, all the places along the eastern seaboard where the Acadians will be allowed to join a French community. A third and more back to

France itself, and each of those to a different port. Of a truth, nobody's falling over themselves to take them in."

Andrew released the stirrup. "What?"

"Not even the other ships know where each is assigned to go. It was intentional." The man's voice roughened. "It's the only way we can ever be sure they'll not gather and attack."

Andrew's knees gave way then, his strength gone. "No, no, it can't be."

The sergeant shouted over Andrew, "You there! Halt, or I'll shoot!"

The vicar ignored the warning and dropped into the mud beside Andrew. "You must be our conduit!" he whispered urgently.

The sergeant slipped from his exhausted steed and struggled through the churned muck. "Get down the pier, you!"

Jean Ricard shook Andrew as hard as his own waning strength allowed. "There is no other way for us to know where we've been sent or how we can regather!"

The sergeant hauled the vicar roughly to his feet. "Enough of that! Get along down the pier or I'll show you the business end of my pike!"

Andrew rose because he had to and stepped to the vicar's other side. "A conduit?" he managed under his breath.

"Let us write to you, please, I beg you. I will pass the word to any I find, all who can be found, all who will pass on the word as well. It will risk your career, but I beg you—"

"I have no career. As of this morning I am no longer a part of the British army."

The vicar accepted this news with only a nod. There was nothing to be said. Nothing at all. "Will you help?"

"I will." They reached the end of the pier. Andrew offered a hand, then as the vicar stood in the boat, Andrew found himself unable to release his grip. "Elspeth is with Louise and Henri. If you—"

"Enough of this, sir!" The sergeant shoved him roughly back. "All right, that's the lot!"

"I will tell them. Of course I will tell them." The priest's voice drifted across the water. "I think I overheard that my ship is going to Charleston. It is a port south of here. Do you know it?"

"The name only." Andrew kept his hand outstretched, as though to lower it would cut off his last remaining thread of contact to his child. "Charleston!"

"Tell any who contact you . . ." The priest stopped then, as though he too was crushed by the weight of loss. "Tell them to pray! To remember to pray for us all!"

Andrew stood long after the soldiers had left the pier. He watched the longboats deposit their final charges. Then the smaller boats were drawn around to the stern and lashed in tandem behind the larger vessel's rudder. He watched the sails unfurl and the anchor be hauled in and the ship begin to make its way toward the bay's mouth, toward the broader reaches of the Bay of Fundy and points south.

And then it began to rain.

CHAPTER THIRTY

Catherine lifted a weary hand and shaded her eyes from the blaze of the afternoon sun. The late summer day was very hot and dreadfully muggy. The rains that had passed through the day before had saturated the countryside, turning the red clay to a deep boggy mire. Shivers of steam drifted heavenward and slowed the wagon's already laboring team. Catherine felt dizzy from the heat, the long jarring ride, and the effort of cradling the baby from the worst of the jolts. The wagon bumped and jostled as the slowly plodding mules and big mud-covered wheels churned the clay trail into gumbo with their passing.

With the rise to the top of each new hill, Catherine strained forward, hoping to catch the first glimpse of something familiar. Some indicator that would confirm they were finally back in their own territory. The homeward journey had seemed to take even longer than the trip out. She pined for home. Back in her own cool cabin. Out of the boiling sun that made her heavy clothes stick to her sides.

Her eyes lifted to the straining team. Sweat rolled from the mules' heaving sides. Foam flecked every spot where the harness rubbed. She was sorry for their discomfort along with her own.

And then she saw the large hemlock that was a familiar landmark. She sat up as high as she could manage, eyes searching the descending hillside. There came a sudden opening in the trees, and down below she spotted the gateway to one French farm. Louise had spoken of the family. The mother had died during the birth of a child. She had been sick with fever, and when the time had come for delivery she did not have the strength to bring another baby into the world. It had happened the previous summer, and Louise's mother had kept the infant for a few weeks until the father was able to make arrangements with relatives.

Catherine settled back with a contented sigh. They would soon be home. Just a few more miles. Surely she could bear that much.

She shifted in her seat, trying again to find a more restful position. At least the baby seemed to be sleeping comfortably. Catherine bent her head and lifted back the blanket for a peak. The baby was flushed and moist but sleeping well, her breathing much more even and strong. It seemed that the doctor's medicine was working. Catherine smiled to herself, thinking of Louise. She would be so pleased. Their prayers had indeed been answered.

It had been a difficult trip—but well worth it. And there had been no questions. For that Catherine was thankful. It was such a shame that the infant might never fully recover, that lovely little Antoinette might remain frail her life long. But at least the child should survive. So long as Louise was careful to give her a good, calm upbringing. Which she surely would. Louise would do her best for this child—of that Catherine was certain.

She shot a glance at her father alongside her. John Price had remained utterly preoccupied with his work that entire journey. Even now he scarcely seemed aware that she was seated beside him.

Thoughts of her own healthy baby brought another smile to her lips. Her little Elspeth. How she longed for her. And Andrew. Soon, very soon now she would be home with them once again.

Catherine replaced the blankets, hoping that the wool's insulation would keep the worst of the heat off the baby. She shifted her position so that her body made a shadow from the merciless sun.

The trees dropped away, and again her eyes turned toward the farmstead's gatepost. She thought of the motherless children. She hoped that by now the man had found another wife, a mother for all the young ones who had seemed to spill out from the door and hang out the windows to check on anyone passing. But she was unable to make out any sign of movement in the fields. She knew the house itself stood beyond a copse of elms, planted as protection against the bitter winter winds and grown tall and hardy over the past four generations. But there was no sign of life there either.

The wagon rumbled over a protruding tree root with a jolt that shook her already stiff and tired body. Automatically she shielded Antoinette, but in spite of her effort the baby stirred and Catherine feared she might begin to cry. At once she began to rock the child back and forth.

When she lifted her head again, they had cleared the edge of the planted windbreak. To Catherine's horror, none of the buildings remained standing. There was only a heap of darkened ashes where the house and barns should have been. Charred bits of log that had not totally burned jutted upward like blackened teeth.

Catherine's face paled. *All those children.* "Oh, God," she breathed. "Please may no one have been in the house."

Everything was burned to the ground. Catherine turned stricken eyes to her father. She saw that he too was carefully studying the devastation.

"A terrible fire," she managed, her tongue suddenly dry. "Everything's gone. It's . . . it's awful."

John Price merely nodded.

"Lightning, do you suppose? In the storm we had yesterday?" It happened, but not often. Usually a large tree was the first to catch the strike. But these trees had been planted well clear of the house, and though there was some smoke damage, none of them looked split or scarred.

"I think not," her father replied slowly.

"Carelessness? But surely—" Was it perhaps one of the Acadian children? But little ones, from the time they could toddle, were taught the serious consequence of uncontrolled fire.

"I would say it was intended." Her father's voice was very matter-of-fact.

His words shook Catherine to the core. "Intended? But the Indians have not been here in years."

Her father was shaking his head.

And then it hit her. She could not have said how she knew, but suddenly she realized what had happened. A coldness washed over her entire body, making her shiver in spite of the scorching day. The army. The *British* army. They had done this. But why?

Her eyes swung back to her father. What would he think when the full truth struck him as well?

But he was standing now, legs far apart to brace himself upright. His eyes coolly observed the scene before him. There was no horror in his gaze. No puzzled expression. Even as she watched she saw him give just the hint of a nod, as though granting approval to the entire scene.

It took her a moment before the truth dawned, before she could allow herself to admit it. She whispered in horror, "You knew?"

Inwardly she prayed that he might deny it. She longed with all of her being to separate him from this terrible event.

But he did not dispute it. She thought she even detected an odd gleam in his eye, much like when he returned to the house with a good-sized salmon to be roasted slowly over the fireplace spit, or a fresh buck that meant meat for their cooking pot.

When he did answer, it was with an acknowledging nod of his head. "I knew it was coming."

Catherine felt the fear wash over her body. She tightened her arms around the blankets bundling Antoinette. "Is this . . . is it to continue?"

John Price turned from the charred remains to look down at her. "Continue? No, I suspect it is all over."

"All over?" What did he mean? What could he possibly mean? All over, like a deed entirely done. "You mean, this one French farmer . . . but why him? Was he some kind of threat?"

"No more than any of the others." His eyes drifted back to where the barn had stood. Little whiffs of smoke still curled upward. Catherine could smell it now. The acrid, sickening smell that all settlers feared as much as the plague. Her father was shaking his head, and his expression told her what he thought of women and their questions. He spoke down to her, "I knew you would be concerned. That was why I agreed to have you accompany me to Halifax."

"You mean . . . might others be affected?" She could scarcely shape the words.

"Really, Catherine, you women simply do not understand the workings of conflict. Of military acuteness. Of what is required to insure that the Crown retains what is rightfully ours."

Elspeth. She had to get to her baby. And Louise. Had anyone been there to warn her? Catherine would have jumped from the lumbering wagon and plunged headlong through the heavy mud had not reason told her that it would be more than foolhardy. Antoinette stirred in her arms, reminding her that she had a responsibility to this little one as well. Her arms tightened until the baby squirmed with the restriction.

"Why?" Catherine flung at her father, her voice wild with demand. "What conflict was there?"

John Price gave her a solid impatient look, but his face now showed weariness. His usually straight shoulders sagged slightly as he lowered himself back onto the seat. When he spoke, even his voice sounded tired.

"Need you ask? The whole situation was precarious. No way to know who were one's allies, and who the enemy. Unwilling to submit, they were. Oh, not openly rebellious. No, too clever for that. The French wanted to pretend neutrality."

"But—"

"Yes. But if push had come to shove, it soon would have been evident whose side they were really on. Upon meeting an Unreliable on the road, one never knew whether to expect a surly nod or a knife at the throat."

"I never heard of knives, or any other such nonsense, except from British soldiers." Her voice was sharpened by her anxiety. She had never spoken to her father in such a tone before.

"Nonsense, is it? Perhaps they were simply not brave enough." There was a spark to his eyes again. "Leave it to the Indians and the troops to wear us down, then swoop in for the final slaughter."

"The French villagers have lived here in peace for years and years," Catherine hurled back, her spine stiffening with the unfair accusation. "And no one has ever proven that the French have attacked us alongside the Indians."

Another wave of fear swept through her, causing her fingers to bury themselves within Antoinette's wool shawl. She had to get to Louise. "What have they done?"

"Look, my dear." Her father noticed her clenched fists and softened his tone. "I know your tender heart makes it difficult for you to understand the deeds of men at war."

"There is no war, not here! Andrew has always said the war—"

"Ah, yes. Andrew. Methinks you have not realized the difficult situation you have placed your husband in. His whole military career has been placed in jeopardy by this absurdly soft side he has been showing toward Minas."

Catherine's fears turned in another direction. "Whatever are you talking about?"

"You shouldn't be running around making friends with the enemy, Catherine. It just isn't done at such a time."

"Making friends . . ."

"Captain Stevenage has had reason to plant some doubts among General Whetlock's staff. His wife has also informed them that you have been seen in the company of some Acadian woman. She even claimed you were over visiting the Frenchy village."

Catherine felt her face grow hot, but this time it was not the work of the scorching sun. Anger burned through her. "And what has that to do with Andrew?"

"Stevenage has hinted—more than hinted, actually—there might be some reason to suspect Andrew would fail to perform his duties as an English officer. The plans were kept from him. Even I was not informed of the details of the maneuver until we arrived in Halifax. Andrew would probably have suspected as much had he not been so determined to ignore what was plain to everyone else."

"That is absurd! Andrew has never given reason for anyone to think he would commit treason! That is the most . . . most offensive charge I have ever heard. Not perform his duties as an officer? I have never heard such an outrage."

"It has gone far beyond protests, I fear. Again, I am not privy to everything, as the boy is my son-in-law. And I must admit, at such a time, I do feel a certain—"

"Stop it! Stop it right now! I will not hear another word!"

"Calm yourself, no need to get yourself further heated. You'll have yourself in a swoon if you're not careful."

Catherine squirmed back onto the wooden seat, but her thoughts still swirled in fear and anger. Priscilla Stevenage, would she never cease to make trouble? Catherine struggled to gather her thoughts. She had to concentrate on the calamity at hand.

"These raids." She fought to control her voice. "You say—they are not to continue?"

"They are not raids," her father responded brusquely. "It was a carefully planned military maneuver to expel the Acadians. Not to harm them. I suspect the burning became a necessity for some reason. It was not a part of the plan as I originally—"

"Expel them?" New horror clutched at Catherine. "Expel them where?"

"Here and there," he answered impatiently. "To several other settlements. Not en masse. That would be too dangerous. A few here, a few there."

"But that is preposterous! How could they even consider such a thing? This is their *home*."

"Not anymore." His eyes were suddenly cold. "Would you have us put them to the sword?"

"Of course not!"

"That is likely what would have happened," he snapped, "had this course not been taken. A number of our senior officers were arguing for it. But no, we are not so brutal as all that."

"But what have they done to deserve—"

"What have they done? Don't talk foolish, child. They are French! They are our natural enemy! Do you think I have ever for an instant forgotten it was a French cannonade that cost me the use of my leg, stripped me of my rank and my career, and relegated me to a pen-pot instead of a sword? Do you think I don't have reason, day and night, with the pain throbbing through my muscles, to remember who my enemies are? I know the French. I have known them longer than you have been alive. They have not changed with the passage of time, and they will never change."

But Catherine remained trapped by his earlier words. The French were to be expelled. All of them. Catherine searched frantically about her. Should she be put down from the wagon? Could she make better time on foot than the tired team? She sank back. No woman could walk through such a mire of red clay. It would suck at her boots and weigh down her woolen skirts until she sank. Especially a woman bearing the burden of a sleeping child.

"This expulsion," she began, her voice not more than a whisper. "When is it to be?"

He swung toward her. "Haven't you heard a single thing I have said? It is accomplished. The maneuvers are over. The British are now in full command of Acadia. We have secured the land for the Crown."

She stared at him, no longer able to comprehend his words. "Over?"

"Over." He seemed enormously pleased. "That is why I so readily agreed to your accompanying me to Halifax. Such a treacherous, miserable journey, but so timely. Under usual circumstances I would have discouraged it. But I wanted you and my grandchild away—just in case things got testy. This request of yours could not have come at a better time. I—"

But Catherine was no longer listening. "Oh, dear God."

Her frantic thoughts tumbled and twisted, coming always back to Andrew. Even if he had not known, at least at first, surely by now he would have been able to do something. Andrew. Her source of strength through so many past troubles. He was there. He would have done something—anything to save Elspeth, protect Louise. Something. Andrew was an officer. Even if the carnage had reached out, had included others, Andrew would have done something.

It was a small hope, but she clutched to it tightly. Surely, surely things were not as black as they seemed. Surely Andrew... surely her precious baby Elspeth . . .

Catherine enfolded herself over the sleeping infant, clutching it and her tiny flame of hope deep to her breast. "Oh, God . . . my baby."

She buried her face into Antoinette's heavy blanket and let the hot tears wash down her cheeks.

CHAPTER THIRTY-ONE

The storm passed after two hard days of wind and rain and buffeting waves. Henri was the only one of those onboard who did not suffer, trapped as they were upon the ship's open deck. He had fished through worse conditions, he assured Louise when she asked him if they were to die. She was so ill and so heartsick, she felt faintly sorry at his assurance.

Louise awoke on the third day to a gentle rocking motion, one which allowed her to rise unsteadily to her feet and walk to the railing. The sea stretched blue and white-flecked in every direction as far as she could see, joining finally with an equally blue horizon. She felt tears drawn from her eyes. Wherever they were, she knew they were far from home, and growing steadily farther still.

By the fifth day they had fallen into an accustomed routine. All around her people were either finding inner strength and surviving, or slowly wasting away. To her great surprise, the sea air seemed to be helping her father grow steadily stronger. It was her mother who suffered, like a plant torn from its roots and unable to settle anywhere again. Whenever Louise looked into her mother's eyes, she saw a shattered soul.

It was her mother's anguish and the baby's needs that kept her from the brink of darkness. She could not afford to succumb to the overwhelming sorrow and loss, much as she wanted to. Much as her own wounds felt as though they would never heal.

Baby Elspeth knew nothing and loved everything about the sea. The ship's gentle rocking sent her cooing to sleep, a blanket upon the deck as comfortable a bed as the baby could ever wish. Every sea gull who came flying in searching for tidbits, every sunbeam that flickered down from between the mighty sails, every flap of canvas overhead, every rattle of rope or hardy seaman's footsteps, all were cause for delight. Elspeth showered Louise with her happiness and her need for attention. Louise nursed and bedded and changed and loved the infant, and in this loving she came to know the first fleeting touches of healing.

And from Henri. The man was a rock, steady and gentle and firm when necessary.

Through the first two endless days he had been everywhere, moving amidst the worst afflicted, carting them up from the holds on his back so they could benefit from the strong sea air, holding them as they were sick over the sides, rigging canvas strips to keep off the wind and rain from those on deck.

When the weather improved he took charge of rations, doling them out, helping the weakest old men to clean themselves after the meals. Through the worst of it he was there for everyone, giving and helping and offering his strength to one and all. When the sun shone bright and the sea sparkled great and blue, he even offered a few smiles and words of comfort to those suffering the greatest sorrow, though Louise could see how much it cost him.

Onward they sailed, steadily south. On the sixth night the wind tasted of a different land, one unseen beyond the horizon yet leaving its distinctive stamp upon the atmosphere. Louise drifted in and out of sleep as always, one ear constantly tuned to the baby lying alongside her, when another sound drew her to the surface. One she had never heard before. Silently she rolled over and raised herself to a seated position to look upon her man. Henri's massive shoulders shook so hard she could see the movement in the starlight. Sobs wrenched his entire body, for he cried as a man cried, one who had never known the luxury of easy tears. He wept with his entire being, a wrenching, gasping groan of unendurable agony.

Louise was weeping herself within an instant of hearing her husband, sharing not only his pain but hers as well. She flung herself upon him and allowed the wounded heart within to melt and flow together with his.

Henri turned over and took her in his arms, for once not offering strength but rather seeking consolation. Yet she had nothing to give. Nothing but her own deep pain, her own empty soul.

They cried themselves to sleep, locked within each other's arms, never shifting the entire night.

Louise woke first, her eyelids tickled by the first glint of sun. She did not move, did not want to waken her husband. She lay in his arms, surrounded by the strength, the scent of her man. And she saw in the deep new lines creasing his face a wearing down, a giving up. She had to do something. She could not help but see his need there in the remnants of the night's sorrow. She had to help him, or risk losing this strength and this goodness along with everything else.

A part of her wanted to give up herself, to give in to the silent cry of agony and bitter anger. Let it all sweep away. Take us all, she wanted to shout at the God who had let this happen to her. Take it all. I don't care.

The two sides of her mind fought against each other through the morning routine. It was only when she moved over with the baby to greet her parents, and she looked into her mother's empty gaze, that she saw and understood. There were others who needed what she could give, and only if she did not herself give into the temptation of hatred. If she could not do it for herself, perhaps she could do it for them.

She sighed, and in a voice still raw from the previous night's weeping, she said to her mother, "Would you like to come and sit with me for a while? We could read the Bible together."

She could see her mother struggling to make sense of the words. The front of her gown was littered with the remnants of what little breakfast she had eaten. "What?"

"We need to find strength for whatever is to come ahead."

She made an effort to focus upon her daughter. "The Bible? You brought the Book with you?"

"God can be our strength now," Louise

said, nodding. "We need Him now more than ever."

Henri chose that moment to join them. "I have just spoken with the ship's second-in-command. He tells me we are destined for the French colony of Louisiana."

Jacques Belleveau brushed the crumbs from his front, took a deep draught of water, and said, "There are Belleveaux in Louisiana. My father's brother and his children. Their children as well by now, I warrant."

"I have heard of this also," Henri said. His dark eyes remained ravaged by the night's struggle, but there was something else to his voice. A first faint hint of something new. "When I was young, my father used to speak of that colony. He said it was a place without winter. My mother never liked winter."

"You never told me that," Louise said.

"I haven't thought of it in years. Not until I heard the lieutenant speak the name. Louisiana. There is a great French city there. Orleans, I think it is called."

Her mother stirred and waved an impatient hand, as though brushing aside all the talk but the one point. "The *Bible*," she said again to her daughter, her voice sharp. "How can you come to me, you of all people, and speak to me about God?"

"Do you know," Henri said quietly, "I woke up this very morning wishing we could pray together."

"*Pray?*" Marie's eyes flashed as she turned to her son-in-law. "How can you even speak the word now, after all that God has done to us?"

"God did not do this to us at all," Henri replied, settling down beside his wife. "It was man's actions, and man will be called to account. I have read the pages, seated there alongside my wife. This I know in my heart, Mama Marie. God did not do this to us."

"We need His strength," Louise murmured, cradling the baby in one arm, freeing her other so that she could reach over and take her husband's hand. "Now more than ever."

"And your child?" But Marie's question lacked fire. "What of little Antoinette?"

Louise felt her heart's wound reopen and threaten to engulf her. But as the shadows loomed, it was Henri who gripped her hand and said in a voice cracked by the same pain she felt, yet a voice that held to a firm calm, "Perhaps it is God's hand here after all. Perhaps God knew our little one would not survive this voyage."

Louise turned to him, amazed by this. It seemed as though Henri had given voice to the gentle whispers of her own heart, voices she had not wanted to acknowledge through these tragic days and nights.

"I think," Henri said, and stopped to take a shaky breath, "I think God is waiting to strengthen and nourish us. Even here, surrounded by strangeness and loss."

"If it is God's will," Louise said, the words for her mother, but the look for her husband alone, "we have a responsibility to this little one."

Henri turned fully to her. Her strong and jesting husband, who always before preferred to meet everything with a smile and a warmhearted turn, now looked at her with such gentle wisdom she felt as though she was seeing him anew. He said, "And a responsibility to each other."

As soon as Louise awoke the next morning, she knew what she was to do. Even before she opened her eyes to the sun and the clouds and the sea and the day, she knew.

She cleaned and nursed the baby, performing exactly the same activities as she had every morning since the tragic voyage began. Only today, everything was different. She could scarcely explain it to herself, how important this difference was. But the mystery mattered little. That the difference, this divine gift, had come was enough.

With a certainty that was not her own, she knew it was divine. Louise had received this gift in the night because of her willingness to open her heart to God and to her family the day before. In turning *away* from bitterness and hatred and despair, she had turned *toward* God's outstretched arms.

There was no great change in her surroundings, in the faces that stared back at her from blank eyes. And yet this gift proved so great that the entire day seemed new. Though her aching, yearning heart remained torn with each mile farther away from her beloved Antoinette, yet there was a message within this tiny gift. A promise of hope. And it was this as much as the gift itself that left her knowing that God was with her. Even here. Even now.

So it was that when Henri came upon her, seated as she was in the forecastle nursing the baby, she was humming a little tune. Quietly, so softly that the wind lifted the notes and tossed them up with the spray and the cawing gulls. But Henri must have heard them, because when he sank down beside her, the look he gave her was filled with wonder.

He asked softly, "What is this?"

"Good morning, my love." She looked down at the infant. "The baby seems fine this morning. But already the heat is so oppressive."

"You were singing. I heard it myself." He reached out one work-hardened finger and touched the side of her face. "And you are smiling."

"Yes."

He seemed at a loss for words. He stared at her, at the baby, and his eyes followed the little hand curling around one of her own fingers. He directed his words and his sorrow at the tiny face. "Do you think you can teach me how to sing—to smile again?"

She shook her head, slowly, loving him so fully it felt that her heart might burst. No sorrow could erase this, not so long as she held fast to God. "No. I can't," she whispered.

He nodded, his face looking hollowed by the asking and by her reply. "I have felt as though I left my laughter there on the side of Cobequid Bay."

"I cannot give it back to you, my husband." She waited until he lifted his dark gaze, then continued, "But God can."

"God," he murmured.

"Yes."

"He spoke to you in the night." It was not a question.

She gave the tiniest hint of a nod, then

asked, "You will meet with the lieutenant later about supplies?"

"As I do every day." There was a young English officer onboard who spoke French and who had confided to Henri that he had studied in Paris. He was the most sympathetic of all the English and had volunteered to act as liaison between captor and captive.

"Ask him for a pen and paper, please."

Henri's eyes widened. "You are going to write a letter."

"Yes."

"It is a good idea, Louise. A very good idea."

"I will make it a journal of our little one," Louise said, pleased that he did not object.

Henri glanced at the officers gathered on the bridge above and murmured almost to himself, "Perhaps he would hide this in his kit and post it when we make landfall."

Louise felt tears sting her eyelids. She could hear a trace of her beloved Henri's strength in those words. She said, "I will tell Catherine of her child. I will try to make the baby live for her upon the page."

"We must set up a chain of communication with the other landings," Henri said, his tone warming with the plan.

"I will make her understand that I am giving her little one all the love and caring I would give to my own—" Louise's voice caught and she took a breath, a long one, and willed her heart to settle. "I will write Catherine and give her all the comfort I am able."

"We will establish contact with all Acadians." Henri was no longer speaking just to her, but to the future. The power of being able to think beyond the moment granted a new spark to his gaze, renewed force to his voice. "Perhaps there is someone still back in Minas, someone who will act as a go-between. Someone who . . ." His eyes widened again.

"Catherine," Louise finished the thought, her heart leaping at the realization. A frail and tenuous thread that might yet connect them with faraway little Antoinette. "Of course. Catherine would be willing to act as our conduit. I am confident of it."

"She and her Andrew as well. I am certain he will want to help us." Henri reached for his wife's hand. "Louise, you have given me hope."

"Not I, my husband," she said, and felt tears course down her cheeks at the sight of her husband's smile. "But God."

CHAPTER THIRTY-TWO

"Evening to you, sir."

"What? Oh, yes, yes." John Price had difficulty recalling exactly who the tall soldier was, though he had seen him day in and day out for these long years. Of course. He remembered now. "Evening, Sergeant Major."

No wonder the man grimaced as he offered a stiff salute. This soldier had held his son-in-law in particular regard. As had so many of the other soldiers, all of whom walked under a cloud these days. The soldier offered, "Grim night of it, sir."

"Indeed." Though there was not a cloud in the sky. Neither man spoke of the weather. "A grim night it is."

John Price left the fort and trudged the dusty lane homeward. A grim night. That day Andrew Harrow's replacement had arrived, bringing with him the papers formally severing Harrow's ties to the regiment. A grim night indeed.

But the fact that his son-in-law, a young man John Price regarded with an affection he would shower upon his own flesh and blood, had left the regiment under a cloud was not the only reason Price walked stooped and burdened. In fact, it was not the principal reason at all.

Overshadowing everything was the devastating news of his granddaughter, a wound still raw after three weeks of torment. They had searched for Elspeth as much as they could, given the fact that their country was now formally at war with the French. But these discreet inquiries had brought nothing but further stains upon Harrow's record.

No one could tell them which ship had taken away the people of Minas village. Vessels from Cobequid Bay were bound for Boston, Baltimore, Washington, Chesapeake, Charleston, New Orleans, Dieppe, Bayonne, Bordeaux, La Rochelle—even one to a colony on the coast of West Africa. John Price had spent the previous nights preparing letters to his counterparts in each of the American cities, then readying himself for the process of going through official channels for the French colonies and ports. Nothing could be done until the hostilities were over, but what little word he had received up to now confirmed that in truth almost nothing would be possible afterward. The ships had been crammed with people so hastily that no record had been made of which families were sent where. The villagers had truly been scattered to the winds. And his baby granddaughter with them.

Yet even the aching void caused by the

loss of his grandchild was not the worst of it.

Catherine had been unable to explain why she had wept so, that day of their arrival in Edward. Her sobs had been her only response to his increasingly irate demands for an explanation. Surely it was not concern over a few French villagers that caused her such brokenhearted woe. Surely not. They had ridden thus through the village, she crying and he shouting, until the din had brought Andrew to the doorway of their cottage. An Andrew he had never seen before.

Mirrored in the young man he had seen a shattered tragedy, one far beyond what was merited by losing his place in the regiment. After all, he was still young, he still had his health. But no. He stood supporting himself with one hand clutching the doorjamb, battered and muddied from head to foot, his dark hair bedraggled and streaming about his face. And his eyes. John Price had shuddered at the first glimpse of Andrew's eyes.

Catherine had taken one look at her husband and screamed with a force that shook her frame. *"No!"*

"Elspeth, she's . . ." Andrew stumbled as he forced himself forward and almost pitched headlong in the dirt at the wagon's side. "She's . . ."

"No!" Catherine shoved the baby into

John Price's arms and spilled from the wagon into her husband's exhausted embrace. "Oh, no, no, tell me it's not so!"

John Price looked down at the wakened fretting baby, then back to the couple clutching each other and sobbing so hard they could no longer speak. And with a rising horror he glimpsed the truth that his daughter had been unable to speak aloud. This small bundle of lightness—this frail, pinched little face—this was not his grandchild that he held in his arms.

But even that was not what troubled him the worst as John Price trudged homeward.

Three nights ago he had walked down to his daughter's cottage, drawn by his loneliness and his need for family. Despite the ire he had showered upon them, the raging, shouting fury he had shown when they had revealed how the babies had been traded, still when he had knocked upon their door, he had been greeted with quiet welcome.

Yes, there had been sorrow. Yes, their gazes had remained as wounded as their voices and their hearts. And yet, and yet. Their welcome had been calm and genuine.

And forgiving. He had been ready for argument, for quarrels, for a banishment he could have carried in stubborn, angry pride. But not this. Anything but this.

Catherine had offered him a mug of cider, seated him by the fire, then returned to her place by her husband. The crib was there at her feet, little Antoinette asleep and beautiful in her frailty in the firelight. They had spoken of this or that for a few minutes, then Catherine had lifted the Book back into her lap.

"You must excuse us, Father. We take the dusk every night for our time of devotion."

"And prayer," Andrew had quietly added.

He had stared from one face to the other, astonished by the admission. Every word became its own question. "You? Pray? Now?"

"It is all we have," Catherine said. She shook her head at that. "No, that is not what I mean, not at all. But we do need prayer now—more than ever."

John Price watched as a struggle went on inside his daughter, one which forced her features to contort with the strain of seeking proper words. Andrew watched her as well, sad yet calm, seemingly willing to wait forever.

Finally Catherine said, "We are weaving

411

together the fragments of our life. And our love. This we can only do with God's help. And His strength. And His light and love to guide us."

Andrew reached across and took her hand. He did not speak, yet there was something in the gaze he turned on his wife, something so warm and overwhelmingly gentle that John Price had been forced to turn away. Shame had burned like acid as it poured over his heart.

The memory still brought pain as it would for all the long and lonely nights he had yet to endure.

"Good evening, sir. May I walk with you?"

"Ah, Andrew. Of course. Of course." John Price paused long enough for the young man to catch up. Andrew carried a heavy bucket in each hand, walking carefully to keep the milk from sloshing over. "Can I help you with that?"

"Thank you, no. The two balance each other out. How are you this evening?"

John could not help but stare. "Not three days ago you were drummed from your regiment under a cloud of dishonor, and you ask *me* that?"

Andrew shrugged as much as the load would allow. "I was going to leave the regiment. I have known that for months now. It was only a question of when and how. Besides . . ."

"Yes?"

Andrew hesitated. "I am not sure you would wish to hear this."

"There is almost nothing about the past few days," John replied grimly, "which I had any interest in hearing."

"No, I suppose not." Carefully Andrew set his pails down upon the earth. "The day of the, well . . ."

The disaster, John found himself thinking, each word a stab to his heart. *The disaster I helped to bring about.* But all he said was, "Go on."

"General Whetlock sent me to round up a French village. He warned me that if I refused his command, I would be sent back to England in chains, there to be tried for disobeying a direct order in wartime and hanged."

John Price clutched at his own throat, a groan all he could voice.

"I'm afraid so. Despite the general's warning, as I was leading my troop down the

413

Annapolis Royal road, I realized I could not do it. Not for Catherine, not for my child, not for my own life. There would be casualties. It seemed inevitable. There are always some resisters. And I can't say I would have blamed them, sir. But to strike them down for defending their homes . . . their families. . . ? It was against everything I had learned in my studies of the Scriptures with Catherine. Faces of the French I had seen in the village flashed before my eyes. I wondered who among them would be left behind for the army to bury the next morning. Which wives heartbroken. Which babies left as orphans. I couldn't do it. It was wrong."

John Price opened his mouth to object, but the words were not there. He could scarcely find the strength to draw a breath through his constricted throat. Yet there was no condemnation in Andrew's tone, and his gaze had become fixed upon a scene so distant only he could see it. Even so, the quietly spoken words rang true. *It was wrong.*

"I reined in my horse, planning to turn myself in to the adjutant Whetlock had sent along for that very reason. Then, out of the thicket ahead, there came another officer, one whose name I cannot for the life of me recall. He had just come from rounding up those very same villagers."

Andrew turned to his father-in-law then, with a gaze whose profound wounding was balanced with a deep and eternal calm. "Why I was granted such a gift of grace while so many others were suffering, I do not know. Yet truly I am certain that grace it was. This conviction Catherine shares with me, and it has helped us mightily to endure these past days, to begin the inner restoration, and prepare for the future ahead."

Birdsong rose from the tree alongside their lane, the sound answered by callings from the next tree, and they from a tree leading to the Harrow cottage. Like heaven's chimes, they were a soft and comforting end to yet another day. John Price forced his voice to function and asked, "What will you do now?"

"Pray." Andrew gave a sad smile. "Pray for guidance, pray for Elspeth wherever she is, pray for our own strength. We pray so much these days, there seems scarcely to be room for anything else." His gaze shifted to the unseen cottage. "Which in truth may not be a bad thing."

John Price could think of nothing to say.

Andrew's gaze remained directed toward the cottage around the bend as he mused aloud, "I have been thinking of perhaps becoming a pastor. But I need to be certain this idea is shared equally by Catherine. After all, it is through her that I have found a voice with which to speak to my Lord, to hear from Him."

John Price had to bow his head. The shame was too great. *It was wrong.*

A gentle hand upon his shoulder underscored the words, "Come home with me, Father Price. Catherine will be glad to see you."

Father. It was the first time Andrew had addressed him thus. It was enough to scald his eyes. He could only nod and follow along as Andrew hefted the buckets and started down the lane.

Catherine was standing in the doorway, there to greet them. The child who was not hers, yet hers indeed, was in her arms. The smile which should not for a thousand reasons be given to him was there as well. Sad and hollowed by all that had happened, but there just the same. "Hello, Father. Welcome."

The scalding grew worse, as though there in the quiet greeting was every accusation he felt the world hurling at him. He hung his head once more, unable to look either at them or the baby. "I have come . . ."

He had to stop and search for the breath and the strength to go on. "I have come to ask your forgiveness."

He had not even known the purpose of his walk until that moment. But once started, he had to say it all. "What happened was wrong. I am sorry. If I could, I would give my own life to take back the role I played." He sighed, and all the breath and all the strength blew from his body. He could only murmur to the earth at his feet, "But I cannot. I am sorry."

"As are we," Catherine said, but there was no indictment in her voice, no bitterness. Only an endless sea of sorrow. "But it is done. And we must now go on the best we can. With God's help."

"With God's help," Andrew agreed. "He has called us to mercy, the living daily act of forgiveness and love. We seek it from Him to give to others."

"Mercy," John Price murmured, tasting the unfamiliar word, asking it also for himself.

"Come in, Father." Catherine turned back inside, stepping aside for him to enter. "It is good to see you."

CHAPTER THIRTY-THREE

Catherine had feared there would never be another spring—but now it was here. New beginnings were everywhere, in the unfurling of tender green leaves on the tree by her window, the call of the robin to the mate already busy with building her nest, the lowing of the roan milk cow as she licked her wobbly-legged newborn, the gentle rain that pattered softly on the stout roof of the little cottage. Catherine had to admit—spring had returned.

It had not been a long nor difficult winter in terms of weather hardship. But it had been a wearying one for Catherine. She had been confined for most of the months, both by choice and by need. She had not felt at ease in the village. Besides, though Antoinette had improved considerably, she was still fragile and small for her age. Catherine supposed that she would always be delicate, and so she kept her from much contact with others who might share illnesses. But the little one was happy. Happy and seemingly content. She adored Andrew, bouncing upon the hearth rug and calling to him the minute she heard his footsteps on the shale pathway.

They could not have called her Elspeth. The pain would have been too sharp each time they spoke the name. Yet they could not continue to call her Antoinette—a French name in an English settlement. So they had chosen Anne, Elspeth's middle name. "Perhaps one day she can have her full name back," said Catherine, in her heart hoping that would mean she would have her Elspeth back as well.

The little girl was not a difficult child to love, and Catherine gave her all the pent-up devotion a mother's love could heap upon a child in the absence of her own dear one. And she prayed—morning and night and oft times in between—that her own precious little one would have Louise's love in full measure as well.

But time moved on. Even Catherine with her grief-stricken heart could not hold it at bay. And now it was spring again. Slowly they had moved past the first birthdays of the child they had lost—the child they had gained.

"The flowers will soon be back in the meadow," Catherine spoke to Anne one morning as she moved about the cottage setting the yeast to rise. "I have not been there for a very long time. I have missed the place. And Louise." She blinked back tears. How much dare she tell this child about the mama she had lost? Very little, she concluded, though she yearned to whisper secrets, to give details about the mother she might never have the privilege of knowing. To share with small Anne stories about her own little girl who could have been—would have been—a friend and playmate.

But it was too fraught with danger. Even now. Catherine dared not disclose any facts about the baby's past. There were still rumors of French refugees hidden in the tall timbers, routed out by vigilante patrols, spotted by outlying farmers as they raided root cellars or hen houses in order to fill empty stomachs. There was still a good deal of animosity on the part of some of the settlers. Still talk about what this Frenchman or that Frenchman had said or done or threatened to do. There was also much talk about bringing in new settlers, ones favorable to the throne of England. These newcomers would take over the deserted farms, rebuild the failing dikes, plant the land that might return to forest if not maintained. Catherine could not help but wonder who those new settlers would be. Would they know that the land they farmed had been watered by tears?

But she pushed those thoughts from her now as Anne pulled at her skirts. "Ma-mama," the child crooned and Catherine reached down to lift her into her arms.

"Well, finally. It is about time you began the Ma-ma-ma." She placed a kiss on the dark head of curls. "Up to now it's always just been Da-da-da."

"Da-da," responded the infant.

"Yes . . . Da-da-da. It is a long time until he will be coming home."

Catherine's eyes moved to the clock. It was only ten in the morning. Andrew would not be home for the noon meal.

"You know," she said, speaking again to the child. "It is a beautiful day. Fresh air would do us both good. I have not left my own yard since I don't know when. Let's take a walk, shall we?"

Once the idea was planted, Catherine could not wait to implement it. She put Anne back on the rug by the rocker and rushed about getting their wraps.

Soon they were on their way up the hillside path. Catherine breathed deeply of the fresh spring air, tilted her head to listen to the song of a house wren, laughingly showed Anne a small frog that hopped its way from their path.

Anne took it all in, small head tipping this way and that, dark eyes darting back and forth as though she wished to miss nothing.

In spite of the child's small frame, Catherine was panting when they reached the last stretch of path leading to the hillside meadow. She lowered Anne to a bed of mossy growth under her favorite stand of pines and pushed back her bonnet.

"My," she exclaimed. "You are heavier than I had imagined." It was a good sign. The child was steadily filling out. "Just let Mama catch her breath and we will finish our journey."

Small Anne reached for a fistful of skirt and cooed up at Catherine.

Catherine could not rest for long. Her desire to be back in the meadow was much too strong to resist. She hoisted the child again and started the last few steps that would take her to the place she had learned to love.

For one bittersweet moment she thought to see Louise resting on their favorite fallen log. The long, flowing dark hair rippled by wind, the bright eyes shining even at a distance, the hand waving a joyous greeting.

But Louise was not there. There was no movement in the meadow except for the flights of birds, dipping from one small bush to another, singing out their springtime song. Or the flash of a bushy red tail as a squirrel scolded that he had been interrupted in some business of importance. A soft breeze nodded the heads of the earliest flowers, seeming to bid Catherine welcome, back to where she rightfully belonged.

"Oh," she sighed. "I have missed this. More than I even realized."

She put small Anne on the ground beside her, steadying her on unsure feet. Her eyes traveled to the spot where messages had often been left in days past. It seemed such a long, long time ago. Almost in another lifetime. So much had changed. So much.

But there would be no message there for her now. Louise was gone. In spite of the French vicar's plea that Andrew be the conduit, there had been no word from any of the Acadians who had been expelled. Where were they? Were they safe? Was her precious little Elspeth safe? If only . . .

But *if onlys* were futile. Andrew had told her that so many times over the months, and Catherine had finally learned to keep her thoughts in check. Almost.

But today, here in the meadow, those thoughts were brought sharply into focus once again.

She lowered herself to the familiar log and lifted the child to her lap.

"This is where your—where my best friend and I used to meet," she began. "We both loved it. The flowers. The birds. And the berries. You've not tasted berries—but you will love them. They are sweet and juicy. You must be careful how you eat them or they will drip down your chin."

Long-ago memories of a Louise with stained lips came back to make her chuckle through her tears. "We will come here again. Often, now that it is warmer. If there is any place where she would return, I'm sure this is it. Who knows—perhaps one day we will find a message here."

The very thought stirred Catherine. She could not resist setting Anne down and reaching under to the place where notes were hidden. But in spite of thrusting her hand into the fallen trunk as far as she could and wiggling her fingers this way and that to feel each inch of the hidden alcove, her hand came away empty.

"Not today," she said, a catch in her voice. She went back over to where the baby sat and played with a pinecone. "See this flower, Anne—*fleur*. And that flash of blue overhead—a bird—*oiseau*. Can you say that? *Oiseau*. And over there—do you see the bunny almost hidden in the grasses? *Lapin*. You must learn the words. I will not be the best teacher, but I will teach you as much as I know. It will be our secret. If your—if my friend comes back someday, she will wish to talk with you. And to do that you must know her tongue."

In the meadow, the canopy of sky so high overhead that the soft, scudding clouds appeared to belong more to heaven than to earth, the birds flitting and darting and whispering their spring love songs, the timid flowers bowing humble heads to the passing wind, Catherine felt closer to Louise than she had for many months.

Closer to God.

"Lord," she began without really thinking about saying a prayer, "wherever Louise may be, take care of her. Oh, God, be with my growing little girl. And even though she cannot—dare not—be told about me, may she feel a mother's love somewhere deep in her heart. Please, God. Take care of my baby girl.

"And take care of the one who is mothering her. Keep Louise healthy, strong, trusting in you. Don't let her grow bitter. Keep her sweet and gentle and growing.

"May she teach Elspeth of you, Lord. So that she will learn to trust. To have a faith that will keep those little feet steady. Keep her strong in her convictions."

Her eyes dropped back to the child, who studiously examined the pinecone held in tiny fingers. "And help me, Lord. You know I have learned to love little Anne. So much.

May Louise know that. Feel that. May she be assured that her child is cherished and cared for."

Catherine stopped and tried to swallow away the lump in her throat. At length she was able to go on.

"And, Father, if it pleases you, may the day come when . . . when two broken-hearted mothers are reunited with their baby girls. Please, God. Let it be so."

Anne reached out to be lifted, and Catherine stopped her prayer to bend down and pick the child up in protective arms. The baby still held the pinecone, but when she looked into the face of the one who held her so closely, she cast it aside to reach up and touch the tear on her mother's cheek.

AUTHORS' NOTE

In researching the material for this story, we have learned a new sympathy for those French Acadians whose only offense seemed to be their land of birth—and the fact that they wished to remain neutral in a conflict involving the homeland. And we also came to appreciate the predicament of those Britishers who found their role distasteful and morally difficult to enforce.

We as individuals may not be able to stop wars. But we can begin by resolving conflicts in our homes, in our churches, in our communities. Let us learn to be people of peace.

"Blessed are the peacemakers: for they shall be called the children of God" (Matt. 5:9).

To Our Readers

Watch for the sequel to Catherine and Louise's story early in the year 2000.

Children's Books by Janette Oke

Making Memories
Spunky's Camping Adventure
Spunky's Circus Adventure
Spunky's First Christmas

CLASSIC CHILDREN'S STORIES

Spunky's Diary
New Kid in Town
The Prodigal Cat
Ducktails
The Impatient Turtle
A Cote of Many Colors
A Prairie Dog Town
Maury Had a Little Lamb
Trouble in a Fur Coat
This Little Pig
Pordy's Prickly Problem
Who's New at the Zoo?